# GRAVELY GAP

## By
## *Raland J. Patterson*

ISBN: 1496064631
ISBN 13: 9781496064639

# DEDICATION

*To my wife, Ann,*
*for knowing what I really meant when I scribbled my notes.*

*And to my West Fannin classmates and family*
*for sharing their stories.*

*And to my Aunt Jewell*
*for her unwavering support and for introducing me to television!*

# CHAPTER 1

Opal Wilson tossed her dish towel on the sink as she finished drying the last of the breakfast dishes. She walked out to the front porch and settled into her rocking chair, where she had a bird's-eye view of the quarter-mile-long curved dirt road from Highway 5 to the two-story farmhouse she called home. Since the war, everyone in the neighborhood knew that's where they could always find her.

Opal had two sons, Bill and Frank. They'd been drafted when the war broke out. Bill had fought all over Europe and returned without a scratch. Frank had been listed as missing in action in 1944. Everyone assumed Frank was dead, but no one could convince Opal it was true. She simply knew that one day her youngest son would return, so every morning she'd sit in her chair and watch for the Trailways bus to pass by the end of her dirt road.

Today was a clear, spring day, and she could see that the two sweet apple trees in the center of the meadow next to the road were in full bloom. Her mind was wandering as she thought it would likely be a good year for apples when something captured her attention. The Trailways bus had stopped at the end of the road. She leaned forward with interest as a tall, thin man stepped off the bus. As he came closer up the dirt road, she could see that he was in uniform. She froze. Then she pushed off the arms of the rocking chair and began to hesitantly move toward the man. When the two were twenty feet apart, Frank smiled. "Momma, I'm home."

In that instant, all the fear and emotions she'd so valiantly held inside over the past few years vanished. She sagged in relief as she scolded him. "It's about time, Frank. Do you know how much I've worried about you? I should break me off a switch."

He was so glad to hear her voice that he just grinned at her tongue-lashing and grabbed up the fragile figure into a bear hug. "Momma, you and Gravely Gap never change. What've you got to eat?"

She desperately wanted to ask where he'd been and what had happened to him, but instinctively she knew it wasn't the right time. So she just placed her arm in his and walked with him back to the house. He slipped into his usual place at the end of the bench between the table and the wall as she opened the oven door and pulled out a leftover biscuit from breakfast and a fresh jar of her homemade blackberry jam, his favorite. Before she could even pour him some coffee, he'd opened one of the biscuits, filled it with jam, and shoved it into his mouth. She watched in amusement as crumbs fell from his lips to the floor.

"Momma, I'd forgotten how good these are. Got any more?"

She opened the oven and handed him the pan with the rest of the biscuits. "Eat them all and I'll fix more for supper."

Finally full, he asked, "Where's Daddy?"

"Over at the Barkleys' helping put up hay."

"Where'd you put my clothes? I'll go on over and help."

Disappointed and unwilling to let him out of her sight so soon, she protested, "They're in your room. I washed and ironed them when Bill came home—but why don't you just wait until Daddy comes home, son?"

"Is Bill here?"

"Oh, he decided to stay in the army. He's at Fort Sill, Oklahoma. You wouldn't know that, though, would ya?"

He shook his head and said, "Good luck to him. I've had about as much army time as I can stand. I dreamed of the day I'd smell fresh cut hay, and I'm not waiting anymore." He rushed upstairs to change his clothes.

When he came down, Opal stood and looked at the shadow of the man who had left home four years before. All she wanted to do was hold him close and protect him from any future harm, but she reluctantly said, "OK, son, just don't overdo it."

"I won't. Momma, you do remember you're my first love," he said as he hopped off the porch.

Frank had a spring in his step as he walked to the Barkley farm. He had been afraid life on the farm wouldn't be like he'd remembered it. But when he heard his momma chewing him out, he'd let out that breath he'd been holding in for the past two years, knowing everything was going to be just fine.

The men in the field stopped work and just stared at the stranger walking toward them. Amos Barkley blurted out, "Tom, if I didn't know better, I'd think that was your boy, Frank."

Tears welled up in Tom's eyes. He swallowed back his emotion in front of the other men and said, "Son, where's your hat? This sun will give you a headache."

Frank said, "I forgot about that, Daddy. It's been a while since I cut hay."

Tom stuck out his hand and said quietly, but with great feeling, "Welcome home, son."

Frank pulled the old man into a hug. He could feel his daddy trembling in his arms. He stepped back and asked, "What can I do?"

As frail as Frank appeared, Amos could see he needed to work. "Get on that haystack and pack it down as we pile it on."

Frank grabbed the sixteen-foot pole and said, "I can do that."

When the hay wagon was emptied and finally placed on the stack, Frank looked over at Amos. He wanted to ask about his two sons, Mike and Jesse, but he stopped himself as he realized that they might not have made it home.

As Frank and Tom made their way back home, Frank asked his question. "Daddy, did Mike and Jesse make it back?"

"Yeah, they both did. They've really grown up from when you boys would pitch horseshoes. Remember that?"

Wistfully, Frank said, "Just like it was yesterday. Jesse was always a smart-mouthed kid, but you couldn't help but like him. If he won, you'd never hear the end of it, but boy was he quiet when he lost!"

"They've changed a lot. Mike came home first, and it was like he'd been snake bit. First, he lost his little girl to strep throat. It wasn't a year later that their son, Michael, came down with polio. He still has to wear a brace so he can walk."

"I'm sorry to hear that. The war was hard enough. How about Jesse?" Frank asked.

"He joined up as soon as he graduated, and boy, did that piss Amos off. You remember how he is." Tom couldn't help but chuckle at the memory. "I think he was really mad because he didn't have anybody left to boss around."

Frank nodded in agreement, "Yeah, he was really hard on both of them."

"Guess he had to be. We were lucky; we owned our farm. They were just sharecroppers. They never knew where their next dollar would come from."

"Is Jesse home, too?"

"No, like your brother, he's making the army a career. I hear he's teaching at that parachute school down at Fort Benning. Mother Barkley says he loves it. Oh, yeah: he married Lorri Hamby from Epworth a couple of years ago. That was after you'd left."

"Sounds like he didn't want to keep following those old mules. Good for him."

"You're right about that," Tom said. "Would you believe Mike is now our mailman? He's got all of Route 1."

"I'll try to catch him. About what time does he come by?"

"Between two and two thirty every afternoon. Son, if you don't mind me asking, what are your plans?"

"Daddy, if it's OK with you, I'd like to just stay right here and help you work the farm."

"Your momma will be tickled to death to hear that. It'll be nice to hear her laugh again."

# CHAPTER 2

Sergeant First Class Jesse Barkley practically quivered with excitement as he shaved. Today was the day his parachute jump class would be making their first jump of five toward qualifying for their silver jump wings out of the new C-119, nicknamed the Flying Boxcar. He finished buttoning his shirt and walked to the kitchen. As early as it was, his wife, Lorri, was fully dressed. He asked, "Why are you so dressed up?"

She gave him the look only wives can and sighed with impatience. "Remember, I told you last night that I needed the truck this morning for a meeting with the NCO wives?"

He didn't remember but knew better than to admit it. "Right, I'll just walk home this afternoon."

"No, I can pick you up. Just tell me when."

"We're taking the students up for their first jump today, so there's no telling when we'll get finished; I'll just walk."

When they arrived at the jump school headquarters, Jesse gave her a quick peck on the cheek and jumped out. She smiled; she'd figured out a long time ago that her macho soldier boy didn't do public displays of affection in front of the men. She slid over to the driver's side, cranked the truck, and gave him a quick wave as she left. A woman driving a pickup was unusual here, but she loved it. She'd been so upset when Jesse had used almost all of their savings to purchase it, and for the next six months she had watched him take his new toy to the craft shop on weekends. It was his first vehicle, and he'd made it a showpiece. He'd brag his five-window pickup would be a classic someday. She had no clue what that meant, but she'd smile back and respond, "I sure hope so, sweetie, with all the work you've put into it."

She felt guilty for telling him a little white lie. She didn't have a meeting with the wives; she had a doctor's appointment this morning at ten o'clock.

The school commander, Colonel Ralph Hill, came out of the headquarters building to give his normal speech to motivate the students: "Men, today you'll make your first jump of the five required. For the past two weeks you've learned how to exit the aircraft and how to land on the drop zone. You have the knowledge; your only threat is panic. When a man panics, he ends up doing nothing, and doing nothing when you jump out of an aircraft will get you killed. Getting killed before your fifth jump means no wings on your chest. If you sense you're about to panic, take action. Just *do something,* and that action will overcome the panic. Remember, do anything, even if it's just peeing in your pants."

The colonel got the laughter he was looking for, so he got serious. "The parachute across your stomach is your reserve." He held up a reserve chute and pointed to the silver handle. "If for any reason your main chute fails, pull this ring. Airborne soldiers have a saying, 'When in doubt, whip it out.'"

The soldiers laughed again as he said, "Remember that saying, and realize that the worst thing that can happen if you pull the ring and don't need it is you just land with two chutes. Take the teasing rather than landing with no chute. Good luck, and have a soft landing."

The group was called to attention as the colonel left, then they were loaded up and taken to the aircraft.

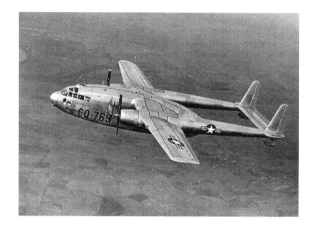

Everyone was excited about the strange new plane. After the equipment check, Sergeant Barkley loaded them on board. The first thing Jesse noticed was the additional head room and how bright it was inside. He liked the way it made him feel. In no time at all, they were over the drop zone and exiting the door of the aircraft. Jesse was last. They were jumping the T-10 parachute, which left the jumper at the mercy of the wind, but thankfully today's wind was calm. Jesse had heard rumors that the army was looking at steerable chutes that would allow jumpers to turn into the wind. Boy that would be a dream. He loved the feeling of drifting after the noise of the aircraft was gone, but soon he noticed he was passing some of his students. He didn't have a sensation of falling, but it looked as if they were going up and this disturbed him. He wondered if he was that much heavier. The jump turned out to be a perfect one for the students—they all landed on the drop zone with no emergency chutes, and no one ended up in the trees.

Lorri sat on the front steps of their quarters anxiously watching for Jesse. Moments later, she admired her tall soldier as he came down the street. She loved the way he looked in his pegged pants. His company commander was an OCS graduate, and while a candidate had had his fatigue pants cut down, or pegged. They weren't authorized, but they looked so good when they were starched that the chain of command usually looked the other way. She had great news from her appointment and couldn't wait to tell him. She stood as he got closer, opening her mouth to blurt it out, when he yelled out, "Sweetie, am I getting fat?"

She studied the muscular frame in front of her and said, "No way! Why would you ask such a crazy question?"

"I noticed I was falling faster than some of the students today when we jumped. That means I'm a lot heavier than they are."

Annoyed, she said, "Jesse, sometimes you blow my mind. Does that mean you want to skip supper?"

He just grinned. "No, today is chicken and dumplings, isn't it?"

She decided to save her news for a better time. "Go wash your hands and I'll put it on the table."

# CHAPTER 3

Life in Blue Ridge never changed. It was Sunday, and the family dinner was just starting. Mike Barkley sat down and looked around the big table at the familiar faces—Ruth, his sister, and her husband, Paul; their daughters, Katherine and Jean; his wife, Martha; their son, little Michael; and his parents, Amos and Mother Barkley. The only family members missing were his brother, Jesse, and his wife, Lorri. There was an air of excitement as Mother Barkley shared news from her letter from Lorri. Jesse's parachute class was graduating soon and it would be a couple of months before the new one started, so the company commander wanted all of his NCOs to use up some of their leave time. Jesse and Lorri would be coming home for a couple of weeks.

Mike looked around in satisfaction. "Sure will be nice to see my little brother."

As she passed the meat around and kept her eye on the girls, who were just pushing the food around on their plates, his mother chided him, "He's a man now, and I don't think he'll like being called *little brother.*"

Mike winked. "That'll make it more fun, won't it?"

"I don't think you'll ever grow up."

Amos interrupted the bickering. "You'll never guess who I saw the other day. Frank Wilson."

Surprised, Mike looked up and nabbed another biscuit. "I thought he was killed in action."

"Everyone did, except for Opal. She's been sitting on that front porch every day for years watching the Trailways bus pass by."

Mother Barkley added, "Don't I always say the hope and prayers of a mother are never wasted? Maybe one day y'all might start believing me."

Everyone got silent and ate. Uncomfortable with silence, Mike changed the subject: "Daddy, I see you cut the meadow. Are you going to start farming again?"

"Nah, I thought I'd get us a milk cow. Now that your momma has an electric icebox, she wants to keep it full of milk and butter."

Mother Barkley asked, "And what's wrong with that?"

"I thought you got your milk and butter from the Davenports across the creek," Mike said as he speared another piece of ham.

She answered, "We did until one of their cows went dry. It'll be almost a year before she drops a calf. I convinced your daddy I'd do all the milking if he'd get me my own cow."

Mike was puzzled. "Daddy, where are you getting it?"

"Tom Wilson has a jersey that had a calf last month, and we made a deal. I'd split the hay from my meadow, help him with his, and give him ten dollars for both the cow and the calf."

Martha looked back and forth at her in-laws. She was concerned that Mrs. Barkley was taking on too much. "Mother, that's going to be a lot of work for you."

Mother looked over at Amos and grinned at Martha. "Would be for a man, but just another day for a woman."

Everyone but Amos laughed. The next week, when Mike sat down at the table, he began talking as usual. "I got to talk to Frank. He needed some stamps, so he met me at the mailbox. Man, is he skinny. He looked like death warmed over. I told him the war sure must have been hard on him, and do you know what he said?"

Martha was fascinated with the story and asked, "No, what?"

"He said, 'Not as bad as it was on that Dockery kid that rode the bus with me. He had a grenade thrown into the hole he'd hunkered down in at Normandy. He told me his back was one big scar and he'd just gotten out of the hospital. He said they made him write out a will because they didn't think he'd make it.' I told him Jesse had been a paratrooper at Normandy, and he just smiled and said, 'Yeah, Daddy told me he was down at Fort

Benning now.'" Mike couldn't help it; his eyes teared up and he looked ashamed. "I couldn't admit I never left the States."

Suddenly, Martha was furious. "Why do you men think you have to be the one getting shot at or you've let the other soldiers down? You don't need to apologize for anything. You did your service. Now shut up and eat." She stomped off toward the stove.

Mike shook his head. He knew her like the back of his hand, and experience told him not to open his mouth when she felt this strongly about something. It was one of her many ways of expressing her love for him, so he took a couple of bites and sipped his coffee. He looked up at her, caught her eye, and winked, saying, "I love you too."

# CHAPTER 4

Jesse got to work early on Wednesday so he could share his news with Staff Sergeant Francis O'Shea. He'd met him in basic, and they'd fought all over Europe side by side. Their friendship was only rivaled by the one he shared with his older brother. He walked up smiling and said, "O'Shea, I'm going to be a daddy."

O'Shea pushed his chair back and shook his head in denial. "Sure, sure. You're not suckering me again."

Jesse patiently waited. "Now, would I do that to you?"

"In a heartbeat! Remember when we were in France and you told me that stream was only ankle deep? I believed you and stepped in a hole—I nearly drowned."

Jesse explained, "Honestly, I didn't know I was standing on a rock."

"OK, then, how about the time you dressed up a mannequin when I was jump master and rigged the chute so it wouldn't open?"

"Hmmm, well, I guess you've got me there. Sorry about that, buddy. But I'm serious. Lorri is expecting in December."

"I still have trouble believing you." O'Shea said as the first sergeant walked into the room.

Jesse said, "Here, I'll show you. Top, I just found out Lorri is pregnant."

The first sergeant laughed and said, "That's just great. So you're going to raise an army brat."

Jesse didn't like the sound of that. "No kid of mine is going to be a brat! I'll warm his little bottom first. I remember Momma used to say,

'Spare the rod and spoil the child.' Trust me, she and Daddy knew how to use a leather belt, and it worked."

O'Shea and the first sergeant bent double with laughter at Jesse. They couldn't believe he had been in the army this long and hadn't heard the term. The first sergeant explained, "*Army brat* is a nickname for kids with military parents. It doesn't mean they're bad, just that their daddy's in the army. I was one, and I've been all over the world."

Jesse asked, "Your daddy was in the army?"

"Made it a thirty-year career. Both of my brothers are in too. One's a marine and the other is navy."

Jesse's first thought was about his siblings and how close they all were. He couldn't imagine not having a home to go home to. "Isn't it hard not seeing your family?"

"As a kid, I never got to know any of my aunts, uncles, or cousins. Dad's family lived in West Virginia, and to be honest I probably wouldn't know them if I passed them on the street."

Jesse couldn't even imagine a life like that. "That's sad. Don't you miss them?"

The first sergeant just shrugged. "Can't miss something you never had. Congratulations, big guy—hope you get a boy."

"Thanks, Top. Now let's go give the students their third jump."

Paratroopers lived the old army saying *Hurry up and wait.* Jesse normally spent time waiting for the air force to show up by shooting the bull with the NCOs. But today he just sat with the students and thought about what Top had said. The fact that he didn't even know his kin really bothered Jesse, and the thought of his child not getting to spend any time with his momma was inconceivable. He'd seen how she'd responded to Jean and Katherine when their real father was killed and how she'd been there for Martha and Mike when Betsy died from strep throat, and again when little Michael came down with polio. Her influence would be with them for the rest of their lives. It worried him because he knew he really wanted his children to be surrounded by his family and people who loved them unconditionally. He felt that was his duty as a father.

O'Shea could tell Jesse was troubled, and he tried to comfort him. "It'll be OK, buddy. You'll make a good daddy. Don't worry."

Jesse flashed him a grin. "Really? That coming from the man who said, 'They can kill us, but they can't eat us.'"

O'Shea said, "Hmm, good point, but this time I'm right. You jump out of a perfectly good aircraft, being a daddy should be a piece of cake."

"That's not my concern. I don't want my kids to join the army just because I did."

O'Shea said, "I see what you mean, but you'll figure it out. Let's go; the plane's here."

Jesse jumped up and said, "Airborne." Thursday evening, Jesse finished his project at the craft shop. He couldn't wait to show off his truck to his daddy. The only problem was there was no place in a pickup to put luggage for a trip. He decided to build a three-by-four-foot waterproof box in the truck bed and paint it the same color so it looked like it belonged.

Lorri was always impressed at how talented Jesse was with his hands. The kid in him came out as he proudly showed off his masterpiece. She couldn't help but laugh at him as he danced around explaining to her what he'd done. Watching him, she remembered what her mother had always said: "Men never grow up. They try to hide it, but the kid inside will always come out when you least expect it. Just love him and the child in him will spend his whole life trying to make you happy."

After the *Jump Wing* ceremony on Friday afternoon, O'Shea slapped Jesse on the back and said, "I'll see you at midnight."

Puzzled, Jesse asked, "What's happening at midnight?"

"We're signing out on leave; what do you think? You know if we sign out before then we lose a day. The train leaves for New York at two o'clock in the morning. How long will it take you to drive to North Georgia?"

"I'm not sure; I've never actually driven it before."

"Well, how've you been getting home?"

"Lorri and I have either ridden the bus or the train, and that takes all day. We usually leave around seven in the morning."

O'Shea said, "Well, now you're leaving at midnight."

Jesse smiled, "You're right, we could. That would mean we'd get home before dark."

Later that day, he asked Lorri, "Are you ready to leave?"

"No, I thought we'd leave first thing in the morning."

As he explained what O'Shea had suggested, she asked, "When would we sleep?"

"You can sleep while I drive, and I can sleep while you do."

She could see how excited he was to go home, so she agreed, "That'll work, and it shouldn't take us long to load the truck; we can leave from the orderly room."

After driving all night, they saw the city limit sign on the outskirts of Blue Ridge around ten o'clock in the morning. It read, *Blue Ridge, Elevation 1700 feet, population, 1700.*

Lorri asked if they could stop at Mike and Martha's first so she could share her news with them. That surprised Jesse. "Thought you'd want to tell your momma first."

"While you were off fighting the war, Martha was the one who kept me from going crazy. She's like a sister, and I owe her big time."

He reached over and patted her knee. "OK, whatever my sweetie wants."

Little Michael was in the dirt playing with his trucks as they turned into the driveway. When he saw who it was, he jumped up and tried to run. Jesse saw the brace on his leg and realized how difficult it was for him, so he rushed over, put his hands under Michael's arms, and threw him high in the air over his head. It was the game they had developed when Jesse came home from Europe. Michael loved being around his uncle, because Jesse never treated him like he was handicapped. Martha came to the door when she heard her son squealing with laughter. She just chuckled and said, "We didn't expect you guys until tomorrow."

Lorri smiled, "Well, that was the plan originally, but my sweetie insisted we drive all night."

Mike walked out on the porch, "Nice-looking truck. I must have a rich brother now."

Lorri shook her head, "You know, Mike, I think he likes that truck more than he does me. I know he spends more time with it."

He laughed and said, "Sounds like my little brother hasn't changed at all."

Jesse said, "Whoa there, you're supposed to be on my side!"

While the boys were looking over the truck, Lorri put her arm around Martha and said, "Let's you and I go get a cup of coffee."

As soon as they were in the house, Lorri blurted out, "Sis, I'm pregnant."

"Congratulations!" Martha said with a big smile. "How far along are you?"

"Two months."

Martha asked, "Have you told Jesse's parents yet?"

"No, I wanted to tell you first."

"I'm honored. What does Jesse think?"

"I don't know. Every time I try to talk about it, he finds something he has to do."

Martha said, "I guess becoming a daddy is a big step for him. I bet you guys haven't eaten."

"You really do know Jesse, don't you? When he starts something, he doesn't stop. I could eat a bear. Do you have anything left over in the oven?"

"How about some biscuits and jam?"

When Lorri finished her snack, they went outside to join the men. By this time they had the hood up on the truck and were checking out the engine. Lorri interrupted their fun, saying, "Jesse, we need to go. I'd like to go see Momma and Daddy before we go to your parents' house."

"Oh, OK. Mike, we'll see you tomorrow, right?"

"Yeah, Sunday dinner should be fun."

As they got on the road, Jesse said, "I sure hope your momma has dinner ready. I'm starving. I wonder why Martha didn't offer us anything to eat."

Lorri didn't say a word. He looked over and accused her, "You did eat, didn't you? Oh, I get it, you're punishing me again. Women don't like to be ignored and we ignored you."

She just nudged him in his side. "See there, becoming a daddy is making you smarter already."

The table was so full for Sunday dinner at the Barkley home that there weren't enough chairs to handle them all. Jesse came up with a solution, moving around the table to the bench and saying, "Slide down, kids, and I'll join you."

Little Michael was sitting between Jean and Katherine, but he quickly scampered over next to his uncle with a shy smile on his lips. As he felt him snuggle closer, Jesse kidded him, "Mr. Michael, was Santa Claus good to you this year?"

"Yeah, he brought me a new steam shovel and candy canes!"

Martha joined the conversation. "His old one got broken when somebody backed over it with a car," she said, giving Mike an accusing glare.

Little Michael was quick to defend his daddy. "He didn't mean to do it, and Santa brought me an even bigger and better one."

Jesse looked over at Mike in sympathy. Mike knew he was guilty and didn't even bother trying to defend himself. Jesse turned back to his nephew and pouted, "Well, you're lucky, I got socks and coal in my stocking. I don't get it either, because I get them every year. You think Santa is trying to tell me something?"

Michael sat up as straight as he could and looked at him in horror. It was a little kid's worst nightmare. "Uncle Jesse! You're on the naughty list."

"I am? Are you sure? What can I do to get off that thing?"

He was very serious as he thought for a moment and then offered, "Momma tells me I need to make my bed and pick up all my yucky clothes off the floor. Oh, and I have to take a bath and brush my old teeth."

Lorri jumped in, laughing, "Well then, Michael, he's in trouble, because he never, ever makes his bed and he leaves his clothes everywhere. I'd say he's definitely on that naughty list."

Jesse looked down at Michael and pleaded, "Michael, if you see Santa, please tell him I'll try to do better next year."

Little Michael just nodded, eager to help. "I sure will, Uncle Jesse."

Amos finally came in the room and noticed the crowd at the table. "I'll eat in the living room. Jesse, you can have my seat."

Lorri jumped up and hugged him. "You big old grump, we love you and want you to sit down and eat with us."

His face flushed as he quickly took his seat. Everyone was surprised at how quiet he was during dinner. Amos's silence allowed the others to chat quietly with each other, and the meal lasted more than an hour. It didn't take long for the kids to get bored and ask to go out and play. Once they were gone, the subject changed to the coming of the new baby. Uncomfortable with that, the men began their own conversations. Jesse brought up

Frank Wilson. Since women can talk and listen at the same time, Martha quickly interjected, "My mother told me about the little girl that lives next to the Wilson farm."

Mrs. Barkley asked, "You mean the one whose daddy was killed in the Pacific?"

"Yeah, that's the one. She used to sit with Opal on her front porch sometimes, but mother said now that Frank is home she sits on her own porch every day until the bus passes by. Evidently her mother has just given up trying to convince her that her daddy isn't coming back."

Shaking her head, Mother Barkley said, "What's that they say? *Little pitchers have big ears?* It breaks your heart to know she is too young to understand."

# CHAPTER 5

The fall of 1949 was a time of change for the Barkley family. Paul had taken a management job with a carpet mill in Dalton and had moved Ruth and the girls to their new home there. Little Michael had his first day at school; Mike had finally come to a tentative truce with his mother-in-law, Irene Burke; and Danny, Jesse's son, celebrated his third birthday on December 2. The most important change, however, was Jesse's. He had to decide if he wanted to reenlist for six more years or return home to Sugar Creek. For four years, since he'd learned Lorri was pregnant, he'd been thinking about what to do. He knew he had to make a decision before his Christmas leave was up. If he chose not to reenlist, he'd need a job, so he decided to check out employment opportunities with the Tennessee Copper Company.

After dinner on Sunday, he pulled Mike aside and said, "I'm thinking about getting out of the army, but I'll need a job. Do you think I can get on at the plant?"

"God, it would be great having you home. Go see Mr. Haymore in personnel tomorrow. It's the first little building you see when you go through the main gate. Tell him what you're thinking about; better still, wear your uniform. He lost his foot in the Pacific and he likes soldiers. If there's a job, I'll bet you get it."

Jesse looked around to be sure no one had overheard. "Keep this between you and me, OK? I don't want Momma to get her hopes up."

"What does Lorri think?"

"She says whatever I decide is with her, but I know she misses her family. Seeing Danny and her with them over Christmas pushed me off the fence."

"It might be selfish of me, but I sure hope you get the job. It would be great to have my little brother home again."

Monday morning, Jesse put on his uniform and headed for the door. Curious, Lorri asked, "Why are you in uniform? We still have leave left, right?"

Caught off guard, he quickly ad-libbed, "Oh, I promised the Stewart sisters I'd wear it for them."

It wasn't a complete lie, but he'd made them that promise before he married Lorri. Since he'd never lied to her and he didn't mean to start now, on his way home from the plant he'd have to pay a visit to the sisters.

"Ah, that's nice. I bet they'll be tickled to death to see you. You know those two old women think the world of you."

He just smiled. "I've got 'em fooled."

She whispered back, "That makes three of us."

He gave her a quick peck on the cheek and said, "Tell Momma I'll be back for dinner."

Sarcastically, she said, "Surprise, surprise—like you'd ever miss a meal."

He was nervous when he drove through the main gate at the plant. He couldn't remember being this unsettled on his first jump from an airplane. A gray-haired lady greeted him as he walked through the door, "Sergeant, what can we do for you?"

"Ma'am, is it possible for me to see Mr. Haymore?"

Haymore had overheard them and poked his head out his door, saying, "Sergeant, come on in and take a seat."

Jesse blurted out his entire story as soon as his bottom hit the seat. When he stopped to take a breath, Mr. Haymore said, "Relax, Sergeant. I'm not your commanding officer; in fact, I never was an officer. Let me see if I have this straight. You're thinking about getting out, but you need a job first?"

Jesse nodded, "Yes, sir. That's about it."

"Well then, this is our lucky day. With the new year, we're starting a project to build more houses for our employees, and when we finish that they have plans for a new company store. So son, the quick answer is yes, we have a job for you. When can you start?"

Jesse sat there speechless. Haymore asked, "By the way, why did you ask for me?"

It was an easy answer for Jesse. "My brother, Mike, told me about you, sir."

"What did he say?" He laughed and continued, "Forget I asked that. I'm not sure I want to know."

Immediately Jesse was at ease. "It was all good."

Mr. Haymore asked, "Then you're Amos Barkley's son?"

"Yep, that's my daddy. He works as a night watchman."

Haymore nodded. "I know, I gave him the job."

Jesse was eager and suggested, "I can start the first week of February if that's OK with you."

Haymore had Jesse follow him out front, stating, "We're a lot like the army. We can't do anything without the correct paperwork. Mrs. Mull will help you with that. Welcome to the company, Jesse."

"Thank you so much, Mr. Haymore."

"No thanks needed. I'm just doing my job."

Deep down, Jesse was still troubled. The only thing that competed with his intense love for Lorri and Danny was his absolute devotion to the army. He agreed that Danny needed to have the same type of childhood they'd experienced, but while the decision to abandon his dream job and move to the mountains was easier knowing he had a job, it didn't ease the ache in his heart. Shaking off his concerns, he went see the Stewart sisters. Elfie came out on the porch to greet him. Delighted, she yelled, "Dora, come out here and see who it is! Jesse has grown into a man."

Jesse tried to pretend he wasn't touched that she felt that way about him, but his heart was in his throat. He'd missed these two old women. Dora led him to the kitchen, then she poured him a cup of coffee and heated him a fried apple pie without even asking. He felt like he'd gone back in time to when he was a teenager and they had paid him for plowing their garden with love and fried pies instead of money.

# CHAPTER 6

New Year's Day was on a Sunday, which meant Jesse had Monday off. He'd taken leave through Wednesday, so when he came through the door Thursday morning, O'Shea met him with, "It's about darn time you got back. Top told me your reenlistment papers are on his desk and as soon as you sign them, he'll take them to personnel. I signed mine yesterday."

Jesse laughed. "I can't believe it. You know what that means, right? You are now a bona fide, certified, damn Yankee."

O'Shea knew he'd heard that before, but he couldn't remember how bad an insult it was supposed to be. "OK, refresh my memory. How am I one of those?"

"Like I told you before, a Yankee comes down south and then goes home. A damn Yankee comes down and decides to stay. Sounds to me like you plan on staying."

He grinned. "Have you noticed all the time we've been here, there hasn't been a single snowfall? A man could get used to that kind of weather. Now go sign that paperwork."

The time had finally come. He knew he had to tell O'Shea he'd decided his army career was over. When he explained, O'Shea didn't believe it. He said, "This is just another one of your sick jokes, right?"

"Not this time. Lorri and I agreed going home is the best thing for our family."

O'Shea abruptly turned and went outside. The news had hit him hard; Jesse was more than just his friend—he was family. Jesse paced the orderly room until the first sergeant came in.

"Sergeant Barkley, are you ready to sign your papers?"

"Not really, Top. Lorri and I decided to raise Danny at home in the mountains."

"Well, I hate to see you leave, but I understand. Maybe it's the best decision for you anyway. Things are really heating up in Korea, and we might just be in another war soon."

"Korea? I've never even heard of it. Where is it?"

"It's a peninsula just west of Japan. Think everybody's going to know where it is soon."

"Let's hope not. Top, when can I get my out-processing paperwork?"

"I'll put the company clerk on it ASAP, and it should be here in a couple of days. Remind me when your reenlistment is up."

"Twenty January."

The first sergeant laughed. "Well then, expect to be on my duty roster a lot between now and then."

Jesse chuckled. "No problem, Top." He knew how the system worked.

O'Shea avoided him the rest of the day, but by the next morning he was ready for a fight. "Listen, Barkley, I don't know anybody that enjoys pushing soldiers out of an airplane more than you do. You love it, and even better, you get paid to do it. I'm sure the first sergeant still has your paperwork. Please change your mind, buddy."

"O'Shea, you're right, I do love my job, but I love my family more. Now seriously, back off."

"OK, I hear you."

Jesse knew him well enough to know that O'Shea didn't give up that easily and would attack from another direction tomorrow, but he and Lorri had made their decision, and he knew it was the right one.

Sure enough, Monday morning O'Shea was at it again. "Barkley, I thought about it all weekend and there's no way I can let you get out. If you want me to, I'll talk to Lorri for you. She knows you're my good luck charm. If I let you leave, I'll break my leg or even worse."

Jesse was surprised by his approach. "O'Shea, I'm beginning to understand what they mean when they say Irishmen are full of blarney."

"Think how guilty you'd feel if something happened to me."

Jesse looked at his friend and said, "My momma would say you're tough as an old pine knot—nothing can hurt them. Trust me: if anybody's a pine knot, it's you."

"All I'm getting is another one of your mountain sayings? Let's go to work. I'll see you later."

The next few days went quickly; and, as promised, Jesse had duty three days. The out-processing paperwork consisted of a list of offices and organizations from which a soldier had to get signatures showing he had returned all of his supplies and equipment. Most areas took less than thirty minutes; but some, like TA50 or web gear, took all day to inventory. The last was the craft shop, housing, and finance for his pay. When they'd finally finished loading the pickup with their meager possessions, Lorri shook her head and said, "I can't believe everything we own fits in the back of this truck."

Jesse hugged her. "And most of it belongs to Danny. Remember when we first moved down here? I had one duffle bag and you had two small suitcases."

She hugged him back. "And now we're a family." She stepped back and looked at him seriously. "Did you tell O'Shea goodbye?"

"Not really. I haven't seen him for days."

"Now Jesse Barkley, that's unacceptable. You two are like brothers."

"I understand why he's avoiding me. It's hard for a soldier to say goodbye. It's always easier to just say see you later, and he did that last week."

# CHAPTER 7

Both families, the Hambys and Amos and Mother Barkley, insisted Jesse and Lorri move in with them. Mother Barkley was lonely since Ruth and the girls had moved to Dalton, and she won the argument because she had enough room that Danny could have his own space. Life was progressing nicely; they had a place to stay and Jesse's paycheck was now weekly instead of monthly. They discovered he was actually making more money here in Blue Ridge, which was a nice surprise.

After having lived on their own for so long, it was hard being back in the family home, and he realized Ruth's comments were true. She had told him, "Jesse, you can't go back, and trust me, you don't want to. "One of the first indications he had that things weren't like they used to be was when he couldn't find one of his most prized possessions.

"Momma, where are my fairy crosses?"

She gave him the typical female response, "Well, where did you leave them?"

"In a box under my bed. The box is still there, but it's empty."

"That was Jean and Katherine's room. I bet they took them out to their playhouse behind the smokehouse."

Jesse went straight there and stared in shock at what his momma had called a playhouse. She'd been pretty creative with her description, and he was impressed with the girls' imagination. The area in question was absolutely flat and was the perfect location. They had taken their poppa's firewood blocks and stood them on their ends. By placing planks on those, they had created the outline of a four-room playhouse. He could see they'd taken one of his momma's brooms and swept the ground completely bare. The red clay almost looked like a carpet. They'd used blocks of stove wood for furniture, which was a good choice because they were half the length of the firewood. They'd chosen carefully, as they were full of knots and couldn't be split. On the top were paper doilies under the pint fruit jars, which contained flowers. From the look of the wilted blossoms, they hadn't played there since early summer. There were remains of honeysuckle vines, jonquils, and a few daylilies. He was relieved and delighted when he noticed the decorations evenly spaced around the fruit jars—his fairy crosses. Not wanting to disturb a thing, he went to get Lorri.

When he got her there, he said, "I can't believe what an imagination they have. Mike and I could never have come up with anything like this."

"That's because you're boys," she said smugly.

Surprised, he said, "You're telling me you used to do stuff like this?"

"I think we came up with some pretty good stuff. I'll show you the next time we're at Daddy's house."

He shook his head; every time he thought he knew everything there was to know about her, she surprised him with yet another talent. Filled with love for her, he pulled her close and asked, "Are you really going to be happy forever with a simple country boy like me?"

Lorri answered, "I promise."

Jesse ran to the house and retrieved a poke, which to nonmountain folks was a brown paper bag. As he began to gather the crosses, he quickly realized he was missing about twenty of them. As luck would have it, his best ones were the ones that were gone. He smiled to himself when he remembered Ruth had always wanted some. She had probably helped the girls decide which ones to take with them to Dalton. That was OK with him, as he loved finding them more than anything. He hadn't been to see the Stewart sisters since he'd moved home, and this gave him the perfect excuse. He looked over at Lorri and said, "I guess I'll go over and see Elfie and look for some more of these."

"Great—Danny and I will go too. He's old enough to look for them. It's time you started teaching him our traditions."

Surprised, he asked, "Are you serious?"

"Let's go. It'll be fun. It's been a long time since we three had a day together. This way Danny will get to know Elfie and Dora."

"That's true. They haven't seen him since he was a baby. Hang on and I'll let Momma know where we're going."

When Jesse stopped the truck, both sisters came out on the porch. Elfie yelled, "We heard you were back! Come on in and let me see that baby."

Lorri put him down and held his hand to steady him so he could walk on the uneven ground. Dora said, "He's not a baby anymore. He's a little man."

Elfie added, "My goodness, he's Jesse made over. He looks just like you did at that age. Let's pray he's not as mean," she said as she winked at him. Both sisters giggled as they remembered the young boy so full of life he'd kept them captivated since the day they'd met him.

Jesse stood a little straighter and Lorri punched him in the side. "Settle down, little rooster. Remember, Mother says he looks just like me."

He just grinned and poked her back. "Don't you ever get tired of being right?"

They stood and watched as the sisters made a fuss over their child. Elfie finally asked, "How long are you here for this time?"

Jesse smiled at her and said, "For a long time. Lorri and I decided to get out of the army and come home for good."

Dora asked, "Where are you going to live?"

"Right now, we're with Momma and Daddy."

Elfie thought for a moment and said, "Why don't you buy the Godfrey farm over there?"

Jesse asked, "Are you talking about the one right across the road?"

"Yeah and that way you could dig up fairy crosses on your own land," she teased.

Seeing an opportunity to amuse Danny, Lorri asked, "Elfie, would you mind showing Danny and me where we could find some?"

"I'd love to. You know, if you two bought that land, you could build a house right up there and we could sit on our porches and talk."

Dismissing the idea, Jesse grabbed Danny's hand. "Come on, little man, let's go find some fairy crosses." He led him across the road and lifted him up on the bank.

# CHAPTER 8

At first, moving in with the Barkleys was like a vacation for Lorri. Mother Barkley spoiled Danny rotten. She'd rock him for hours and kept him occupied for most of the day. But after a few months, Lorri began to miss their days at Fort Benning when it had just been the three of them. Mother Barkley wasn't the problem; it was Amos. He'd been the man of the house for so many years, as the father of two strong boys, that he felt the need to exert his dominance and show them all who was in charge every now and then. At first Lorri didn't mind it so much, but as time passed it got harder and harder to remain quiet as he threw his little tantrums. Unfortunately, he worked the night shift, so he was there all day and most of the evenings.

Frustrated with the situation, Lorri allowed Elfie's comments about buying the land to gnaw at her inside. It was beginning to sound like heaven, but she wasn't sure how to bring up the subject to Jesse without hurting his feelings or making herself sound ungrateful. She decided to just be prepared to plead her case if the subject ever came up. Managing the money in the family had fallen to Lorri while Jesse was in the army and out on maneuvers, so she'd continued to perform that function since they'd returned to the mountains. They were comfortable with the arrangement, and because their expenses were low since they lived with his parents, each week Lorri was able to set aside money and hide it in the secret compartment in her music box. It had been a Christmas present from Jesse their first year at Fort Benning. Before today, she'd been saving for a rainy day, but suddenly she had a purpose—saving for their first home.

The next Saturday when Amos came in for breakfast, he told Jesse, "I told Paul Davenport you'd help him fix his fence where the storm blew down those trees last Tuesday."

Jesse just nodded and agreed. It didn't seem to bother Jesse at all, but Lorri was furious. She didn't say anything and wondered if she was just being overly sensitive where Amos was concerned. However, it seemed Amos had Jesse doing something every Saturday.

Several months later, Jesse was helping Tom Wilson clear his field of sprouts so he could plant corn for his cattle. They had worked tirelessly all day, and it was nearly dark before they were finished. Tom stood and admired the day's work. Jesse and Frank made a good team. This kind of work had always been rewarding to Jesse because he could see the results of his labor when he finished, but he was startled when Tom said, "Jesse, thank you. We couldn't have done it without you. I've already paid Amos. Let's go home and get some supper."

Jesse couldn't believe his ears. It was a good thing it was a five-mile drive home. The entire time he had flashbacks to when he was a teenager and Mr. O'Neal wanted to pay him for the mule but not for his labor when he finished plowing. It was clear his daddy thought he was still just a kid in his house. He was madder than hell, but he wasn't sure what to do. That night when he and Lorri climbed into bed, he shared his secret that his daddy was hiring him out. The news was almost too much for Lorri to process. Her first instinct was to tell Jesse how she had felt about Amos over the past few months; however, she knew that wouldn't accomplish anything. She just squeezed his hand and said, "I think it's about time we find our own place, don't you?"

He whispered back, "I wish we could."

"I think we can," she confided. "I've been putting aside money just for that. We've got enough for a down payment."

He sat up in the bed. "You're amazing."

Excited, she asked, "Then you'll go to the bank next week and buy the Godfrey farm?"

"Yes, I promise." He pulled her toward him. "I'm wide awake now."

She teased him back, "Well, what should we do to kill the time?"

Lorri could see the joy on Jesse's face when he came in from work Tuesday afternoon. She could hardly wait to get him alone, and as soon as she could close the bedroom door behind them later that night she whispered, "Well, tell me what you found out."

He folded his arms and looked at her, thinking that she was acting like the Lorri he'd fallen in love with in high school. The longer he delayed, the more she fidgety she became until she finally just punched him in his chest and demanded, "Tell me!"

"The bank is more than happy to sell it to us, but there's a problem. The land has a grocery store on Highway 5 included in the parcel. I'm just not sure what we can do with that."

She cocked her head to the side and logically asked, "Who's there now?"

It was an obvious question, but he didn't have an answer. "I don't know, but somebody is running the store, because I drove by there on the way home."

"Maybe he'll want to buy it from us. What do you think?"

"It wouldn't hurt to ask him. I'll go by and see him tomorrow if you're sure you still want to do this."

"Absolutely. I haven't been so sure about anything since the day I agreed to marry you. Does it have a house on it?"

"Not sure, but I saw a couple of buildings. I don't know if any of them are livable."

She squeezed his hand and suggested, "Well, we'll just have to check it out on Saturday."

After work, Jesse stopped by the store and asked for a dollar's worth of gas. An older gentleman put in the gas for him as Jesse asked, "Are you the owner?"

"I'm not the owner, but I run the place with my wife. Why do you ask?"

"I'm Jesse Barkley, and I was thinking about buying the Godfrey place. I understand this store is part of the package."

"Well, my name is Billy Darby, and that's right, son. I just rent the place from the bank. Come on in and have a Coke on me."

Mrs. Darby was behind the counter as they entered. Billy opened the cooler and handed the drink to Jesse as he said, "Cathy, Mr. Barkley here is thinking about buying the place."

Jesse stuck out his hand and said, "Just call me Jesse. I want the farm, but I don't want the store."

Darby laughed. "We want the store, but we don't want the farm."

Cathy just shook her head and laughed at how silly men could be sometimes. "Sounds to me like you don't have a problem, you have a solution."

Her remark caught them completely off guard. Billy questioned, "Cathy, what do you mean?"

"Jesse, you buy the farm and then sell the store to us."

Jesse said in relief, "What a great idea."

Billy was pleased. "That would work. I told the bank I wanted the store and a couple of acres for a garden, but they didn't think they'd be able to sell the farm without the store. I'll pay you what I agreed to pay them, if that's OK." He wrote the amount on a piece of paper and handed it to Jesse. "Take this and tell me what you think. I hope we can become neighbors."

Jesse didn't look at the paper as he stuck it in his pocket and promised, "I'll talk to my wife and let you know what we decide."

Later that evening, he pulled out the paper and read the amount to Lorri. She did some quick math and said, "What he wants to pay for the store is three-quarters of the total cost. That way we could pay for it in a couple of years. Let's do it before he changes his mind!"

He leaned back against the headboard of the bed and smiled. Lorri asked, "What are you thinking?"

"I haven't felt this good since I bought that single shot .22 rifle from Mr. Collins a couple of years before I met you."

She just grinned right back at him and said, "The good old days, huh?"

"You said it; I didn't."

Breakfast on Saturday began normally, until Amos told Jesse he needed him to go help Mr. Barnes with his fence. Jesse set his cup down and said, "Can't do it today, Daddy."

Amos bristled with anger. "How come? I've already told him you'd do it."

For the first time since leaving the army, Jesse felt like he was in charge of his life again. He took a deep breath and said, "Lorri and I bought the old Godfrey farm and have plans to go check it out today."

Amos was furious. "Why in the hell would you do something so stupid?"

Even as a kid, Jesse had always stood up for himself, and he didn't hesitate as he defiantly snapped back, "Because I'm married now with a family, and it's time I started taking care of them like a man should."

His younger son had never been as malleable as Michael, so Amos changed his approach. "Well, then, what am I supposed to do about Barnes?"

"You made the promise, so go help him yourself," he said as he stood. "Momma, good breakfast as always. Lorri, are you ready to go see our new home?"

Lorri ran to get her sweater and asked if Momma could watch Danny for a while.

Mrs. Barkley had always been secretly proud of the fact that while Jesse never sassed his daddy, he didn't exactly take any stuff off of him either, so she said in satisfaction, "You bet I will. You kids go have some fun."

Amos stomped off into the living room and Mother Barkley said to her son, "I'm really proud of you for buying that place. Don't worry about your daddy; you know how he is. He'll calm down later and regret what he said."

Jesse gave her a big hug. "Thank you, Momma. You're the best. I know how he is, but sometimes he's really hard to live with."

As they headed out, Lorri could see how excited Jesse was as he chattered on about how huge the place was. He turned the truck down a dirt road that ran through a big farm that he knew connected to GA Highway 2, and went right by the home of the Stewart sisters. It was in such poor condition that no one could believe it was maintained by the state. As they traveled west and passed a white house on the left side of the road, Jesse blurted out, "That belongs to the Dills family. Our land starts with those trees." He pointed.

"This road is the northern boundary, and it's seven-tenths of a mile from here to Highway 5. That's more than twelve football fields long."

Lorri teased, "Yeah, sure was a good idea—you had to buy it. I can't believe you're so smart."

His face turned red. "Help me look for an opening we can drive on."

After about fifty yards, Lorri pointed and said, "Look, in that old field— it looks like there're five apple trees."

Jesse glanced over and said, "That's an old home place. See the chimney? I bet it was one of the first houses built on this property. You know, it might even be the original Godfrey home."

Lorri looked over at him, quivering with excitement. "I already love our farm."

"Me too—now let's find a road."

They couldn't find one, and after a quarter of a mile they were in front of the Stewart home. Lorri laughed. "Doesn't look like much of a farm. It's all woods."

A hundred yards later, Jesse passed a small stream and pointed toward an open field. "That used to be a meadow. When we clean it up, it will be again."

Lorri craned her neck. "Oh, Jesse, look at that gorgeous apple tree right in the middle."

"There's another one on the stream bank. Bet if we pruned them, they'd produce a good crop for us. If you look up the hollow, you can see the old house. Frustrated, he complained, "There's got to be a way to get back there to it. Let's keep looking."

After another quarter mile, they arrived at Highway 5 next to the grocery store. Jesse turned left on the pavement and slowly drove about two hundred yards. Lorri leaned forward, pointing eagerly. "There's a road going down that hill."

He turned down the dirt pathway, followed it straight for about two hundred yards, and then turned to the left into a small pine thicket, where the road abruptly stopped. He turned off the engine as he looked around and said, "I guess we walk from here."

She looked around and frowned. "I can't see the house. Where is it?"

He nodded to the southeast and said, "Across that little hill."

Once they approached the house, Lorri turned and looked in all directions. "Are you telling me there's no road to this place?"

"I can see a faint trail going down the hollow through the meadow, but I guess because no one has lived here in a while it's all grown up, just like the meadow."

Then they looked at the house, which was facing west on the slope of a hill. It was about forty feet wide, and the rear was two feet off the ground.

Because of the slope of the land, the front porch was about ten feet above ground. The steps were on the right side of the porch, and Jesse decided to try them first. He sighed with relief when he reached the top and held out his hand for Lorri. "They're in good shape. That top hand rail needs to be replaced, but I can do that."

The front door was padlocked, so he looked around for a tool to use to break it open; he hadn't been given a key from the bank. He checked behind the house and under the floor and found a four-foot steel bar, which he put between the hasp and the door and broke loose the lock. He opened the door and looked inside and then had an idea. "Come, Lorri, and look."

When she got next to him she cautiously bent around him and looked into the big, open room. Without saying anything, he reached around and picked her up in his arms. "I can't let you walk into our first home; I'm supposed to carry you across the threshold."

She kissed him on the cheek and said, "My prince charming."

He carried her inside and turned slowly so they could take in their surroundings. There was one large room, which would serve as a living and dining room. There was a kitchen area and two small bedrooms. The studs were exposed, and you could see several cracks in the sheeting on the outside. His first thought was how hard it was going to be to keep them warm during the winter. The previous owners had left a wood heater in the right corner of the big room, and there was a wood stove and small table in the kitchen. One bedroom had a bed frame with a corn shuck mattress. Lorri pushed down on it with both hands and grimaced when it rustled and crackled. "I don't think this is going to work. As much as you toss and turn, you'll wake Danny up."

He grinned devilishly. "That's true. Just think how much noise we'd make trying to give him a sister."

She came right back at him, "You think he needs a sister?"

The one thing he'd learned from being married to Lorri was to quit digging when he found himself in a hole, so he asked, "I wonder where the outhouse is?"

She loved how quickly he could change the subject. "While you check that, I'll look at the stove."

He figured the best location for the outhouse would be downwind, so he headed south, and about fifty feet away, next to the wood line, was the building he was seeking. He grabbed the rope opener and cautiously pulled. He had a flashback to his childhood, when opening the door too quickly meant being stung by a wasp or hornet. The tall weeds around the building and lack of any type of odor told him no human had been anywhere around to disturb the insects. He could see it was a two-holer, and in the top left corner he found a wasp's nest. It was about eight inches across and covered with wasps, their wings spread preparing for attack. There was a larger one in the right-hand corner. He continued to look around, and in the corner next to the door hinges he saw what he had been dreading the most: a black hornet's nest. It was the size of a basketball. Usually he'd just burn it, but due to the size and location that wouldn't work. Any fire large enough to do the job would also take out the outhouse. He already had too much work to do without having to build a new one. He thought for a moment and then realized that a nest's biggest enemy was a raccoon. Due to the nest's location, the coons hadn't been able to get to it. He went back to the house, grabbed two planks, and carried them to the outhouse. He stuck the boards inside and leaned them against the wall just below the nest. He propped the door open with a stick and smiled in satisfaction. The boards would give the raccoons easy access. Then he used a long stick and knocked down the two wasp's nests. In a couple of weeks, they would be able to use it for its intended purpose.

He walked back toward the house to share his adventure with Lorri and noticed a wisp of smoke coming from the kitchen chimney. She greeted him with a smile. "The stove is OK. With a little stove black, it'll be just like new. Where do we get the water?"

"I didn't see a well, so I bet they got water from that little stream. I'll check it out." He wandered that way, and just inside the woods he could see a well-used path to the stream. He followed it and discovered where it came out of the ground. The previous owner had dug out a hole and lined it with rocks. It was a couple feet deep but filled with leaves from years of neglect. He returned to tell Lorri, and when the stove burned down they walked to the truck. Instead of getting in, he walked to the edge of the pines and said, "Lorri, this is the place we're going to build our house. See the power lines on Highway 5? We'll only need to buy one light pole to get our electricity. I'll dig a well first to make sure we have water. What do you want our home to look like?"

From their location, they could see the Darbys' grocery store. About one hundred yards behind the store was a pretty white house. She pointed to it and said, "I want it to look just like that one."

He just chuckled; his bride didn't have any trouble making a decision. "Well, that's settled; I'm hungry. Let's go eat."

# CHAPTER 9

Martha rushed Michael to get ready for church Sunday morning. "I need to get there early, so let's go."

She'd taken him the day before for his scheduled doctor's appointment. It was supposed to be a simple visit, and she thought they'd just adjust the brace on his leg. He'd been stricken with polio at age three, and they had the routine down after all these years. When they had arrived they'd been greeted by the new doctor now treating him. Dr. Johnson was much younger than Dr. Hyde and had an easy way that had immediately put Michael at ease. He greeted him with, "Hello, Mr. Michael, how are you today?"

Shyly, Michael had whispered, "Fine."

"Well, that's good. Hop up here and let me have a look at that leg."

The doctor had unbuckled the brace and let it drop to the floor. He began at the ankle and slowly moved up the leg, squeezing the muscles as he went.

"Mr. Michael, I think it's time you threw this old brace away. What do you think about that?"

Martha saw the gleam in her son's eyes as hers had filled with tears and cautiously asked, "Doctor, are you sure?"

He lifted Michael off the table and kneeled down to his level and coaxed, "Michael, how about walking to the door and back?"

He did as instructed; he had a slight limp, but he was walking. Martha exclaimed, "He's walking! How can that be?"

"The brace helped him at first to walk, but he's reached the point that it's now preventing the muscles from gaining strength. It'll take a while, but the more he walks on it, the stronger it'll get. The best thing you can do is not baby him."

Michael heard that and quickly protested, "I'm not a baby. I'm a little man; just ask my Mamaw."

Dr. Johnson smiled. "We men know that, but you may have to keep reminding your momma. She might forget." Then he turned and whispered to Martha, "He will go through some pain in the next month or so, but if you don't let him, he'll be using that brace for the rest of his life."

She thought about it all night long and decided she wanted them to get to church first so Michael could greet her parents as they arrived. Mike parked next to the one oak tree in front of Barnes Chapel Church. As he started to get out, she stopped him and said, "Wait a minute, not yet."

Clueless as usual, he asked, "Why?"

"Just wait," she snapped. Five or ten minutes later, her parents drove up and parked near the front door. "OK, we can go now."

It quickly became clear to Mike what all the fuss had been about. Obviously, she wanted to surprise her parents when they saw Michael walking unaided. He got out and stood at the front of his car and proudly watched as his son limped toward the Burkes.

"Grandma, look! I don't need that old brace anymore," Michael proudly announced.

She ran and grabbed him up in her arms. He immediately squirmed, trying to escape her tight grasp. "No, Grandma, let me down. I can walk."

She turned him loose. "Yes, you can."

They all moved into the church and took their customary pew. When the minister told everyone to turn to page 142 in the hymnal, the loudest voice in the church that morning was Sam Burke.

Afterward, Mike drove straight to his momma's for the regular Sunday dinner. He couldn't wait to surprise her. They were all waiting, and Mike figured Amos would be fussing to eat, but his daddy knew better than to break the cardinal rule of the house—no one ate until everyone was seated.

Mike parked the car and let Michael crawl out first. He reached out his arm and stopped his son's progress, yelling, "Momma! Come out on the porch."

She opened the door. "What's wrong?"

Michael proudly exclaimed, "Look, Mamaw, I can walk."

As he slowly limped his way across the uneven ground toward her, she called out, "Well, look at that. My little man is walking."

His face lit up. He loved it that his mamaw understood he wasn't a baby. Jesse and Lorri stuck their heads outside to see what all the fuss was about, and when Michael saw them he broke out in a peal of laughter and shouted, "Uncle Jesse, I can be a soldier now!"

His son's comment reminded Mike about the letter he had in his truck. It was lucky he worked at the post office, or it never would have found its way to Jesse. It was simply addressed *SFC Jesse Barkley, Blue Ridge, Georgia.* The return address was *SFC Francis O'Shea.* Since Jesse was occupied playing with his nephew, Mike just stuck it in his shirt pocket to pass along later.

When they entered the house, Jesse said to Michael, "Well, kid, you and me get the bench to ourselves today."

Michael slid down to give Jesse room. He'd never felt so special. Mother Barkley filled Michael's plate first and slapped Jesse's hand as he reached across the table for the fried chicken. Mike couldn't hold back and gave out one of his belly laughs, and everyone joined in. Mother Barkley flushed with embarrassment when she realized they were really laughing at her. To Amos it was just another dinner with the kids playing, and he demanded, "You kids cut out all this nonsense. Let's eat!"

Jesse asked, "Daddy, what do you think about Michael walking?"

He looked over at his grandson and said, "I told everybody when he got that polio he'd be walking again. Now Martha, didn't I tell you that?"

She smiled. "You sure did." She picked up his plate and filled it with food for him as everyone watched in awe at her generosity. For the next few minutes, the only sound was that of forks hitting the plates.

Finally, Momma said, "Jesse, tell your big brother what you and Lorri did."

Mike looked over at Jesse in amusement. "OK, kid, what kind of trouble did you get into now?"

"We bought the old Godfrey farm," Jesse said proudly.

"Did you now? What is it they say, once a farmer always a farmer?" Mike said. "How big is it?"

"About two hundred acres."

"My God, you're not a farmer, you're a land baron. Daddy, did you hear that? Two hundred acres!"

Amos just slid his chair back and grunted. "A waste of money if you ask me." Then he wandered off to listen to his radio.

Jesse ignored him. "Mike, I need you to help me dig a well next Saturday."

"Can't help you there, bud. Remember, I deliver mail on Saturdays, too."

"Hmm, guess I'll have to work with Wesley again. He's my next best choice."

"I don't think he'll be much help either," Mike said. "He fell off a truck a couple of weeks ago and messed his shoulder up. He can't even move his right arm. Why don't you call Mr. Kincaid? He can do that water-witching thing and show you exactly where to dig. For a few dollars a foot, he and his boys will even dig it for you."

Jesse thought for a moment and then asked, "How do I get in touch with him?"

"If it's OK with you, I'll see him on my route this week and set it up for you."

"Well, big brother, guess you're not completely useless. At least you do deliver the mail."

"That reminds me," Mike said as he reached up and pulled the envelope from his shirt pocket, "this is for you, but you need to give this guy your address. Looks like he's overseas. I noticed he has an APO address."

Jesse ripped the envelope open and read:

Hi, Mountain Boy,

You can tell by my APO address I'm back overseas. I want you to know I'm still a damn Yankee because I'm in SOUTH Korea. Would you believe it? I'm now a platoon sergeant. The CO makes us write our family at least once a month. I've got a smartass from New York in my platoon. The other day I dropped him for twenty and when he finished he yelled out, "You can kill us, but you can't eat us." I immediately thought of you. The answer is no, we didn't have a blanket party. Tell Lorri I send my love, and I'll see you later.
O'Shea

Monday morning, Michael asked, "Mother, is it time to go to school yet?"

"Not yet, I'll let you know."

Mike expressed confusion at his son's odd behavior. "I can't believe he's so excited about going to school. He's got an hour before he has to leave."

She just chuckled. "He just can't wait to show Craig Foster he doesn't have a brace anymore."

"Oh, that explains it." The name pushed a button with him, but he knew better than to open his mouth. He'd fallen into that trap way too many times. He had no respect for Craig's father, Bobby Foster, and assumed the apple didn't fall too far from the tree. Martha didn't particularly like Bobby either, but his wife, Amy Jo, was her best friend from childhood. They'd had a few words before about how Michael seemed to look up to Craig and it really concerned Mike. Craig was a couple of years older, and from what he could tell, seemed to be a bad influence. Instead of saying something he might regret, Mike took the easy route this morning. "Honey, I'm going to work. I need to see Mr. Kincaid for Jesse."

He wasn't fooling her for a moment, so she just grinned and replied, "Sure, sure. You be safe out there."

When Jesse got home from work, Lorri met him at the door. "Mike left a note in the mailbox. Mr. Kincaid will meet us at the Darbys' store at nine o'clock on Saturday morning."

He was pleased. "Looks like things are starting to fall into place. Like they taught me in the army, make a plan and then work the plan."

She was glad to see the change in her man. Ever since he'd joined the army, he'd had a mission and had gone from one to the next. When they got back last January, he'd lost that motivation and gone into hibernation. The purchase of the land had woken him up and given him something to work toward.

He asked her, "You want to go with me Saturday?"

She crossed her arms and gave him the look. "What do you think? Have you forgotten who started this adventure?"

"I just figured you'd get really dirty."

She just snorted, "Unlike you, I'm not allergic to soap and water."

When they entered the store, Mr. Darby laughed and said, "Hello, neighbor. This guy says you owe him money."

"Not yet, but I soon will," he replied. He stuck out his hand to the other man and said, "I'm Jesse. Are you Mr. Kincaid?"

"Yeah, I'm Charles, but call me Chuck. Understand you're looking to find water."

"That's it, sir. Lorri and I want to build a house across the road, but we need to be sure we'll have plenty of water before we get started."

"Well, let's stop wasting time. Show me where you want to build."

Jesse grabbed Lorri's hand and said, "Follow us."

They quickly drove to the small pine thicket. When Jesse got out, he pointed to the north side and said, "We're thinking the house should be on the rise of the hill, if we can find a place to dig a well."

Chuck laughed and said, "Guess that's where I come in." He walked to the rear of his truck and pulled out a twig in the shape of a Y. "I cut this thing this morning from my peach tree. Let's see what she does."

He took the branch in both hands, put pressure on the twig, and began to walk slowly across the ground. As he started down the back slope of the little hill, the twig dipped and pointed toward the ground. He walked away a short distance and began again. When he came to the same area, the stick seemed to quiver in his hand. He grunted in satisfaction and asked, "Jesse, how's this spot?"

Jesse looked down and then back toward the site for the house. "It's absolutely perfect. I can put an outside faucet right there," he said, pointing at Chuck's feet. "Mike said you'll dig the well, too."

Chuck handed him a three-by-five-inch card and said, "My son and I charge by the foot. Here are the rates. If you're OK with them, we can get started on Monday."

Jesse looked at the card. The deeper the well, the more it cost. He did some quick math and realized that if they managed to hit water before they were one hundred feet deep, he could swing it.

"How deep do you think the water will be?" he asked.

Chuck looked at him. "It's hard to tell, and I can't promise, but my dowsing stick reacted pretty strongly to this site. I'm guessing we'll hit before sixty feet. Not sure how deep it'll be, but I can promise you there's water."

Jesse stuck out his right hand. "Chuck, looks like you've got the job."

"Great. I'll move my equipment over here this afternoon so we can get started Monday."

Jesse had been so fascinated by Chuck's talents that he hadn't noticed Lorri had left the truck. She was nowhere in sight. He knew exactly where she'd be. He waved goodbye to Chuck and jogged to the poor excuse for a house that would serve as their temporary home.

Lorri had covered the small table with a cloth and moved it into the big room. Jesse looked around, impressed with her creativity. She'd found a couple of wooden crates and used a board to create a two-person bench. She grinned as he entered and asked him, "Ready for our picnic?"

"How in the world did you do all of this?"

"I know you. When you get interested in something, you wouldn't notice a herd of cattle stomping by. I had to make two trips to the truck, and I bet you didn't even know I'd gotten out." His look reinforced her theory. "See, I knew it, Jesse Barkley!"

He changed the subject by asking, "OK, what's in the basket?"

She had him right where she wanted him. "Sit down and I'll show you." She took out a gallon fruit jar filled with sweet tea and poured it into two glasses. Then she asked, "Do you want a tomato or a banana sandwich?"

Jesse grinned impishly. "How about both?" He hadn't realized how hungry he was until he bit into the first sandwich. He almost inhaled it.

Lorri laughed and admonished him, "Slow down or you'll choke." She pointed to the bedroom. "I think it's time we christened this little house. If you choke, that might get in the way."

He pulled her close and whispered, "Why don't we eat later?"

Monday after work, Jesse headed straight for the well site. Chuck was placing something in the back of his truck as Jesse approached. He yelled, "You nearly missed us! We've got to get another bucket. How's that old song go? 'My bucket's got a hole in it and doesn't work anymore'? That's what I get for leaving my tools outside in Copperhill," Chuck complained. "Anything made of iron doesn't seem to last long around that plant. I remember Eric and I were digging a well there and tasted the sulfur every morning. It was really strong where Fighting Town Creek runs into the Toccoa River. The bucket was doing OK until we started hitting rock, and one heavy load was more than that rusty old bottom could take. Eric was lucky because it broke loose before it got above his head."

Eric just grinned as Chuck continued, "We got down about seven feet today and hope to do better tomorrow."

They'd already covered the well, so Jesse just stood and looked at the new pile of dirt. He turned and retrieved an axe from the back of the truck, figuring he may as well get something done while he was here. Looking toward the open field and meadow, he decided on a route to the old house for the driveway. He cut back the sprouts and bushes and threw them to the side. In less than an hour, he'd cleared almost to the little stream on the other side of the meadow. When he came to the point of the ridgeline between the well and the house, he could see a flat area between the hill and the stream. It would be a perfect place for the driveway, but because it was so near water the sprouts were larger and thicker. He worked as if his life depended upon it as he visualized what the path should look like. He was impatient and wanted it done today. When he finally finished the turn-around area beside the house, he realized he was working in the dark. He'd been so focused, night had slipped up on him; it was almost eight o'clock.

When he drove up in the yard, Lorri was sitting on the front step with the porch light on, waiting for him. As soon as he opened the door she began, "Where have you been? I was worried sick something had happened. Don't you ever do that to me again! I had to put up with you being gone and me not knowing where you were when you were in the army, but mister, you don't have that excuse anymore!"

Jesse realized she had been scared. "I'm sorry it's so late. I love you too."

The next day he realized he'd better stop and pick up his woman before he headed to their new home in case he got distracted again. Chuck and Eric were loading their truck when they arrived. Chuck called out, "We had a good day today and nothing broke!"

Jesse could see the pile of dirt was twice as large as it had been the night before. He waved and said, "We'll see you guys tomorrow."

Lorri walked over to the hole and peeked through the crack in the boards covering it. "It's getting deep."

"Chuck said we should have water at about sixty feet. Get in the truck and let's go."

"We're going home?" she complained.

"Just get in the truck."

"You're up to something, aren't you?"

He just grinned and drove behind the pile of dirt down the newly trimmed road to the house. When he turned right, and she could see the path had been cleared all the way to the house, she blushed and said, "You're trying to make me feel guilty for yelling at you last night, aren't you?"

"Is it working?"

She laughed and said, "Darn it, you know it is."

Saturday morning driving to the farm, Lorri reminded him, "Did you ever write O'Shea back? You know he loves you like a brother."

He just mumbled, "I know, I'll do it tonight."

"OK, that's good. You can give it to Mike tomorrow at dinner to mail."

Jesse was uncomfortable. He didn't know how to explain that he just didn't have anything to say to O'Shea. Their lives were totally different now, so he just changed the subject. "You know what would be great today? On Saturdays, Mike and I used to always get an RC and a Moon Pie. Why don't we stop at Darby's before we go over to the house?"

"OK, but I'm not forgetting about your promise to write O'Shea."

Jesse drove in silence the rest of the way; he knew when he'd lost an argument with his woman. He breathed a sigh of relief and stopped next to the gas pump as Lorri jumped out and went into the store. Mr. Darby greeted him and asked if he needed gas.

"Yeah, a dollar's worth. No, make it two. That way I won't need more until next weekend." He laughed. "I bet I spend ten dollars a month on gas now."

Mr. Darby just nodded in agreement. "Everything is getting expensive. I have to charge twelve cents for a loaf of sandwich bread. Can you believe that? What's really bad are state taxes. It's three cents on every dollar." As he put the gas in Jesse's truck, he nodded toward the farm. "I can see Chuck has built up a nice pile of dirt. Is that where your house is going?"

Jesse looked that way and was surprised what a clear view there was. "The house will be about fifty feet closer to this side."

"Nice. How big will it be?"

"Lorri wants it to look like that house behind your store. She loves that long front porch. I can already imagine myself sitting in the swing."

Darby smiled. "It's nice to hear young people dream." He was replacing the hose when a flatbed truck came up and stopped on the opposite side. Recognizing the driver, he called out, "Dooley, what are you up to?"

The driver got out of the truck and said, "Not much. I'm making a delivery of blocks to a guy in Blue Ridge. Will you go ahead and fill it up?"

Darby said, "I might have you a new customer here," as he pointed to Jesse.

Dooley looked him up and down and said, "And who would you be?"

Darby introduced them and pointed over to the pile of dirt at the farm. "Jesse plans on building a house down there. He'll be needing some of your blocks."

Caught off guard, Jesse said, "Yeah, I might need a few."

Dooley warned him, "You'd better make your mind up quick. With this stuff going on in Korea, I can't get any cement mix. It's so bad I might have to find a new line of work. Jesse, got any kids?"

"Yes, sir, one boy. He turns five next month."

"I've got two. A girl seven and a boy four—he's a tough little bugger," he said laughing. "You know something about kids? They want to eat every day. I'm beginning to worry about putting food on the table. I guess that's why my hair's turning gray."

Jesse smiled. "Well, I guess I can help you out some. I'm going to need those blocks. Where do you live?"

He pointed north. "About a mile as the crow flies. My house is the first house on the left past Barnes Chapel Church."

Curious, Jesse asked, "Was that church named after you?"

"Nah, it was named after the family. Not many people would go to a church called Dooley's Chapel." He looked over at the pump as Darby finished filling his tank. "Two dollars and seventy-eight cents? How much are you charging for gas now?"

Darby replied, "Eighteen cents a gallon."

Dooley complained, "If it goes up any more, a poor man won't be able to buy gas and eat!" Dooley paid Darby, who walked back into the store. Then Dooley asked Jesse, "How long have you known Billy?"

"Only a few weeks, why?"

Dooley chuckled. "Well, let me warn you, boy, don't ever bring up politics when you're around him unless you really want to hear everything wrong in this county."

"Thanks for the advice; I'll remember that."

"See that you do, or you'll regret it," Dooley assured him.

Jesse liked the man; he reminded him of O'Shea. Now he had something to say in that letter to his old friend. As Jesse walked back into the store, Lorri handed him an open bottle of RC Cola and pulled out an apple pie from a little brown bag. He complained, "I wanted a Moon Pie."

Lorri said, "OK." She took the pie from him and handed him what he wanted. "I'll eat the apple pie, no problem."

As she took it away, he started to protest, and she laughed and said, "Gotcha." She took another apple pie out of the bag and handed it to him. He loved how she messed with him; it made him love her even more. He gave her a big hug and almost made her drop her pie.

Lorri gave him the look. "Be nice, we're not alone."

When they left, Mrs. Darby looked over at her husband wistfully. "Remember when you used to love me like that?"

He put his arm around her waist and whispered, "Old woman, I couldn't love you any more if I tried."

Jesse stopped the truck next to the thicket and just sat there finishing his drink. Lorri started to open her door but stopped when she realized he was deeply in thought. "What's that brilliant mind of yours up to now?"

"I'm thinking it's time we laid out our new home, don't you agree?"

"What do you mean, 'lay out'?"

"I'll show you," he said. He got out, opened the box in the bed of the truck, and handed her some wooden stakes and string. He pulled out a hammer, a six-foot folding ruler, and some more stakes. "Let's start with the front porch."

After they'd been driving the stakes and pulling the strings for a while, Lorri said, "This reminds me of Jean and Katherine's playhouse."

Surprised, he stood and stared at their work. "It does, doesn't it? Don't think theirs had a bathroom, though. Looks like I'm gonna need to cut some of these pines before we start."

"Yeah, you might be able to leave the one in the living room, but that one in the kitchen has got to go!" she giggled.

"We're going to need some lumber. Guess Mike can tell me where to get it tomorrow."

Lorri reminded him, "Make it the cheapest place. We've got a house payment now."

He scratched his head and said, "That reminds me. I know you'd like to move into the little house so we can be a family again, but I don't think the time's right. It's October already, and I'm not sure I can cut enough firewood to keep us warm all winter. How'd you feel about staying with Momma and Daddy until spring?"

"As much as I hate to admit it, I think you're right. I wasn't looking forward to running out to the outhouse in winter."

He burst out laughing. "Sooo, guess I've been pampering my sweetie with the easy life?"

She poked him in the side. "No, I'm agreeing with you; just don't let it go to your head."

He stood back and stared at his woman. She asked, "What?"

"I'm so glad we came back to Sugar Creek."

Later that evening his daddy met them at the door. "It looks like your hero, General McArthur, is kicking butt over there in Korea. The newsman said the Americans have taken Seoul back from North Korea. The politicians may call this a police action, but McArthur is going at it like it's World War III. Son, I'm glad they're doing it without you."

Caught totally off guard by his daddy's words. Jesse forced a smile. "Me, too, Daddy."

# CHAPTER 10

The new farm was the topic at Sunday's dinner. Everyone was fascinated with the water witching. Even Amos told stories of when no one ever dug a well without first dowsing. He elaborated on how he'd even known people who used dowsing to find gold. Curious, Jesse asked, "Why on earth don't people do that now?"

Amos was happy to share his knowledge. It wasn't very often anyone listened to what he had to say. "Because Roosevelt made it illegal to own gold back in the thirties. Said it would help us get out of the Depression."

Everyone turned and looked at Amos in awe. Mike asked, "How in world did you know that?"

Momma looked at him and smiled. "Daddy, if you don't tell them, I will."

When Amos stayed silent, she continued, "When your daddy was a youngster, he and his buddy, George, came up with a scheme to go to Dahlonega, dig gold, and get rich. Now tell them when your dream ended, Amos."

"Mr. Roosevelt did it on the third of April, 1933."

Mike couldn't help himself; he'd never heard this before. "And how on earth do you remember the exact date?"

Jesse answered, "That's easy. That was his tenth birthday, right, Daddy?"

Amos glared at his wife and said, "Now why in the world did you bring that up?"

"Because I wanted them to know you were telling the truth and not just making stuff up."

Everyone laughed. They could see he was uncomfortable but enjoying the attention. As it got quiet again, Mike turned to Jesse and asked, "OK, little brother, what's next?"

"I need to find some lumber."

Lorri jumped in, "Martha, isn't Amy Jo's husband in the lumber business? Do you think he could help us out? We're on a pretty strict budget."

Mike snorted, "Lorri, you don't want anything to do with that guy. Deal with him and he'll take you for everything you've got."

Defensively, Martha said, "He's not that bad, Mike. Just because you don't like him doesn't mean he can't help."

Mike's opinion of Bob was an ongoing problem for her and made her friendship with Amy Jo awkward at times. Mike took a moment and chose his words carefully. "Sweetie, you know his help always comes at a pretty steep cost. I'm not sure they can afford it. Remember how during the war he helped the merchants in Blue Ridge by loaning them money and then took part ownership of their businesses? Besides, I don't like how he treats Amy Jo."

Martha just bit her lip, and as she opened her mouth to respond, Mike said to Jesse, "Let me ask around; there has to be a better option. I'll ask Bill and Adele Mercier where they got their lumber when they built their new house. I know it wasn't from Foster."

Eager to cut the tension, Jesse asked, "Who's Bill Mercier?"

"You know. He's the county agent who bought that apple orchard on Highway 5 from the druggist in Blue Ridge."

"I know where that orchard is, but I've never heard of him," Jesse said.

Then Mike remembered that all of this had happened while Jesse had been gone in the army. "I guess you're right. They moved up from Jasper in 1943."

Jesse said, "I was only gone for eight years, and I can't believe how much Fannin has changed and how many new people have moved in."

Mike chuckled and assured him, "I'll let you know what I find out."

"That's good. We've got plenty to keep us busy for now. I want to fence in some acres and raise a few cattle and get a couple of horses."

Lorri gasped and gave him the look. This was the first she'd heard of this. Seeing her expression, he quickly tried to recover. "Mike, I just thought of that while you were talking. What do you think?"

From experience, Mike knew his little brother had waded into a pretty deep hole. "You've got the space. Sounds like a good idea to me, but Lorri, what do you think?"

# CHAPTER 11

Martha's favorite radio show came on Wednesday night, and she always rushed Mike and their son through dinner so she could get the dishes done in time. Mike's retelling of this weekly event at the post office was a hilarious source of entertainment. He'd give one of his big belly laughs as he complained, "Lord help us if she doesn't get to listen to *Our Miss Brooks*." Every Thursday morning, the group would gather to hear the latest installment, and his laughter was like a tonic to the workers, because they all knew this was the one show he absolutely hated. It reminded him of his fifth grade teacher, who now happened to be his mother-in-law. Currently they had a fragile truce, but it was tenuous at best and could easily shatter over even the most innocent imagined slight. Every Wednesday, he'd come up with elaborate excuses why he couldn't listen to the program, and today he had a good one. It was important that he and Jesse talk, so he said, "Sweetie, after supper I need to go over to Jesse's. I talked to Bill Mercier and he told me about a man who has a saw mill."

Martha knew this was just the latest of his excuses, but she couldn't care less. She'd enjoy the show a lot better if he wasn't sitting there making his stupid noises and smart comments the whole thirty minutes. She waved him off. "Just make sure you're home by nine o'clock."

"I promise," he said. It was a subtle reminder that *The Whisperers* came on and she wanted him home. She loved the program, but it frightened her. It fascinated him that she actually enjoyed being scared to death. She also loved *The Shadow Knows*. It was a Friday night program, and Mike was hap-

- 61 -

py to reap the rewards because she always snuggled all night afterward. He knew exactly how lucky he was to have found and married his perfect mate.

When he walked into his momma's kitchen, she and Lorri were sitting at the table drinking coffee. He asked, "Where are the guys?"

Lorri pointed with her head to the living room. "Listening to *The Cisco Kid.*"

He walked into the living room calling out, "Oh, Cisco!"

Jesse responded, "Oh, Poncho!"

Irritated, Amos held up his hand letting them know he wanted silence. Mike smiled as he remembered his father's routine warnings—first, came a raised hand; next came, "Boys, be quiet," and there was no third warning, just action. Amos would show them how much a leather belt could hurt. If they were stupid enough to make noise during their daddy's favorite radio show, *The Lone Ranger,* he'd eliminate step two and go straight to the whipping. From experience, Mike chose to wait until the Cisco Kid caught the bad guy before saying anything.

When it went to commercial, and the man on the radio was trying to sell Martha White Self-Rising Flour, Mike motioned for Jesse to follow him and said, "The old man hasn't changed at all." He gave out one of his belly laughs.

Jesse responded, "And neither have you! What did you find out?"

"I saw Bill, but first tell me how the well's coming."

"They ran into solid rock at around twenty-five feet. Chuck said it was solid blue granite and he'd need dynamite to get through it. They've been drilling holes for the last couple of days to break it up into small pieces. He said it would make it easier for them to get it out of there. I think he's going to blast tomorrow, and believe me, I'm glad he's doing it and not me."

"What is it they say?" Mike asked. "If it were easy, everybody would be doing it."

Jesse said, "Yeah, I hear you. So what about that lumber?"

"Bill said a guy from Cherry Log was cutting timber on Pedro Anderson's farm. Do you remember where that is?"

"On the other side of the road from Sugar Creek Grocery?" asked Jesse.

"That's it. The guy who has the sawmill is Kell Weeks. Bill said his younger brother, Taft, bought the farm from Anderson. He and his wife, Mildred, are planning on building a house and moving here from Cartersville."

Perplexed, Jesse shook his head. "I can't believe how many people are moving to the mountains. I remember when we knew everybody within five miles by their first name. I'm feeling like a stranger in my own hometown. Oh well, how do I get in touch with Mr. Weeks?"

"He lives on a farm just south of Cherry Log. Bill said the road to his house is straight across Highway 5 across from Rock Creek Baptist Church. When we get on the road, ask anyone and they'll know where he lives. If you want, I'll go with you Sunday."

Jesse said, "I was thinking about going on Saturday, but it'll be like old times for us to do it together."

Mike grinned. "Great. Who knows, I might even buy some more of your fairy crosses."

"You took advantage of me when I was a kid. I should have charged you double."

Mike was amused at his kid brother. "And the more I think about it, I'd have paid it, too."

Groaning, Jesse said, "Oh, now you tell me. Let's plan on leaving after Sunday dinner."

Jesse and Mike drove to Cherry Log while Martha, Lorri, and the kids went to visit Amy Jo. Jesse updated Mike on how he'd cut down all the sprouts in his future meadow and pruned the large apple tree located in the center. After that, he'd gone over to visit Elfie and Dora. Jesse told him, "Dora really surprised me with everything she knew about apple trees. She said the one in the middle of the meadow is a June apple tree and the one on the stream bed is a wine sap. She said we'd have apples to eat from the June apple tree by the middle of July."

Sarcastic as always, Mike let loose with his deep laugh and quipped, "Then why don't they call it a July apple tree?"

When Mike finally stopped laughing at his own joke, Jesse continued, "Mike, I noticed the sisters only had a small stack of firewood. Do you know how they've been getting their wood since we left for the army?"

"You know, Jesse, I'm ashamed to admit this, but I have no idea and to be honest, I never even thought about it. Boy, do I feel small. I know it's not an excuse, but I work six days a week and am in my own little world."

Jesse shook his head and commiserated. "Me too. What brought it to my attention was Elfie giving me fairy crosses she'd found for me while I was in Europe. She had them separated by the year she found them, and it gave me flashbacks of when we would cut firewood for them by Pleasant Grove Church. What are we going to do about it?"

Mike thought for a minute and said, "I don't know, Jesse. I deliver mail all week and on Saturdays. Elfie and Dora would wring our necks if we cut wood on Sunday. You got any ideas?"

Jesse grinned and suggested, "We could do like we did when you were courting Martha. Cut every afternoon right after work. I know four or five red oaks have blown down on my land. What do you think?"

"I don't know about you, little brother, but a little hard work wouldn't hurt me for a change. Supplying those sweet ladies with wood would be good for my soul."

As they drove through the little community of Cherry Log, Jesse answered, "Good, let's do it next week. Now help me find the road."

"Seems like Bill said we'd cross Rock Creek and take a right on the first road. That looks like the bridge just ahead."

As they turned onto the dirt road, they saw a young man walking toward them. Jesse stopped the truck and rolled down his window. "Sir, can you tell me how to get to Kell Weeks's place?"

The young man replied, "I sure can. That's my daddy—I'm Otis Weeks." He pointed across the pasture. "See that house? That's it."

"Thanks. Is your daddy home?" asked Jesse.

"Yes, sir, sitting on the porch listening to the radio."

When they drove up, Kell didn't even move from his chair. He just hollered, "Can I help you fellows?"

Jesse opened his door. "I sure hope so. I bought a little farm in Fannin County and need some lumber cut. Bill Mercier said you have a mill and do good work."

Kell laughed. "I'm not sure you're talking about the Bill Mercier I know. He didn't sound all that pleased the last time I saw him."

Mike added, "Well, he's singing your praises now. My name is Mike Barkley and this is my brother, Jesse. He just got out of the army and needs a house built by next summer."

"Well you boys come on in and have a cup of coffee. We'll see what kind of trouble we can get into."

After about two hours of tossing around ideas, they finally came up with a plan. They decided it was too close to winter to begin the job now, but as soon as spring came, Kell would move his sawmill to Jesse's farm. He'd cut house pattern for Jesse and then pay him ten dollars per thousand board foot on the stump for the additional lumber he'd cut. He'd use that for cross ties to sell to the railroad. Jesse loved the idea; he could get the lumber he needed with no cost to him and maybe even make a little profit. They shook hands to seal the deal.

On the way home, Jesse kept talking about how nice it was to do business with an honest man. He reminded Mike of Butch O'Neal and how he'd tried to pay Jesse for the mule but wouldn't pay *him* because he was a kid.

Mike laughed. "Daddy told me what you and Wesley did! Once you guys refused to do the work, no one else in the area would do it. You really took the wind out his sails."

Jesse was still mad about it. "Hard to believe that's been almost ten years ago. He's probably still trying to bully people."

Mike agreed. "Bullies do it as long as they can get away with it. The biggest bully around here is Bobby Foster."

"Is that why you hate him so much?" asked Jesse. "I noticed you got a little hot under the collar when Martha brought him up the other day."

"He always sticks his nose where it doesn't belong. Remember I told you Bill Mercier moved up here in 1941 as the county agent? A couple of years later, he and his wife bought that orchard from the local druggist in Blue Ridge. When Foster found out, he went to the druggist and told him to give Bill his money back. He demanded he only sell to local people, not outsiders like the Merciers."

"You're kidding me. What did Bill do?"

"He told him a deal was a deal and if he had to take legal action, he would."

Jesse asked, "What did the druggist do?"

Mike said, "Nothing. He was really happy with the deal, and Bill's threat was all he needed to get Foster off his back."

"Mike, you were right. I really don't want to do business with a bully. But I do think I'd like to get to know Bill."

"He's a big man like you," said Mike.

Jesse just nodded. "Sounds like he's a big man inside and out."

Martha watched Danny and little Michael interact as Lorri drove to Amy Jo's house. She could see Michael was already protective of Danny and treated him like a little brother. She couldn't help but feel regret that she wouldn't be able to give him a little brother of his own. She'd suffered two major losses as a mother; first the death of Betsy, their daughter, and then the news from her doctor that she would never have any more children.

Lorri was surprised at how neat and clean the house appeared when she pulled into the driveway. It wasn't the largest house in the county, but it was situated to maximize its appearance and give the impression of size. It took up a full city block. There was a yard in front and a two-story house at the rear of the lot. A six-foot walkway split the lawn and led to the house with its five grand white columns. It looked more like a plantation than a typical house in the mountains. She whispered to Martha, "Boy, it looks like Bobby has really cleaned the place up. He must spend a lot of time in this yard."

Martha looked around and agreed, "Yeah, the grass and hedges look like they've been manicured. It's hard to believe he'd have worked this hard on anything, though. He likes sitting behind that big desk of his too much."

"Well, you can't argue with success. It looks great. Let's go see your friend."

When Amy saw who was at the door, she immediately hugged Lorri. "My goodness, how long has it been?"

"Years," said Lorri, and when she noticed little Margaret, she said, "My, how she has grown."

Margaret ran straight to the boys, grabbed Danny's hand, and led him into the living room just like a little mother. Lorri asked, "How old is she now?"

Amy answered, "Would you believe she's seven?"

Indignantly, Margaret said, "No, Mommy! I'm seven and a half."

Lorri went over, snatched her up, and gave her a big hug and kiss. "And you're a big girl to only be seven and a half."

Margaret nodded in approval, and a new friendship was born. Lorri stepped back and noticed a band aid on Margaret's arm. She kneeled and said, "Oh, you have a boo-boo."

"Yeah, but mine's not as big as mommy's."

Curious, Lorri moved her eyes to Amy, and Martha quickly intervened to save her friend the embarrassment of having to explain. "Boy, Bobby sure does have this yard looking good."

Amy rolled her eyes. "Yeah, he's got three guys who do all the work and he just tells them what to do—his favorite pastime. I wanted him to put out some plants, but he insists it looks more impressive with just a manicured lawn across the front of the house. Martha, did you bring any of your world famous sugar cookies?"

Martha just smiled. "What do you think? Is the coffee hot?"

The girls settled in for a long-overdue visit. Mike and Jesse made a simple plan for their upcoming week. Mike would meet Jesse at their daddy's house to pick up the saw and axes, and they would convoy over to the farm to start cutting firewood for the sisters. As they drove up at the same time and exited their vehicles, Mike laughed and said, "We couldn't have timed this better if we'd tried."

Jesse impatiently answered, "Let's get the tools and get started. It gets dark earlier now."

They walked side by side to the shed like they'd done hundreds of times as teenagers. When they opened the door, they could see the tools were still exactly where Wesley and Jesse had placed them just before leaving for the war. They glanced at each other in dismay at their condition.

Disgusted, Jesse said, "Looks like no one has touched them since I left."

Mike gave out one of his laughs. "You sure didn't think Daddy would be using them, did you?"

Jesse laughed, too. "I'm guessing this door hasn't even been opened since I left."

"You'd lose that bet. When I was fixing my house after I came home from the war, Daddy, Paul, and I came in here to get buckets so Daddy could teach us how to make whitewash out of lime. That's all I could get to paint the house with. Before you say anything, Martha has already told me we need to repaint it. I plan to redo it this summer with real paint this time."

"Isn't it funny how wives always find some kind of fix-it-up project just to keep us busy?" Jesse complained.

Mike was eager to share his theory on the subject: "I actually think there's some kind of secret school that teaches them how to do that, and we men just stumble through it."

"When did you become a philosopher?"

"You'd be surprised what you see and learn on a mail route," Mike responded. "Jesse, why don't you go get some kerosene and rags to clean the rust off the crosscut and I'll start sharpening the axes?"

"I guess getting them ready is all we'll get done today," Jesse grumbled.

Mike said, "Remember, papaw always said you never waste time sharpening your tools."

"At least we won't have Daddy supervising us. Thank God he's on the evening shift these days," Jesse said as he got started.

Tuesday evening, they met at Darby's to save time. Jesse had identified five red oaks that had been blown down next to the meadow earlier in the spring. They worked like beavers and cleared away the limbs and brush until they could comfortably begin working with the crosscut saw. They soon fell into the old rhythm they'd developed after years of practice. The saw seemed to pass through the twenty-inch log like a knife through butter.

Jesse looked at the blocks and could visualize perfect logs for splitting. They'd each split into six equal sticks of firewood. He smiled at the thought. "I didn't realize how much I'd missed just being a farm boy. You know we had a perfect life and didn't even know it."

Mike contemplated this for a moment. "It's like Momma says, 'You never know just how good things are until you lose them.'"

They got back to work and soon started on their second tree. After a few minutes, Jesse noticed a change in Mike's rhythm. It reminded him of when he used to saw with his daddy, so he knew Mike was riding the saw, just like Amos did. He'd begun to put more weight on the saw, hoping it would cut faster. Mike probably didn't even realize he was doing it, but Jesse knew it meant Mike was beginning to tire. Obviously, the easy life of delivering mail hadn't prepared him for physical labor. He'd always thought Mike was invincible, and it surprised him to see he wasn't perfect after all. When he was a teenager, he'd have told Mike to stop riding the saw, but now he realized it would just hurt Mike's feelings. Their daddy had done that to them way too many times in their lives, and he refused to fall into that trap.

When they finished cutting the log, Jesse suggested, "Let's split some of these blocks so we can see how much we've gotten done."

Tired and out of breath, Mike jumped at the idea. In order to hide it from Jesse, he pointed up the valley and said, "Look at all those dead chestnut trees. There must be more than a dozen of them. Look how they stand out. They look like twenty-foot light gray toothpicks. They're about ten inches in diameter, but they don't have any branches or limbs. It's a shame that blight that came through and killed them all."

Jesse asked, "How long do you think they've been dead?'

"From looking at them, some of them were dead before you were born. We should cut a couple of the bigger ones for kindling for the sisters. That should last them all winter."

Jesse laughed. "Start splitting those blocks. Let's get one project finished before we start another one."

Neither of them said it, but they were glad when darkness fell.

Wednesday afternoon, Chuck was waiting for Jesse next to the well. "We finally got the rocks cleaned. Most of the time we were bailing out water. It's down to twenty-seven feet, and the bottom six is water. This has to be the best well we've ever dug. When we dynamited that rock, it was like we tapped into the river. I don't think you'll ever have a water problem."

Mike drove up and asked, "How deep is it?"

Jesse answered "Twenty-seven feet with six feet of water."

"Only twenty-seven feet, huh? I've got a good water pump I couldn't use on my well because it was too deep. I'll bring it over tomorrow, but you'll need electricity before you can use it."

"Leave it to you to give me something that means more work."

He gave a big belly laugh and reminded Jesse, "That's what big brothers are for."

Jesse snorted. "Let's go cut some more wood."

Chuck asked, "Are you selling wood? I sure could use a couple of cords if you are."

"Nah, we're just cutting some for a friend," Jesse said. "I'm sorry, but we'll be using all we cut this year. Let's go, Mike, we're burning daylight."

By Thursday evening, all five of the oak trees were cut into blocks, and they'd split most of them. Friday, they cut two of the dead chestnuts and split the blocks into kindling until dark. Jesse planned to deliver the firewood on Saturday to the sisters around 2:00 p.m., which was about the time Mike usually delivered their mail.

The plan worked out great, and just as Mike was about to put the mail into their box on Saturday, Dora, Elfie, and Jesse walked out to greet him. He handed Dora two letters, and she handed him a glass of sweet tea and a fried apple pie. "Here's your payment for the wood. Jesse's already eaten his," Dora said.

Mike said, "I bet he wanted to eat mine, too, didn't he?"

Elfie laughed. "You really do know him, don't you?"

Jesse was indignant. "I only ate two pies." He knew the sisters loved making a fuss over them, and he enjoyed the time spent with them. He'd told a lot of his secrets to these old women when he was young.

Dora smiled and said, "Thank you, boys. It feels like old times." That keyed a memory and she asked, "Did you hear Frank Wilson came home after all these years?"

Mike smiled, "I see him about every week on the route. He's gaining some of his weight back. When he first got home, he looked like death warmed over."

Dora just sighed, "Thank God Opal's prayers were answered."

# CHAPTER 12

It was nearly dark on the first Friday of November when an old army jeep pulled up into the Barkleys' front yard. Jesse recognized the vehicle, so he went out to greet his guest. The man got out of the jeep and yelled, "Sarge! Get your lazy butt out here and let's go coon hunting."

Nick had been promising to take Jesse hunting ever since he'd gone to work at the Tennessee Copper Company. Once Jesse had worn an old fatigue shirt to work with the imprint of sergeant stripes on the sleeve, Nick had been calling him Sarge ever since. The other workers warned Jesse to steer clear of him, saying Nick was a strange duck. But from the first day Jesse worked with him on a project, they'd just clicked, and eventually they became good friends. Nick was always coming up with ideas that would allow him to spend time with his only friend, and coon hunting was the latest.

Jesse started down the steps, rehearsing all the reasons why he couldn't go, but Nick headed him off with, "Have you already eaten supper?"

Jesse just chuckled. "Yeah, an hour ago. You want something to eat?"

"Just making sure you didn't have something else you had to be doing."

Jesse just shrugged. "OK, let me put on some hunting clothes."

"Sarge, you better put on some long johns too, it's getting down to freezing tonight."

"Nick, do you have any good news?" Jesse teased.

He boasted, "I've got three of the best blue-tick hounds in the county. They find something every single time we go out."

Jesse got into the jeep, fascinated by how creative Nick was. With half-inch plywood and two-by-fours, he'd made a watertight cab that covered the entire jeep. He'd removed the backseat to make a space to haul around his dogs. On the ride to Higdon's Store, the noise and rough bouncing gave Jesse flashbacks to his army days.

The dirt road was so bumpy that conversation was out of the question. After a short ride, they turned left onto a little dirt road that led to Cashes Valley. When the road began to lead up into the mountains, they forded small streams across the road. After the fifth stream, something ran across the road ahead of them. Nick stopped the jeep and yelled, "There goes one! Let the dogs out."

As soon as Jesse opened the doors, the three howling dogs picked up the trail. Jesse and Nick got out of the jeep when it sounded like the dogs had the animal treed, but instead of barking up the tree as usual, they began to whimper and whine like they were being beaten. When the first dog got back to the jeep with his tail between his legs, it was obvious what had happened. "Oh, my God. They caught a skunk."

Jesse gagged and held his nose. "You've got that wrong. Smells like the skunk caught them. Still believe they're the best dogs in the county?"

Nick just grinned. "Maybe not the best. Do you think they'll follow us home?"

"They're your dogs. What do you think?"

"No such luck. They've got to ride inside with us."

The three hounds came back to the car, and Jesse had to laugh—they looked like naughty kids. They didn't hesitate as Nick said, "Load up."

The bad thing about that waterproof cab was that it was airtight, too. Anyone who's been near a skunk when it's defending itself remembers how the odor takes your breath away. About halfway home, Jesse insisted, "Stop this thing. I have to get out and get some fresh air."

Nick got out laughing. "Sarge, you have to admit it was funny."

Jesse shot him a glare and then grinned. "I'm not sure you know what funny is, Nick."

"Now Sarge, didn't you ever have something go wrong in the army?"

"Nothing that stunk like this."

They got back in the jeep and Nick drove as fast as he could to get them home. As he drove away, Jesse realized there was no way he could go inside his momma's clean house smelling like a skunk. He vaguely remembered an old mountain tale that tomato juice would take away the smell. He went to the root cellar and got two jars of canned tomatoes. He stripped and hung his clothes on the line, and then he poured the tomatoes on his hair and worked it in. He continued to use the tomatoes down his face and shoulders, and then rinsed with the garden hose. He continued this process as long as he could stand it and finally went into the house and took a hot bath. It was well after midnight before he finally got to bed.

At breakfast the next morning, Danny turned up his nose and whispered to his grandfather, "Papaw, Daddy stinks!"

Everyone at the table recognized the smell and burst out laughing. Jesse just sat there with a guilty look and crimson face.

Later, Jesse and Lorri were removing stumps from their future home site when Nick drove up. Jesse ducked his head and snickered as he looked over and saw that Nick had removed the two doors.

Nick jumped out and yelled, "Thought you were cutting fence posts today."

Jesse rested his arms on the top of his shovel and replied, "I am, but I had to get rid of these two stumps first. Nick, this is my wife, Lorri. She's heard me talk about you enough; it's nice she finally gets to meet you."

Sticking out his hand and bowing slightly, Nick said, "Nice to meet you, Mrs. Barkley."

Lorri smiled. She recognized his accent but couldn't place it. Nick turned and picked up the mattock and started digging around the base of the stump Jesse was working on. She watched him work, and it became clear they were a good team. When Nick would stop digging, Jesse would begin to shovel, and they continued this process without saying a word. The stump fell over and Nick leaned his tool against the side of the hole. They both sat down to take a break, and Lorri said, "Nick, you're not from around here are you?"

"What gave me away, my good looks or my southern charm?" he teased.

She came right back at him: "No, maybe it's because you hunt skunks."

He blushed and mumbled, "Tillman's Corner, Alabama, ma'am."

Then she realized his accent was the same as the local people she'd met at Fort Benning. "It must be a small place, 'cause I've never heard of it. How in the world did you end up here?"

"An old army buddy told me about it, and after the way he described it, I had to see it for myself."

"Who is he? We might know him," she replied.

"Doubt it, he was killed two months before the war ended."

"Well you know, Blue Ridge is a small town. We probably would at least know his family," she persisted.

He smiled. "That's just what Troy used to say. We would argue about who came from the smallest town. The best story Troy he ever told me was his town was so small both city limit signs were back-to-back on the same pole in front of the post office. I had to see that for myself. You know, when I went to Turtle Town, I realized all his stories were true."

"How did he die?" Lorri asked.

He paused as tears welled in his eyes, "Saving my worthless butt, ma'am. I got hit and he pulled me right out of the path of a Nazi tank. They shot him dead just as he got me behind cover."

"I'm sorry about your friend. What was his last name?"

"Troy Bearden, but I haven't been able to find any of his kin," Nick answered.

The tension was so thick, she asked, "Did he know where your town was? What's close to it?"

He smiled and returned to telling his story. "You go as far south in Alabama as you can, and then you find yourself Tillman's Corner. We're so far out in the country we don't even have a post office."

She thought about it for a minute and then smiled. "Tillman's Corner?" Then she teased, "Must be a grocery store, like our Higdon's Store. You know, that place where you and Jesse go skunk hunting?"

"Sarge, you married a woman too smart for me or you. Let's go cut some fence posts."

Jesse was in awe of the conversation. Lorri had gotten more out of Nick in ten minutes than anyone at the company had gotten from him the entire time he'd been there. No one had even realized he was old enough to have been in the army during the war.

Sunday, when Mike's family arrived for dinner, little Michael scrunched up his nose and asked, "What stinks?"

Mike placed a hand on his shoulder and laughed. "That, my little buddy, is a skunk. Somebody must have scared one. That smell is how they defend themselves."

Martha just looked around trying not to gag Yeah, but where's it coming from?"

"By the way the wind is blowing, it must be from Momma's clothesline."

Little Michael ran into the house, eager to share what he'd learned. "Mamaw, somebody scared a skunk and it sure does stink!"

Mother Barkley just laughed. "It sure does. You can blame your Uncle Jesse for that smell. Why don't you give him a talking to and tell him he shouldn't play with skunks?"

He ran into the living room where Jesse and Amos were listening to the radio, put his hands on his little hips, and glared at his uncle. "Uncle Jesse, Mamaw says you shouldn't be playing with skunks! You'd better stop or you'll get a whipping!" He lowered his voice to a whisper, "They really hurt."

"Trust me, little man, I don't plan on ever getting close to another one. What have you been up to?"

He stood a little taller. "I've been collecting money for the March of Dimes so they can stop that old polio."

Jesse put his hand in his pocket and pulled out two quarters and a half dollar. "Will this help?"

Michael grinned and grabbed it up faster than a blink of an eye. "That's just great, Uncle Jesse. That's the most I've ever gotten from one person."

"How much do you have?"

Michael had been hoping someone would ask. He thought for a minute and then proudly stated, "With your dollar, Uncle Jesse that makes eight whole dollars and seventy-five cents."

Amos was listening. He unbuttoned the top of his overalls and pulled out his change purse. He pulled out one quarter and two half dollars and extended them to Michael. "Son that should get you to ten dollars."

Michael hugged Amos. "Thank you, Papaw."

Pretending to be offended, Jesse grabbed him. "And where's my hug?"

Michael struggled to escape. "Men don't hug, Uncle Jesse."

"Oh yeah, I forgot about that."

Sunday dinner was painful for Jesse, as everyone had a joke about a skunk. He was relieved when Michael and Danny went outside to play and the conversation turned to the March of Dimes drive. Martha bragged, "Would you believe he's collected more than anyone else in his class? I didn't know a child could have so much determination."

Mother Barkley asked, "Aren't there other kids in the class who had polio, too?"

"Yes, but I think the difference is they're still wearing their braces."

Amos interjected, "I bet Michael feels a little guilty that he's well."

Jesse glared at him. "Now Daddy, a nine-year old kid doesn't think like that."

"Your Daddy could be right," said Mother Barley. "He might not even know he feels guilty; he just knows it makes him feel better to help someone else."

Lorri had been listening quietly. "Martha, Mike, you should be so proud of him."

Martha got up and looked out the window at Michael playing. "You wouldn't believe how full my heart is."

Thursday after work, Mike walked in and immediately noticed his wife was upset. She handed him his usual glass of sweet tea, and he sat it down, turned to her, and asked, "OK, what's wrong? Did someone die or is someone sick?"

"No, nothing like that. I saw Miss Anderson today and she told me was disappointed in Michael that he didn't collect any money for the March of Dimes. She said he was so excited when he'd heard about it, but he was the only one in the class who didn't turn in any money. Mike, what did he do with that ten dollars? You don't think he kept it, do you?"

"Did you ask him?"

"No, I thought I'd wait until you got here." She went ahead and set the table for supper. She'd made all of Michael's favorites; creamed corn, pan-fried potatoes, cornbread, and peach cobbler. Once he'd almost cleaned his plate she quietly confronted her son, "I saw your teacher today, and she told me she was surprised you didn't collect any money for the March of Dimes. What happened to that ten dollars?"

Between bites of his cobbler, he said, "Craig said somebody might take it, so he took my money and Margaret's so we wouldn't lose it. He said he'd give it to the teacher for us. Did I do something wrong?"

She and Mike were speechless, and she finally said, "As long as the March of Dimes gets the money, I guess that's what's important." She and Mike exchanged looks and then she wisely changed the subject. "You want some more cobbler, son?"

"Yes, please."

Later that evening, Mike whispered to Martha, "Why don't you walk Michael to school and have the teacher check on Craig Foster?"

Mike had fumed over the situation all day and could hardly wait to get home and hear what Martha had found out. Walking through the door, he asked, "Well, what did he do?"

"Hello there. I love you, too," she teased.

"Sorry sweetie, I love you more. But I just couldn't wait to hear what that little red-haired hellion has been up to this time."

"He did turn the money in, but he took credit for all of it. So it looked like he collected eighteen dollars, which was the most for the fifth grade."

Mike's face flushed with temper. "Well, ten dollars of that was Michael's!"

She cautioned, "Don't you dare say a word to Michael about this. Now promise me."

Determined to have the last word, he agreed. "OK, but I'm giving that darn Bobby Foster a piece of my mind."

Saturday, he sat a record delivering the mail—no conversations and no deviations, just mail in its assigned box. Then he was off to Bobby Foster's office with fire in his eyes, just itching to pick a fight. When he got there, Bobby's car was the only one in the lot. He walked in as Bobby was removing the cap from a Coca Cola. Seeing Mike, he sarcastically asked, "And to what do I owe this honor?"

Mike was hot and not in the mood for chit-chat. "I want to talk to you about Craig."

"What's my number one child up to now?" Bobby crowed.

"Do you know he took the money Margaret and Michael collected for the March of Dimes and then turned it in as his own?"

Bobby burst out laughing, almost gloating. "That little rascal! Boy is he a chip off the old block. I didn't realize he was so smart."

Mike just stood there in disbelief. "You think it's OK he stole money?"

"He gave it to the teacher, so what's the harm?" Bobby rationalized.

Mike shook his head, fighting the urge to put his fist in that smug face. "You don't see that he did anything wrong, do you? I knew you were a little man, but I didn't realize you were corrupt as well." Mike turned and left, slamming the door as he departed.

Bobby was chuckling and yelled after him. "Come back anytime, Mike. Especially when you can stay longer."

# CHAPTER 13

At dinner on Sunday, Mike tossed Jesse a letter and said, "Thought you were going to give your friend your address."

"I did, but knowing O'Shea he probably lost it," Jesse said. He ripped open the envelope and began to read.

Hi again, Mountain Boy,

Just wanted to let you know things got a little exciting last month. We were kicking North Korea's butt until their big brother, the Chinese, came to help. Those guys are really tough bastards. They nearly had our company overrun and would have if it hadn't been for a South Korean company next to us. Just as we were about to surrender to the Chinese, they came in like Hannibal and his elephants. Their CO, Captain Hung, is just like you—tall and ugly, but one hell of a leader.

Real reason I'm writing is I got to see General McArthur up close and personal. He came down when they were reorganizing our company. There were only nineteen of us left when the battle was over. He had the leadership of the South Korean company come over and held an award ceremony right then. I watched him pin a bronze star on Captain Hung's chest. If it had been up to me, I'd have given him the Medal of Honor!

Buddy, have I told you this is the coldest place on earth? The ground is so cold it makes my knees hurt and I can't even feel my feet and toes anymore. God, do I miss Fort Benning.

I cut a picture out of the *Stars and Stripes* so you can see. Now tell me, doesn't it look just like Europe, just thirty degrees colder? Write me back. How's that plantation coming? Did you ever dig that well? Can't wait to hear.

Your damn Yankee friend,

O'Shea

Jesse studied the picture, and his mind raced back to his last winter in Germany. Those memories made him shudder. The entire time he'd been at war he felt like he was living a temporary life. That thought made him uncomfortable, as in some ways he was feeling the same way now. He needed to find a way to move out from his parents' house and start living a permanent life with his family. All of his life he'd been planning for something in the future, and he now knew that wasn't what life was all about. He made a silent promise to himself that from now on he and his family would put their emphasis on the present. He needed to move them to their own home. He looked over at Mike, and it was clear to him that they lived every day to the fullest. They enjoyed the present. It had been a long time since he'd heard Mike say "one day" he'd do something. Now that he knew what the problem was, all he needed to do was fix it.

The rest of the family had all taken their seats at the table. Amos hated waiting for anyone, especially his youngest son. Lorri asked, "Is O'Shea OK?"

"Yeah, he was bragging he'd met General McArthur and was freezing his behind off over there. He says it's colder than Germany, and that's hard to believe."

Martha interrupted, "We're talking about Thanksgiving dinner on Thursday. We'll eat at two o'clock, and we expect you guys to come."

Jesse's thoughts returned to O'Shea's letter and his promise to himself. "Sorry, I can't. Nick is coming over to help finish the barbed wire fence we've been working on. Maybe next year."

He filled up his plate and looked around. Everyone was so surprised by his response they were all speechless. For a while the only sound was that of forks hitting plates. Momma Barkley shook her head at the little boy she'd raised—independent and always quick to avoid family events. She hadn't seen this reaction since he'd been home. The rest of the family may have been disappointed; however, secretly she was pleased to see him returning to normal.

At 2:00 a.m., Jesse woke up filled with new ideas and motivations to live life to the fullest. Little did he know this would become his normal routine. After a couple of nights, he began to keep a pencil and paper by the bed to capture his thoughts.

Unloading his tools Thursday morning, Jesse waved as Lorri and Danny headed out to spend the day with Martha. Lorri was excited about helping Martha cook. It was just like it had been when Jesse was off fighting the war. He turned as Nick drove up and got out with a big grin on his face.

"Sarge, look in the backseat. I found something every farmer should have," Nick said.

Jesse opened the door and saw two young dogs. "How old are they?"

"About eight months, I think. They're purebred saddleback beagles and just the right age to train to hunt rabbits."

Jesse was secretly pleased. "And just how much are they going to cost me?"

"A couple of days hunting every year will just about do it," Nick stated.

"Are you sure?"

"Let me see, you train them, you feed them, and I get to hunt with them? Can't get any better than that the way I see it."

Jesse scratched his head and asked, "Nick, do you know how to train a rabbit dog? All the ones we had were squirrel hunters. I'm afraid I might ruin these two purebreds."

"Sarge, I'll take care of you. That's all my uncle would own. I used to drag dead rabbits all over south Alabama. Guess it won't hurt me to drag a few in Georgia. When do we start?"

"Not today. I need to get that fence done so I can work on the old house. We're moving in the first sign of spring." Jesse smiled as he articulated his plan for the first time.

They worked until noon, when Jesse opened the backpack and took out the sandwiches his momma had packed for them. He handed one to Nick, and when he opened it, he said, "This one must be yours. It's got a note that says Jesse on it."

Jesse took the note and opened it, reading, "Son, enjoy your first Thanksgiving dinner on your own farm. It's always been my dream that you boys would have land of your own. You know your daddy and I have been sharecroppers and rented all our lives. You and Mike have made an old woman's dream come true. Your families will have a better life. Happy Thanksgiving, Momma."

Jesse was silent while Nick devoured his food. Finally finished, he shook his head in gratitude. "My God, she made peach pie. Sarge, how did your momma know that was my favorite?"

"Ah, nice try, friend, but she made it for me," teased Jesse. "Tell me how to train rabbit dogs, Nick."

"It's easy. You kill a rabbit, drag it through the fields and briars, and let the dogs track it."

"There's got to be more to it than that," protested Jesse.

"Nah, you just gotta know what a rabbit does when you jump them," Nick explained earnestly.

"Now you're telling me you think like a rabbit. Nick, you're so full of it I can't tell when you're lying and when you're telling the truth."

"Sarge, I don't lie, but Mother said I bend the truth until it almost breaks. Seriously, though, rabbits are creatures of habit," Nick explained. "When a hunter jumps a rabbit in a field, it'll keep running. The strange thing about it, though, is if it's pursued, it'll run in a big circle and return to within ten yards of where you jumped it. All good rabbit hunters know this, so they don't get too mad if they don't see the rabbit right away. You want it to run in a complete circle. Only a really good dog can make that happen. If it's too slow, the rabbit'll sit down, and when the dog jumps him again he'll start a new circle from that point. That could be two hundred yards away from the first place. If you have a big, fast dog that pushes too hard, the rabbit will find the nearest hole and disappear. You have to have just the right size dog, and those two pups are sixteen-inch Beagles, the perfect size for hunting here. Sarge, how's that for rabbit thinking?"

Jesse thought for a minute and said, "Maybe you aren't completely full of bologna. Let's get back to stringing this wire and we'll start training the dogs next Saturday."

When Lorri and Danny drove up, Nick had the pups hidden behind his Jeep. When Danny got out and began to run toward his daddy, Nick turned them loose. The dogs joined in the game and began to chase the child. When he saw them, he stopped and gaped at them. Both jumped up on him and knocked him down, licking his face. As he watched the boy scream with delight, Nick turned to Danny's parents and asked, "Think he likes them?"

Lorri asked protectively, "Will they hurt him?"

Watching the two dogs and his son rolling around on the ground, Jesse asked, "The real question is will he hurt them?" Then he laughed out loud and joined the three on the ground.

Lorri could see she had just inherited a new job: feeding dogs.

Nick walked up to Jesse Friday morning and slapped him on the arm. "Sarge, guess what I found on the way home last night?"

"I don't have a clue," responded Jesse.

"Road kill. It was a rabbit someone had run over. I skinned it out so we won't have to waste any time looking for one tomorrow."

"I believe you were born with a horseshoe up your butt."

Nick chuckled and asked, "What time do you want to start in the morning?"

"Let's shoot for ten. Should be a little warmer by then."

"You bring the dogs and I'll bring the rabbit skin," Nick confirmed.

The next morning Nick was waiting on him as Jesse drove up. He shook his head when he saw how excited Nick was. He yelled out to Jesse, "Let's go! I've already dragged the skin around the meadow."

"OK, Nick, where do we start?"

"Just lead them down to the edge of the meadow and we'll go from there," Nick suggested.

When the beagle pups got near the meadow, they got excited and tried to pull loose from Jesse. He let them go and they took off howling when they caught the scent. The men stood, looked over at each other, and grinned in delight. It only took the dogs about ten minutes to find the end of the drag trail.

Nick suggested Jesse hold the dogs while he made another trail up through the woods. It took almost half an hour for him to complete the task, and when he returned he said, "I bet they don't find this one as easy as they did the last one. Let them go."

But Nick was wrong. The dogs loved this new game and were quicker this time. This went on for a couple of hours. Just before they were ready to call it a day, a small miracle happened. The dogs went into a briar patch, jumped a rabbit, and the chase was on. Jesse saw where the rabbit jumped and quickly moved toward that location. After about thirty minutes the rabbit responded just as Nick had said. Jesse could see it headed toward him, and he couldn't believe his eyes as he stood perfectly still. The bunny got within five feet of him and started another circle. He caught the pups when they arrived.

Nick screamed with excitement, "See, I told you what would happen. Now ain't them dogs a perfect size?"

The rest of the winter was spent chasing rabbits. Lorri was glad he'd been having so much fun, but she was secretly pleased the day Jesse told her Kell Weeks was moving his sawmill from Cherry Log up to their farm. That night she whispered, "How many rooms will our house have?"

"Let me see, a kitchen, a dining room, living room, a bathroom, and two bedrooms. That makes six, right?"

She rolled over closer to him. "You'd better make that three bedrooms."

It went right over his head as he continued, "I was thinking about two more upstairs when we need them."

As usual, being subtle didn't work with him, but she enjoyed playing the game anyway. "Sweetie, we'll need one of them in a few months."

She'd finally gotten through to him. "Another baby?" he asked. "When? Are you OK? Do you still want to move into the old shack?"

"Whoa! One question at a time. Yes, another baby in about six months, I'm OK, and I definitely want to move into our little brown shack."

"What can I do?" he asked as he pulled her close. "Tell me what I should do."

"Maybe we could have someone come help a little when it gets close," she suggested.

Knowing how eager Jesse was to get into his home, Kell Weeks made the lumber cuts for the house a priority. Thursday afternoon, Jesse was surprised to see that there were three stacks of lumber already. Two were two inches by eight inches and the last was one inch by eight inches, to be used to complete the flooring. Jesse almost wrecked his truck in his hurry to get home and share the news with his bride. After supper, he loaded up the box he'd built in the back of the truck before he left Fort Benning. Instead of items from the move, this time he loaded it with tools he'd need to work on his new home.

Eight o'clock Saturday morning, Nick drove up and Lorri handed him a cup of coffee from the thermos she'd brought. He took the cup and nodded his thanks. "OK, little lady, let's build you that house."

The men worked all day as Lorri fetched tools and water, doing whatever they needed. The fact that she felt as big as a house wasn't going to slow her down. When dark slipped up on them, Jesse stood back and surveyed their progress. "Nick, we've done a good day's work. I can't believe we have the floor joists done."

"We can go ahead and put the flooring in tomorrow if you want," Nick suggested.

Jesse shook his head. "Nope, tomorrow is Sunday. We don't work on the Sabbath. I'll do a little after work next week. Can I expect to see you again next Saturday?"

"As long as Lorri keeps feeding me like this, you won't be able to run me off," he insisted.

Jesse woke the next morning sore and stiff. Every muscle in his body hurt. The green, red oak two-by-eights had been a lot heavier than he'd expected and made him remember he wasn't eighteen anymore. Lorri watched him struggle to get his clothes on and scolded, "I told you both you were overdoing it yesterday."

He wearily looked over at her and said, "You do want that house done, don't you?"

"You know I do, but it's not worth it if you kill yourself in the process."

He'd planned to put down the flooring Monday afternoon, but his body was screaming at him to take a rest. In fact, he didn't work on the project until Wednesday. As he drove up, he noticed a new pile of lumber waiting. This was all two-by-fours. It was apparent Kell knew exactly what was needed in each stage of the build. Even with sore muscles, Jesse worked hard to get the flooring down so he and Nick would be ready to start on the walls on Saturday.

Friday night he whispered to Lorri, "I think it's time we moved to our little brown shack. That way I can work until dark, and with any luck we can move into our house by Thanksgiving."

"I'm ready, but that means we're going to have to hire someone to help me until the baby is born."

He asked, "Do you have anybody in mind?"

"I was thinking we might get Marie Galloway. She's the oldest of five girls, and since her mom passed away she's practically raised her sisters."

"Well, why don't we go talk to her Sunday afternoon?" he suggested.

She was relieved. It was obvious he loved her as much as she loved him. She asked, "And when are you going to tell your momma? You know you can't put it off any longer."

He pulled the blanket up under his chin. "I'll tell her after we talk to Marie."

"You promise? I'm with her every single day, and when she looks at me with those big old blue eyes, I feel so guilty about hiding our secret," she confessed.

"Yes, now let's get some sleep. I'm planning on working Nick's butt off tomorrow."

"I wouldn't be so frisky, old man, remember how you felt last Sunday?" she teased.

# CHAPTER 14

Spring exploded in the North Georgia Mountains. It seemed everything was in bloom. As usual, mountain people became inspired to plant and build just like those who'd come before them. Once Marie agreed to stay with Lorri during the week, they quickly moved to their little brown shack. She was scheduled to stay Tuesday through Saturday every week. With Nick's help, the house was soon framed and ready for the roof.

Marie and Danny were with Lorri when she brought lunch to the boys around noon. Seeing them approach, Nick scrambled down the ladder ready to begin his easy banter with Lorri. As soon as his feet hit the ground, he looked up into Marie's face. For once in his life, he was speechless. He couldn't believe his eyes or his luck. Where on earth had this beautiful creature come from? He held out his hand and said, "I'm Nick."

Marie tentatively placed her hand in his and introduced herself. She said shyly, "You guys are doing a great job."

Nick just held onto her hand and stared at her in fascination. Jesse couldn't stand it any longer. "Say something. The lady paid you a compliment."

"Oh, yeah, thanks. We try," he stammered.

Not sure how to proceed, she added, "Looks like you know what you're doing."

He just continued to stand there and stare. Marie gently pulled her hand loose. Lorri and Jesse just looked at each other in silent communication—Nick was smitten! Lorri winked at her husband. It was obvious no work would be done until the ladies and Danny returned to the shack. Once they departed, Nick babbled about Marie the rest of the day. He was curious if she was married or had a boyfriend. Jesse just smiled. He could tell next week would be fun. He'd be able to tell everyone at work how big mouth Nick had finally bit the bullet and fell in love.

Later that evening, when he told Lorri how Nick had acted, she told him it was pretty obvious that Marie felt the same way. "You know, she asked me what Nick's last name was and I was so embarrassed—I have no idea what it is. Do you?"

"Turner. Thought you knew. And by the way, Nick isn't really his name."

She looked at him, shocked and said, "Are you kidding me? Why am I not surprised?"

"His full name is Jedidiah Nicholas Turner."

Putting her hand on her hip she complained, "Why in the world would a man do that to his kid?"

"Lorri, think about it: Nick is the perfect name for him. It just fits. Jedidiah is an old man's name, and he's acting more like a kid right now. You know this is kind of fun."

"I remember one of those guys back at Epworth," she teased.

"Yeah," he said, "he chased the girl until she caught him."

"Are you complaining?"

"No way, but I can't wait to see what happens with those two," he laughed.

"Wonder how long it will take him to ask her out."

"Knowing Nick, it might be after we finish the house," he said.

"I sure hope not. I don't think I can stand the suspense. We might have to give them a little push if it looks like it's heading in that direction," she said.

He just laughed at his woman. He knew exactly how she thought.

Jesse wasn't too surprised to see two new stacks of lumber next to the new house on Thursday afternoon. They were one-by-tens, perfect for covering the rafters in preparation for shingles.

When he passed along the news to Nick, he had to choke back his laughter. Nick's immediate response was, "Do you think Marie might stop by?"

"I have no idea. Maybe she will and maybe she won't. You know how women are," Jesse said casually, all the while watching Nick out of the corner of his eye.

Not even bothering to hide his disappointment, Nick replied, "Oh."

It was all Jesse could do to refrain from ribbing him. Nick beat Jesse to the worksite on Saturday morning. As Jesse walked up, he looked at his watch and saw it was only seven thirty; Nick had already carried one of the stacks up to the roof. Amused, he decided to just keep his mouth shut. Nick's enthusiasm was working out just fine for Jesse's end goal, and he didn't want to take a chance on hurting his feelings. They quickly set up a system. Nick measured the lengths needed, and Jesse cut it to size. While Nick nailed it into place, Jesse would cut the next one. It worked just fine until around noon. The closer it got to lunch time, the slower Nick nailed boards into place. Realizing production had almost come to a halt, Jesse wondered if Nick was getting tired. Just as he started to ask if they needed to take a break, the problem became obvious. Nick was driving in a nail, and then he would turn to check out the trail that led to the shack. Jesse innocently asked, "See anybody coming yet?"

"Nope," Nick grumbled. Embarrassed, he began to drive in the nails faster. That didn't quite work, though, as he was bending or missing the nails entirely. Jesse just shook his head in frustration and sent out a silent prayer to Lorri to please put Nick out of his misery.

Soon the answer to his prayers slipped around the corner of the house with her picnic basket. Watching Nick searching frantically for Marie, she ducked her head to hide her smile and called out, "It's just me today, boys. Hope these fried bologna sandwiches will hold you until supper. Marie is cooking tonight. Nick, would you like to join us for supper?"

He perked right up. "If you're sure it won't be a bother."

"No bother; in fact the company will be nice," she assured him.

The men climbed down from the roof and quickly devoured the sandwiches. When he'd finished, Nick whispered to Lorri, "Can I ask you a favor?"

"Are you kidding me? After all you're doing for us? What is it?"

"Would you go up to my jeep and smell inside? I need to see if that skunk smell is gone or if I've just gotten used to it. Sarge said it had, but I'm not sure I trust him. He might just be saying it to make me feel better. Being a woman, you'll know if it's still there," he explained earnestly.

Even knowing how important it was, she couldn't help herself and asked him, "Why on earth do you care about that smell, Nick? You've been riding in it for months."

He flushed and Lorri almost felt guilty. Then she just cocked her head and said, "You wouldn't be planning on asking a girl to ride in there with you, would you?"

He gave her a saucy grin. "Just maybe."

Before she walked back home, she went over to the Jeep, opened the door, stuck her head inside, and inhaled. She closed the door and waved to Nick. When she had his attention, she gave him a thumbs-up. He yelled back, "Thanks!"

The rest of the afternoon, Nick pushed Jesse to hurry, until about four o'clock, when Jesse decided to take pity on him. He handed Nick the last of the one-by-tens and announced, "Guess this is a good quitting point. I'll pick up some shingles this week. It sure will be nice to have the house in the dry. Seems like it rains every other day in April and May around here. I don't want to have to worry about the weather slowing us down. Nick, you will never know how much I appreciate all of your help."

Shrugging, Nick asked, "Sarge, what else is there for me to do on Saturday?"

"Well, let me see. You could go fishing, or to the movies, or to the supper club. Surely a single man can find a way to stay busy on the weekend."

Nick thought about it for a minute and then calmly explained, "Well, I don't have a boat for fishing and fishing from the bank isn't any fun. I don't have a girlfriend, so going to the movies by myself isn't any fun. I hate beer and being around a bunch of drunks isn't any fun."

Jesse slapped him on the back. "Well, let's do something about that. You're eating dinner with us, aren't you? I know for a fact that Marie doesn't have a boyfriend right now, but a pretty woman like that won't be alone for long. You'd better make your move pretty quick."

Nick looked down for a minute and asked quietly, "Sarge, do you think she'd go out with somebody like me?"

"Hell, boy, you'll never know if you don't ask her. You remind me of Mike when he first met Martha, and you know how that turned out. Let's put these tools away and go eat."

Nick saw Danny as soon as he entered the little shack and immediately engaged his friend. "Hey, there. How's my little rabbit-hunting buddy?"

"Hello, Uncle Nick. Come look at my new bed," he said as he led Nick by the hand to a pallet in the living room next to the wood stove.

"That's fantastic. Bet you didn't know I had one just like it when I was twelve. But mine was in a bathtub."

Danny looked at his friend in total disbelief. "No way. You're just fooling me."

Nick raised his right hand. "Honest Injun. My uncle Olin, Mother's brother, had just died. We had so many people in our house they were hanging out the windows. Mother had insisted my Aunt Betty and her kids come live with us in our little bitty house. Once she figured out we didn't have enough beds, she put the dirty clothes in the bottom of the bathtub and then laid blankets on top of them. They looked just like your bed. I slept there all summer long, and I liked it. I felt safe. There was no way I could fall out of bed!"

Danny laughed in delight. "Did your legs stick out the ends?"

"Naw, I was a little fellow just like you."

Shaking his head, Danny said, "I bet that was fun. We don't have a bathtub."

"You will soon. You can bet your daddy and I will make that happen."

Hearing Nick's voice, Marie had crept toward the door and listened as he talked with Danny. She had wondered why Nick spent so much time helping Jesse. She knew he wasn't getting paid, and it just didn't make sense to her that he would do so much work for no money. But after listening to his story, she respected him and realized he was just doing as his mother had taught him. She decided she needed to get to know this man better.

As they sat down to supper, Danny monopolized the conversation, trying to impress his uncle Nick. Marie sat politely with a wooden smile. Lorri watched for as long as she could stand it, and then she snapped, "Nick, when do you plan to take Marie to a movie?"

He was shocked and blurted out the first thing that came to mind. "We don't have a movie theater in Turtletown."

Always eager to get his friends in trouble, Jesse suggested, "How about Copperhill and McCaysville?"

Marie spoke up hesitantly, "There's a new one next to the Rexall Drug Store, and I hear it's pretty nice."

Whirling his head around at the sound of her soft voice, he asked, "Would you go with me tomorrow afternoon?"

"Yes, I'd be pleased to, Mr. Turner," she replied with great dignity.

Lorri and Jesse exchanged pleased glances, and Jesse said, "Well, now that that's settled, what's for dessert?"

His reward was Lorri's famous stare down, or the stink-eye, as he called it. The rest of the meal was a little awkward for Nick, so when he finished he thanked the ladies for the wonderful meal and made his escape.

After church, they were surprised to see Nick's jeep parked next to the shack. He looked concerned as they approached and asked, "Sarge, where is Marie?"

Jesse whispered, "Nick doesn't know she goes home Sunday and Monday."

Lorri scolded Jesse, "Well, tell him so he won't think she doesn't want to go out with him."

Jesse explained they always took her home on Sunday morning before church. As he tried to explain, he figured out the problem. Nick didn't know how to get to her house, and he didn't know enough about the area for Jesse to give him good directions. Not sure what to do, he pleadingly looked to his wife for help.

She just shook her head. "Men! You always make things so complicated. Have him follow us to her house on the way to your momma's."

It was such an easy solution, Jesse was embarrassed he hadn't thought of it. He relayed the plan, and Nick followed them to Marie's father's house. As they rode along, Lorri complained, "Getting those two together is turning out to be a lot harder than I thought. But come hell or high water, we're going to make it happen."

Jesse just smiled at his little matchmaker. She noticed his grin and asked, "Are you telling me to stop meddling?"

"Lord, no. I learned a long time ago to pick my battles, and this ain't one of them."

"You're right about that. I'll fill Martha in and she can help me set those two straight. She's really good at this stuff."

When they got to their destination, Marie was waiting in the swing on the front porch. Lorri fussed at Jesse, "Don't stop! Just point to the house and leave them alone. They're uncomfortable enough as it is."

Jesse slowed and stuck his arm out the window pointing to the driveway. He was relieved Nick understood his directions. He shook his head in exasperation. When on earth had courting gotten so complicated? Those two were beginning to make him feel old.

Marie met Nick at the jeep. He got out apologizing, "I'm so sorry I'm late. I thought you'd be at Jesse's. I guess I wasn't listening if you'd told me you wouldn't be there."

She gave him a sympathetic smile. "You're not late, and no one told you I'd be here. I just assumed you already knew I only worked there Tuesday through Saturday."

He walked around and opened her door. "Let's go. I don't want to be late for our first movie date. Do you know what the movie is?"

"I think it's *The African Queen.* That's what the paper said."

As he drove to Blue Ridge, he focused on his driving and didn't say much. Marie instantly relaxed. She had always been shy, and small talk made her uncomfortable. Here was a man she could be with who would be OK with silences and not feel threatened.

On East Main Street, Nick asked, "Have you been here before?"

"No, how about you?" she replied.

"Naw, this is the first time I've been to a movie since moving here."

The theater was packed. Nick could only find two seats together near the front of the theater, and he turned to her and whispered, "Think it's always like this on Sunday?"

"Maybe, but it's probably because this is the first time they've showed this movie. It has Humphrey Bogart in it."

They took their seats as the lights dimmed and the cartoon began.

# CHAPTER 15

Lorri couldn't wait to ask Marie if Nick had liked the movie. Marie was eager to share everything and they sat down to chat. "To say he didn't would be a stretch. Actually he couldn't take his eyes off the screen."

Lorri just chuckled, because it sounded just like him. "What did you do after the show?"

"When we came out, he said he was hungry as a bear and asked where we could go. I wasn't sure how much money he had, so I told him about Harry's out by the lake. He almost wrecked going around Dead Man's Curve next to Weaver Creek. I could tell it embarrassed him, but he didn't say a word until after we ate."

Now Lorri was really curious. "OK, come on, girl, spill it. What did he say?"

"It was kind of personal," she said evasively.

Lorri couldn't believe it. "You better tell me! After all, I'm the one who fixed you two up. You know I won't tell a soul."

Marie wrestled with it for a minute, then she decided it couldn't hurt to get Lorri's opinion. "He said, 'Can we start over? Ever since I met you it's like I have two left feet. I nearly killed us on that curve back there, and I can't seem to do or say anything right when I'm around you. I find it so hard to believe that a beautiful woman like you would even give me the time of day, much less go out with me. But I'm finding the more I get to know you, the more time I want to spend with you.'"

Back at work, Jesse couldn't wait to ask Nick how the date went. Nick deflected, "Sarge, it was fine."

Jesse was flabbergasted. "Just fine? That's all?"

Finally Nick volunteered, "Well, we went to Harry's and had the best steak I've ever had. Both meals cost me nearly a day's pay, but I guess it was worth it. The steak came with a baked potato. God, it was good. Have you ever had one of those?"

Realizing he wasn't getting any information, Jesse gave up his quest. "Yeah, Momma would make sweet potatoes at least once a month."

"No, I'm talking about Irish potatoes!"

Not sure where Nick was going with this, he said, "I remember when Mike and I were kids, Momma would put them under the ashes in the fireplace. That was our snack when we were listening to the radio. Didn't you ever do that?"

"Yeah, but I didn't like the way they tasted. It was like they were burned or something," Nick protested. "The ones at Harry's were great, especially with butter and salt and pepper on them."

Jesse laughed. "Nick, when you were a kid you left the potatoes in the fire too long. I bet the peelings were black, weren't they?"

"Yeah, they were."

"The best way is to cover them at least an inch deep with ashes and only leave them in there about an hour tops. Or you could just go back to Harry's with Marie. You're not going to tell me about your date, are you?" Jesse said.

"Nope." He grinned. "What are we doing on the house Saturday?"

"Nothing. I'm going to Rome and pick up some windows. Mike got his there. He says that's where they make them. I can get what I need at a price I can afford."

Nick asked, "Want me to tag along?"

"OK, but don't you have a date? If you don't, you should, and it'll be after dark when we get back. You'd be doing me a favor if you take her home Saturday night. Then I won't have to do it on Sunday morning. I'll have a truckload of windows, and that way I won't have to unload them."

Nick jumped at the chance to see Marie. "Think it will be OK with her?"

"Don't worry about it; let Lorri handle that. Let's get back to work before the boss sees us goofing off. Remind me at lunch to go find that electrician," Jesse suggested.

"What electrician?"

"Mike said Scott Newman and his son wired his house and did a great job for a good price. They work on the weekends. Scott used to work in the carpenter's shop, so that's where I'm heading at lunch," Jesse said. "I sure hope he's still there. If he is, can you show him around on Saturday? I'd really appreciate it."

"Sounds like a plan; just let me know when he'll be there," Nick said.

Jesse rushed to catch up with Nick after lunch. "Scott said he'd be there between nine thirty and ten o'clock on Saturday."

Nick nodded and said, "I'll be there with bells on."

Later that night, Jesse told Lorri and Marie that Nick would be showing Scott around on Saturday because he planned to head to Rome. Lorri was pleased to see a twinkle in Marie's eye when Nick's name was mentioned. "How many outlets did you tell Mr. Newman we wanted?"

By the look on his face, she could tell Jesse hadn't even thought about it. "Don't worry, Marie and I will meet him on Saturday morning. If I didn't learn anything else from living on post, I learned where not to put outlets and light switches."

Jesse realized he'd messed up and quickly countered with, "That's exactly what I was thinking. You know what you want."

She just looked at him and said, "It's amazing how you read my mind. That's probably why I love you so much."

"What's for dessert? Let's celebrate," Jesse suggested.

Marie just watched them spar back and forth. Lorri had gotten the best of this situation, but they were both happy with the end result. She was too young to understand how her own parents had resolved problems. Her mother's death had robbed her of that experience, but watching the Barkleys had given her some insight into what a happy marriage should look like. She smiled to herself and wondered if Nick was as strong a man as Jesse seemed to be. Scott Newman and his son were surprised by the small group of people waiting for them on Saturday morning. Scott called out, "Are you Nick?"

"Yep, that's me."

"Jesse said you'd show us what was needed," Scott said.

Nick deferred to Lorri. "This is Lorri, Jesse's wife, and she knows better than I do what she wants."

Scott was pleased. "That's even better. It's always better when the woman is involved."

Lorri introduced Marie and Danny, and Scott introduced Roy, his son, who moved closer and said, "Hello, Marie. Long time no see."

"Nice to see you too. Are you still dating Grace Ann?" Marie asked.

"Nah, we broke up a couple of years ago. She's engaged to a guy from Ellijay. You still single?"

She smiled shyly. "I'm afraid so."

Lorri watched Nick watch Roy and Lorri. She could tell Nick was wishing he could blast old Roy right back to Copperhill, and it was all she could do not to burst out laughing. She looked over at Marie, and coughed to hide her glee as she saw that young Miss Marie knew exactly what she was doing. Roy noticed his dad was getting red in the face, and he knew this meant he was wasting valuable time flirting with the girl. He quickly said, "Guess we can catch up later; nice to see you again."

Lorri took control. "If you'll come inside with me, I'll show you exactly what we need."

Finally able to draw a breath, Nick stepped forward. "Mr. Newman, before you go inside, Jesse wanted me to show you the well house. He wants an electric line from there to the kitchen with a switch inside."

Lorri was busily pointing out where she wanted switches, but she kept an eye on Nick and Marie. Nick was as busy as a bee trying to herd Marie as far as possible from Roy. She could hardly wait to tell Jesse what he'd missed today.

When Scott was comfortable with what was needed, he and Roy left to get materials for the job. Marie and Danny started up the trail toward the little shack, but Lorri stayed behind. Once they were out of earshot, she counseled Nick, "What in the world are you waiting for? Aren't you going to ask her out for tonight?"

"It sounded like she wants to be with that old Roy!" Nick sounded like a kid.

"Nick, you know she thinks the world of you. Why on earth would she want that pretty boy? Now get your butt up that path and ask her before she gets back to the house," she encouraged.

Without hesitating, he took off running. Danny saw him coming and thought he was coming to play. "Uncle Nick, hold on. I'll go get the ball."

"Not this time, little man. I need to ask that pretty lady if she'll go to the movies or something with me tonight."

Marie smiled. "Or something would be nice. When will you pick me up?"

Caught off guard, he improvised. "Seven o'clock?"

"Good, I'll see you then." She took Danny's hand and led him into the house.

Nick just stood and watched. He was so excited he thought he'd explode.

# CHAPTER 16

The remainder of the month of June was a nightmare for Jesse. The construction was going great, but Nick was driving him nuts. He was so eaten up with jealousy he was behaving like a guard dog, making sure Marie and Roy didn't have a single moment alone together. Lorri and Marie were enjoying his antics. It became such a source of entertainment for them that Lorri would meet Jesse at the door every afternoon to discover what Nick had done and Marie made it a practice to be close by so she could overhear. Exasperated, Jesse would just shake his head. "The only good thing about it is that Nick works his butt off all day just to impress his rival. Scott told me Roy had never worked like this before, so I guess he's experiencing the rough patches too."

Lorri asked, "Didn't they finish the wiring last Saturday? What do they have left to do?"

Scratching his head, Jesse said, "Yeah, they're done, so I guess life should get back to normal next week. God, I sure hope so." He craned his neck so he could see Marie and begged, "You've just got to put this guy out of his misery. Tell him he's your beau or at least give him something. I'm growing old here."

Lorri looked at him in irritation. "She will do no such thing. It's the man who has to take that kind of step."

Jesse was bewildered "Was I that slow?" He was so frustrated with it all.

"Let me see, two years in high school, four years at war, and another year after the war. I'd say you were even slower."

Jesse's face turned red when Marie asked, "It took you seven years to ask her to marry you? I like Nick a lot, but I'm way too old to wait that long."

Lorri and Jesse burst out laughing, and Jesse asked, "Do you like him a lot?"

It was Marie's turn to be embarrassed. "Maybe."

Life on the work site became bearable again with Roy's absence. Jesse and Nick were learning how to install sheetrock. It was an improvement over putting boards up, and the four-by-eight-foot sheets went up a lot faster than one-by-six-inch planks. The days were getting longer and they could work almost three hours every evening. On the last Thursday in June, Mike dropped by to check on the progress and deliver a letter from O'Shea.

Inspecting their work, Mike noticed all the outlets and was envious. "How many of those did you put in?"

Jesse just snorted. "I had nothing to do with that. Lorri made that call."

Mike said, "It's a great idea. I only had Scott put one in each room, and I still hear about it every single day."

Jesse followed as Mike wandered around the house looking at all the changes since his last visit. He mentioned, "Oh, yeah, I talked with Frank Wilson the other day. He bought himself a new tractor from Coot Mason. He said to tell you it plows a field ten times as fast as a mule and you ought to get yourself one. That thing has all kinds of extra stuff: a hydraulic lift on the back that makes it easy to lift plows, discs, and even a mowing machine for hay. Here's the thing he tore out of the newspaper for me to give you."

Jesse just shook his head. "Frank said he promised himself if he lived through the war, he'd never set foot off his daddy's farm again. Looks like he's living up to it. I can't afford a tractor. I'll just have to hire him for a couple of years. Think he'd be up to cutting and raking my hay?"

"Boy, are you slow, little brother. I'm pretty sure that's why he told me to tell you about the tractor in the first place," Mike said with one of his big laughs. "He said he was buying it on time. He thought working for his neighbors would earn him some extra money. You should drop by before he gets too busy."

Jesse was glad his big brother had visited. He'd been so focused on building the house, he'd forgotten all about the farm. If he was going to raise cattle, he'd need all the hay he could get. Next week would be the Fourth of July, and the meadow should've been cut by the first of June if he was going to get two cuttings. He'd need to cut it next week. He looked at the calendar in his truck and saw the fourth was on a Wednesday. Since everybody would be off, he decided to ask if Frank could do it this Saturday or Monday. That way he could stack it on Wednesday. He told Mike his plan. "You're off that day, right?"

"Yeah, and unfortunately I don't have an excuse. Get in the car and we'll go see him now. We might even get Daddy to help us if we're lucky."

It was dark when Jesse got home, and Lorri was sitting on the porch in her rocker. It was the only place she could get comfortable now that she was in the last month of her pregnancy. She could tell her man was excited as he relayed the events of the day and how they'd soon be able to have cattle.

Wednesday morning, a small crowd gathered in the meadow. It was Mike, Amos, Nick, Tom, and Frank, but no Jesse. They stood around and looked at each other for a while, and then Amos spoke up, grumbling as usual. "Don't know where that boy is, but if we're going to get this hay in we need to get started."

Everyone laughed, grabbed a pitchfork, and went to work. Amos yelled out, "A couple of you boys ought to cut a pole for the haystacks."

Nick answered, "Sarge and I did that already. They're at the north end of the meadow. We put in three of them."

Amos was getting madder by the minute and snapped, "At least he did that much. Where in the hell is he?"

At about ten thirty, Marie walked into the meadow leading Danny by the hand. When he saw Amos, he jerked loose and ran toward him, yelling, "Papaw, what are you doing?"

A smile came over Amos's usually stern face. "We're making haystacks for your daddy. Where is he?"

"He went to the hospital with Momma to get me a baby sister. It must have been a long ways because they've been gone all night," he complained.

Realizing Jesse had a good excuse, Amos soothed the boy. "Don't worry, they'll be home before you know it."

Mike decided to take advantage of the break and handed Nick some money. "Why don't you go over to the store and get us something to eat and drink?"

"Anything special?" Nick asked.

Frank yelled out, "Get me a couple of those fried pies and an RC."

"Sounds good to me too," chimed in Mike.

Amos just handed Nick a couple of dollars and said, "Get me and Danny a couple of Coca-Colas, two packs of salted peanuts, and two moon pies. I want to show him a trick."

Danny perked right up. "What kind of trick, Papaw? Is it hard? Can I do it?"

"Patience, boy. You don't want to spoil the surprise."

Nick whispered to Marie, "What do you want, pretty lady?"

She ducked her head and said, "A peach pie and an RC would be good."

Everyone went back to work. They'd just finished offloading the hay from the wagon and placed it on the second haystack when Nick returned. Danny was dancing with excitement, "Show me the surprise, Papaw!"

Amos took his pocket knife out and opened the blade designed for soda bottles. He snapped off the cap of one of the Cokes and tore the top off of one of the packs of peanuts, pouring them into the bottle. When they hit the liquid, it began to fizz and foam up. He handed the bottle to Danny. "Take a swig of this. It tastes great and makes those peanuts taste even better."

Danny did as he was told but wasn't prepared for the foam that ran out of his mouth and down his chin. He wiped it off on his hand and grinned with delight. "Marie! Did you know you can put peanuts in a Coca-Cola?"

She laughed. "Yeah, we did it all the time when I was your age. Tastes good, doesn't it?"

He had the bottle up to his lips so all he could do was nod his head and mumble, "Uh-huh."

Pitching hay was something none of the men had done in a while, and the midmorning treats really hit the spot. No one talked, they just found a spot to sit, rest, and enjoy their food. Marie and Nick took advantage of the empty wagon and sat on the tailgate. They were busy whispering back and forth when Mike walked up, stuck out his hand, and said, "I'm Jesse's brother."

Marie laughed. "Mike, I know who you are. When I was a little girl, I would see you and Martha at the grist mill. Daddy would take me on Saturday."

Mike just shook his head. "You're that Marie Galloway? What happened to the pigtails?"

Tears came to her eyes. "I haven't had them since Momma died. She always did them, and after she passed there was no one to plait them."

"I'm so sorry," he apologized. "I didn't mean to bring up bad memories."

"You didn't; those were great ones. I just hadn't thought about it in a long time."

"Well then, let me ask you another question," Mike said. "When are you and Nick getting married?"

Nick had just taken a large bite of apple pie when Mike asked the question. He tried to swallow, but choked instead.

Knowing exactly what had happened and feeling guilty for causing it, Mike slapped Nick on the back. "Easy now, Nick." He gave one of his big laughs and said, "I didn't mean to scare you or let the cat out of the bag. Jesse and Lorri are always talking about how the two of you make such a wonderful couple. If I'm being nosy, just tell me to butt out."

Still unable to catch his breath, Nick just stared at him stupidly as Marie smiled and said, "We haven't decided yet."

"Oh," said Mike. He decided to change the subject before poor Nick died from shock. "Did Jesse take her to the company hospital?"

"Yes, sir, they left right after supper last night," Marie said.

"Think I'll drive on over when we finish with this hay," Mike said.

The last load went up just after two o'clock. Not much was said as everyone headed to their vehicles. Amos turned and yelled at Mike, "Let me and your momma know how Lorri's doing on your way home, boy."

"I will, Daddy. Thanks for the help. I'm sure Jesse will get around to telling you that later."

"Ah, it won't nothing. He's thinking about that baby right now. You know this makes our sixth, counting sweet Betsy." As soon as it came out of his mouth, he regretted bringing up the subject.

Remembering the agonizing loss he'd experienced with the death of his daughter, Mike looked sad, but he tried to reassure his daddy. "She would be thirteen now if she'd lived."

The silence was awkward as everyone quickly left and drove off.

Mike drove through McCaysville near the water and was surprised to see decorations up all along the river and across in Copperhill. Then he realized it was the Fourth of July. Both border towns were filled with locals ready to celebrate. He and Jesse had entered a horseshoe pitching contest one holiday in Epworth, but for the life of him Mike couldn't remember if they'd won. He'd have to ask Jesse if he remembered. As he left Copperhill, he crossed the railroad tracks near the Tennessee Copper Company and turned up the narrow road near the headquarters. He'd only been to this hospital a handful of times—some of them good and most of them terrible. One of those times he'd entered those doors and lost his baby, Betsy, to a severe case of strep throat. This was also the place where young Michael had been diagnosed with polio. Recalling how helpless he'd felt, he prayed Jesse would only have good memories of this white, wooden structure.

Jesse was the only one in the waiting room when Mike entered, and he could tell by the expression on his face that he was glad to see him.

"How's she doing?" asked Mike.

"Nurse said her contractions are every five minutes, whatever that means."

Mike tried to reassure him, "What that means is it won't be long now. Have you picked out a name yet?"

"Yeah, if it's a girl, it will be Nicole. If it's a boy, it will be Nicky."

Mike just howled with laughter. "Boy, will Nick like that! We got your hay put up. Two stacks, and Daddy even helped."

"Yeah, and I'll bet he complained every step of the way, didn't he?"

Mike gave another of his famous laughs. "Yeah, well, he can't help himself. But I have to admit when Marie brought Danny to the hayfield, Papaw Amos took charge and calmed him right down."

Jesse shook his head. "I'd like to have seen that."

A nurse entered the room with a big smile. "Mr. Barkley, you have two beautiful little girls."

Shocked, Jesse stammered, "What?"

Mike slapped him on the back. "Well, little brother, looks like you better be coming up with another name and a lot more money!"

Jesse ignored him and asked the nurse, "Can I go see her?"

"They're moving her to a room and want to keep her overnight. I'll come get you when she's ready."

As she left, Mike said, "Daddy asked me to come by and give them an update, but I feel like this news should be delivered by the proud daddy himself."

It was only a few minutes until the nurse led Jesse to Lorri. He asked, "Is it OK if my brother comes, too?"

She smiled. "Yes, sir, it's a special day and should be shared."

Lorri looked exhausted but welcomed them both with a big smile. "Have you seen our girls yet?"

"Not yet," said Jesse.

Mike gave her one of his laughs. "Girlie, you sure are full of surprises. Jesse said you had names picked out for a girl or a boy. Got another one picked out for the little surprise yet?"

Lorri said, "Yes, I'm changing it. Cindy and Mindy. What do you think?"

Jesse hugged her. "I like it."

# CHAPTER 17

Work on the house came to an abrupt halt after the twins were born. Jesse bought a cow and calf from a man at work and was forced to build a shed for shelter. By now, Nick was taking his evening meals with Lorri and Jesse. The two men would work until dark. Even though it was temporary, Jesse was thinking ahead and designed it to be expanded later into a two-story barn. Things soon got back on track for the remainder of the summer, until Marie left. Lorri and Marie had already agreed she would return home the first week of September to get her siblings ready for the first week of school. That plan seemed fine with everyone but Nick. He'd grown real comfortable with things just the way they were. He was able to spend time with Marie every day. When things changed that first week of September, Nick's attitude changed with them. He tried to be his usual self, but he had a major hole in his heart, and his depression was obvious to Jesse, who'd been trained in the army to recognize the symptoms.

When the last of the asbestos siding went up Saturday morning, Jesse said, "Let's go to Dooley's house and get those cement blocks for the front porch. When they hook up the electricity in a couple of weeks and we finish laying those blocks, we'll be ready to move in."

Surprised and horrified at the same time, Nick asked, "Sarge, are you saying we'll be finished?" He had no idea what he'd do with himself. He'd really liked being around Jesse and Lorri all these months.

"Yep, my man," said Jesse. "Bet you'll be glad to get your life back."

Looking around, Nick said, "Hell, Sarge, you're right. This place is looking good. You know, we ought to start our own construction business."

"I've got a much better idea," Jesse said. "Why don't you get married and we build your house?"

Nick flushed. "I've thought about it, but I think I'm too young to settle down."

"Really, or are you just scared?" Jesse challenged. "I know you'll be twenty-six or twenty-seven on your next birthday, so let's be honest. You're scared, aren't you? I'll bet if Marie liked Roy the way she does you, he wouldn't hesitate to put a ring on that girl."

Wide-eyed, Nick asked anxiously, "Have you heard something you haven't told me?"

"Nah, there's nothing to hear. Nick, get off your lazy ass and ask the girl."

When they got to where the dirt road met Highway 5, Jesse turned the truck to the left. Nick asked, "Thought we were headed to Dooley's. Where are you going?"

"Blue Ridge."

"What do you need there?" Nick asked suspiciously.

"It's not what I need. It's what you need," Jesse said.

Not a word was spoken until the truck came to a stop in front of Andy's Jewelry. Nick looked around and asked, "What's this?"

"This is where you're buying Marie a ring. Any questions? But before you say a word, know I'd hate to have to kick your butt."

Nick just nodded. "Want to help me pick it out, Sarge?"

Andy's wife met them at the door. "Can I help you fellows?"

Jesse took the lead. "Yes, ma'am. Nick here needs a nice engagement ring. Can you help him out?"

Hearing it said out loud had a good impression on Nick. Suddenly he felt the weight lifted from his shoulders and got excited.

She directed them to a display in the center of the room. "Do you want yellow or white gold?"

Nick looked over at Jesse and whispered, "What's white gold?"

Jesse whispered in return, "Kind of a silver color."

Nick pulled out his wallet and took out a piece of paper. He unfolded it and asked, "Do you have Keepsake diamond rings, like the one in this advertisement?"

She smiled and sat out five rings in front of him, asking, "Which do you like the best?"

While Jesse had been only mildly surprised Nick was carrying around the advertisement, he was absolutely stunned with what happened next. He picked up the one in the center and turned it over to look at the price. "I'll take this one," he said. He immediately pulled his wallet out again, counted out the bills and handed them to the smiling salesperson.

Jesse couldn't believe his friend was walking around town with that much cash on him. The lady asked, "Do you want it gift wrapped, sir?"

"No, ma'am. Does it come in a box or something?"

She opened a drawer and brought out a deep blue velvet ring box. Seeing it, Nick smiled. "That one is perfect. How much?"

"Nothing, sir. It comes with the ring," she reassured him.

Nick placed the ring in the box and held it like it would break if he so much as breathed on it. "Thank you, ma'am," he said, turning toward Jesse. "Guess we can go get those blocks of yours now."

Jesse opened his mouth to speak, but he really had nothing to say, so he followed Nick out to the truck. As they were riding along, Nick asked, "How did you ask Lorri to marry you?"

Jesse shook his head. "No way—you'll have to come up with your own plan, buddy. I asked Lorri in a letter from Germany just after the war."

Those words reminded him of the letter from O'Shea. He flipped down the visor and the letter dropped out. Jesse cursed himself, "I can't believe I forgot about this letter. It's been here for a couple of months. What a lousy friend I turned out to be!"

In order to make his friend feel better, Nick said, "Lorri having those twins hasn't had anything to do with that, right?"

"That's just an excuse. In the army, the answer is always 'no excuse, sir.'"

"But you ain't in the army now," Nick argued.

"O'Shea sure is."

Nick could tell the unread letter was eating at his friend. When they got to Dooley's, Jesse was all business. As usual, Dooley wanted to use the time to catch up and chat. Realizing that Jesse wasn't holding up his end of the bargain, Nick began chattering a mile a minute. Dooley was venting about how the Korean War was putting him out of business, so Nick listened while Jesse loaded the blocks. Once home, Jesse ripped open the letter.

Hello, Mountain Boy,

Believe it or not, spring is here in Korea. I made a promise to myself I would never complain about hot weather again, so I won't go there. I guess you heard the president fired General McArthur. That took a man with steel balls. The joke is it only took an artillery captain to put the general in his place. He sure had a hard-on for the Chinese, and I guess he thought if the nuke was good enough for the Japs it would be great for the Chinese. Next month I'll have been in this army for ten years. That puts me halfway to retiring. Enough about me. Have you finished that plantation house yet? The real question is, do you have another kid yet? Write more. Later,
Your damn Yankee friend,
O'Shea

When he finished reading, Jesse just sat and stared across the empty meadow. Nick kept busy offloading the blocks, as it was clear Jesse's mind was thousands of miles away. When he'd finished, he hit Jesse on the shoulder and said, "Sarge, I'm done, what's next?"

Jesse just looked up in surprise. "Let's go eat."

When he saw Nick drive up, Danny took off to greet him. "Uncle Nick, a lady brought Momma a crying rose!"

"Don't think I've ever seen one of those. Why don't you show me?" Nick said.

He ran to the porch and held up a pot with a twelve-inch plant with three white blossoms. Nick took it and looked it over. "They're beautiful, but I'm not seeing any water."

Lorri walked out after overhearing their exchange and handed Nick a card labeled, "Cherokee Rose."

No better symbol exists of the pain and suffering of the Trail Where They Cried than the Cherokee rose. The mothers of the Cherokee grieved so much that the chiefs prayed for a sign to lift the mother's spirits and give them strength to care for their children. From that day forward, a beautiful new flower, a rose, grew wherever a mother's tear fell to the ground. The rose is white, for the mother's tears. It has a gold center, for the gold taken from the Cherokee lands, and seven leaves on each stem that represent the seven Cherokee clans that made the journey. To this day, the Cherokee Rose prospers along the route of the Trail of Tears.

"I read it to Danny and explained the Trail of Tears meant a lot of people were crying," Lorri said apologetically.

Nick laughed and tossed Danny into the air. "Little man, you're going to grow up to be one smart cookie. What happened was President Andrew Jackson made all the Indians that used to live here in Georgia move to Oklahoma. That's a long way, and they had to walk every step of it. It took months, and along the trip some old people and children died. That's why they call it the Trail of Tears."

Danny frowned. "That president was a mean old man."

Surprised at Danny's statement, Jesse said, "A lot of people thought so, but the settlers moved in here and they wanted the land and its gold. The president was just trying to make them happy."

"But Daddy, he was mean to the Indians," Danny protested.

Lorri smiled with pride. "Out of the mouths of babes."

Nick joined in, "It was a horrible thing, Danny, but while I was in the army I met a Cherokee from Oklahoma, and he told me the Indians being sent there saved the tribe in the end. I was surprised and asked him to explain. He said the Indians and the settlers' lifestyles were so similar that a lot of them married each other. Because of that, after a hundred years or so, there wouldn't have been any full-blooded Indians left. Disease and marrying outside of their race destroyed a lot of tribes in the United States. He said the suffering they endured on the trail saved their lives in the long run. So don't be sad, little man."

Jesse looked at his friend in amazement. "Well, by golly, aren't you a wealth of knowledge? My great grandpa Carpenter used to tell us kids about the Indian braves returning from Oklahoma and digging up their family treasures that had been hidden before they left on the march. They hid them under rocks, in small caves, in small holes in trees, and all kinds of places. A lot of them were hidden at Talking Rock and also where Blue Ridge Lake is now. We kids used to go turn over every rock in the creek looking for the stuff, but we never got lucky enough to find any."

A light bulb went on over Nick's head as he realized that a treasure hunt was the perfect way to propose to Marie...as long as he could figure out how to make it happen. Then it hit him. "Danny, how would you like to take Marie and go on a treasure hunt?"

Danny's eyes danced with excitement. "Can we? You promise? We'll find all kinds of stuff! Just you wait."

"Sure we can. Let me talk to Marie and see when she can go," Nick promised.

Jesse cut his eyes over to Nick. "Does that mean what I think it does?"

Nick just grinned. "Could be."

"What are you two plotting now?" Lorri asked suspiciously.

"Just men talk," said Nick.

"Don't give me that stuff," growled Lorri. "I'm not stupid."

Jesse realized Nick had pushed Lorri's buttons. "Sweetie, I'll tell you later. Right now we have little ears."

Later that evening, Nick opened the top drawer of his bureau, the one his sister used to call his goodie drawer. When he was young, he'd always tease Sharon and make fun of her hope chest and how silly it was to put things in there she wouldn't use for years. One day she'd told him, "If it's so silly, why do you have your goodie drawer full of rocks and ribbons?" Needless to say, after that he didn't tease her much anymore. He emptied the drawer out on his bed and found the three arrowheads and a tortoise shell necklace he'd bought from the Indian store in the Smoky Mountains. He'd found the store shortly after he'd moved to the area. That should be treasure enough for Danny; now he needed to come up with treasure for Marie. He looked around his three-room apartment, which had been an addition on an old country store. It only cost him forty dollars a month and wasn't any place to keep a woman, but that was a problem to be solved on another day. Right now he needed to find something small and watertight to hold a ring and a note, and he figured he'd know it when he saw it. He opened his medicine cabinet and there it was: a small Alka-Seltzer bottle. It was perfect and would be easy to hide. His next problem was what he'd say in the note asking her to marry him. He destroyed his first four attempts, instinctively knowing he could do better. The ninth try met his expectations. He rolled up the paper and slid the ring over it, and then he placed both inside the bottle. He was concerned Danny might think it was for him, so he returned to his drawer and found the perfect solution: nail polish. Someone at work had told him once the best solution for chigger bites was to cover the bite with the polish, so he'd bought the first bottle he could find. At first he worried that the bright red color of the polish would be noticeable, but that turned out not to be an issue. Chiggers always bit him in a place no one else would ever see. He took the little brush and neatly wrote "To Marie" on the cap. He sat it on the nightstand to dry and was surprised to see it was almost three o'clock in the morning. He went to bed but tossed and turned, thinking about what he'd planned.

He woke early, too excited to just lie there. He placed all the stuff in a shoe box, gathered up his rubber boots, and put them in the floorboard of the passenger side of his old Jeep. He left Turtletown and had breakfast at the New York Hotel and Restaurant in Copperhill. The plan was to wait until Jesse's family left for church, then he'd hide the stuff under one of the rocks in the stream that provided them with water. He was floating with coffee by the time he left and headed to Jesse's house. He got out of the Jeep and was so excited he practically ran. He followed the trail to the spring house, where he noticed another small trickle of water that fed off the spring house stream. He walked it and noticed rocks and leaves were slowing the flow of water. Just when he was starting to get concerned about finding just the right spot, he saw a long, flat rock that was absolutely perfect. It was shaped like a shark's fin and about three feet long. He eased it up out of the water and was thrilled to see it was flat on both sides. He carefully moved it in order not to disturb the earth around it. Three spring lizards scampered off into the water, and their movement startled him. Holding it steady, he placed the three arrowheads and the necklace near the large end of the stone. Then he dug a shallow hole with his fingers toward the smaller end for the bottle. He eased the stone back in place and was satisfied—it didn't appear to be have been tampered with. He picked up the empty shoe box, walked back to the Jeep, and went to pick up Marie from church.

Driving back to the Barkley house, Marie asked, "Now tell me again what kind of hunt we're taking Danny on today?"

"Jesse told Danny about how the Indians hid their stuff before leaving on the Trail of Tears. I suggested we take him to see if we could find some of their stuff. I put some arrowheads under a rock near the spring house so he'd have something to find."

She smiled. "That's wonderful. It should be fun. Thanks for letting me go along." Nick never ceased to surprise her. He was a little rough around the edges, but she had no doubt he'd make a wonderful husband and father.

Nick was practically quivering with excitement and trying desperately not to show it. He didn't want to spoil the surprise.

Jesse and Lorri weren't there when they arrived, and Nick reminded her of the Sunday dinner at the Barkley house. Moments later, they pulled up next to the Jeep. Jesse was apologizing as he got out. "I'm sorry we're late. Momma insisted we stay for her 'Nanner pudding."

"Well, did you bring us some?" Nick teased.

"Nah, we ate every bite of it," Jesse said sheepishly as he rubbed his stomach.

Danny jumped out of the truck and ran to the corner of the house. He picked up an empty lard bucket, then he turned back and yelled, "Can we go hunt treasure now?"

Lorri and Jesse were each headed toward the house with a twin in tow, and Lorri looked over at Danny and said, "Young man, you'd better go get out of those good Sunday clothes first."

Danny didn't need to be told twice, as his mother's voice told him she was dead serious. He ran in the house, slamming the door behind him, and before the adults could carry all the baby stuff inside he was back in his play clothes. Marie just chuckled. "Well, I guess we're looking for treasure now."

Danny impatiently shifted his weight from one leg to the other, holding the bucket in front of him, praying the stupid old people wouldn't want to stand and talk all day. Nick directed him, "Little man, lead the way. We'll follow you."

Danny took off at a dead run, but Nick and Marie walked at a normal pace. At the edge of the woods, Danny stopped and waited on them. At the edge of the stream, Danny sat down his bucket and waded in, flipping over rocks. His third rock uncovered a spring lizard, and he caught it and placed it in his bucket. Nick was a little concerned the hunt might be in jeopardy, as he could see the boy had been distracted by the lizards. Fortunately, when Danny went to place the second lizard in the bucket, he noticed the first one had escaped through a small hole. Seeing the disappointment on his face, Nick suggested, "Why don't we turn over that big rock? I'll help you with it."

Marie remembered the hidden items so she joined in. "I'll help, too."

When they flipped it on its side, Danny immediately spotted the white, flint-rock arrowhead. He got so excited he stumbled and fell face-first into the mud. Nick and Marie held their breath, thinking he would cry, but he did just the opposite. When he fell, his face had landed next to the necklace. He became so elated at his find that he scrambled up on his knees and yelled, "Uncle Nick, we're rich! We hit the jackpot! They left a bunch of stuff here!" He scooped up the rest of the arrowheads and the necklace and held them out for inspection. All Marie could see was the muddy little boy standing in front of her, jumping with excitement, and she realized she'd better clean him up before Lorri saw him. As Danny moved down the stream flipping over more rocks, the sun glinted off the Alka-Seltzer bottle. She saw her name in bright red letters painted on the bottle. She bent over, picked it up, and turned to Nick, saying, "Another surprise, huh?"

She unscrewed the cap and pulled out the note. The ring had slipped off and had settled in the bottom of the bottle. Nick hadn't planned it that way, but he was pleased with the results. She handed him the bottle to hold while she opened the note. While she was reading, he emptied the ring into his hand and patiently waited.

Dearest Marie,

Once I left the army and moved here. I thought having close friends, like Jesse and his family, was the best I could ever hope for in life. Then I met you and started to dream. By our second date I knew I couldn't live without you. We just fit and can be together without having to talk about anything. You fill all those empty places I didn't know I had and have made me want you and our own family. I love you. Will you marry me and promise to be there forever?

Nick

# CHAPTER 18

Danny didn't know or care what Labor Day was. All he knew was the holiday was on Monday and he got to start school the next day. His mom had gotten him paper and two pencils, saying that was all he'd need. She explained that if he listened to the teacher she would show him how to use them.

Lorri led Danny along the path leading from their house to Darby's on Tuesday morning. When they arrived, she was shocked at how many kids were waiting for the school bus. She recognized the Barnes children, but the others were strangers. She approached the oldest girl and asked if she would mind making sure Danny got on the bus in the afternoon, saying, "He's starting the first grade."

One of the older girls stepped forward. "I can do it; it's my little sister's first day, too."

"Thanks. I'm Lorri Barkley."

"I'm Molly, and this is my sister Lucy."

As they were talking, the bus approached and stopped. Everyone lined up hurriedly, and Lorri stood back watching Danny climb aboard. He'd made it clear to her the night before that he was a big boy now and didn't need any help. While she stood there fighting to keep her emotions in check, Billy walked out onto the porch. "Hi, Lorri. Seeing Danny off to school?"

She grimaced. "Yeah, and it's killing me. He doesn't want to be seen with me. I asked that Molly girl to make sure he got on the bus this afternoon. Where did all these kids come from?"

"Oh, that's right, you were born and raised in Epworth. Most of them come from the road that runs next to Barnes Chapel Church."

"I knew the Barnes children lived there, but I didn't realize the road went any farther," she admitted.

He laughed. "Molly and her sister are the last house on that road, and it's more than a mile from here. In fact, I bet they could throw a rock from their porch and hit Sugar Creek."

She was shocked and concerned. "They walk that far every day?"

"I'm afraid so; there are nine of them living down that road, so they have lots of company."

"I guess that helps. I better get home and feed the twins. I'm guessing my mom will be glad to see me back," she said, giving him a little wave.

"Tell Jesse I said hello. Oh yeah, the bus gets here about three thirty every afternoon."

"Thanks, Billy."

At three thirty that afternoon, Lorri was anxiously standing on the right side of the porch so she could see the bus when it stopped. She sighed with relief when she saw Danny jump off and start running full speed all the way home. When he hit the porch, he said, "Momma, it was fun. My teacher is Miss Waters. She looks just like Mamaw Barkley and has white hair, too!"

"That's great. She was my first grade teacher, too. Does she have you sit in alphabetical order?"

"I don't know what that means," Danny frowned.

"Did you pick a seat, or did she tell you where to sit?"

"She said we had a special desk," he explained earnestly.

The meal was long that night as the proud parents listened to their new student tell them all about his day.

It had also been Michael Barkley's first day in the fourth grade and the first full year he didn't have on the dreaded leg brace. Supper that night was exciting at the Barkleys' too, as it was clear Michael felt entirely differently about this new phase of his life. His classmates finally saw him as normal, not handicapped. Everything was going well until Michael brought up Craig's name. He was now in the sixth grade, and Michael still worshiped him for some reason his daddy couldn't even fathom. When the name came up, Martha furtively glanced over at Mike and noticed the fire ignite in his eyes. She touched his hand and shook her head to let him know this wasn't the time to express his feelings about the Foster family. Later that night, he whispered to her, "You know how I feel about Craig; he's a bad influence and you darn well know it."

"Just relax. In a couple of years, he'll be in high school and their relationship will be over," she reasoned.

"God, I hope so. Just the thought of that kid upsets me so much I won't sleep a wink all night."

"Oh," she laughed, "that's your excuse for needing a glass of buttermilk and cornbread?" She got up and headed to the kitchen.

"Don't forget the onions!" He grinned.

# CHAPTER 19

On Saturday, Jesse was surprised when Nick failed to show up. He couldn't remember the last time he hadn't been there. Lorri was feeding the twins, and he said, worried, "Wonder where Nick is. You don't think he's in trouble, do you?"

"He might be, but not the kind you're thinking of," she laughed. "You know he asked Marie to marry him, don't you?"

"I thought he was doing it on their treasure hunt, but I didn't see the ring when they came back and I was afraid to bring it up in case she'd said no."

"You really thought she might say no? Why didn't you just ask? I can't believe you've been wondering all this time. They don't want anyone to know until Nick asks her dad for his blessing. I bet that's what he's up to today."

Annoyed, Jesse said, "And to think I've been feeling bad for him all this time. For sure, they're getting married?"

"Wild horses couldn't keep them apart. Nick wanted her father's blessing since she's been the woman of the house since her momma passed. I was really impressed that Nick understands that her family's support matters," Lorri said.

Jesse grinned. "I guess that old saying 'still waters run deep' is true. I just saw him as a kid all this time. Guess I won't make that mistake again. Sweetie, how do you feel about us giving them a couple of acres of land as a wedding present?"

"I think that's a great idea. He helped you all this time and wouldn't take anything for it but meals."

Jesse continued, "I was thinking about that land between our driveway and Billy's four acres."

Lorri didn't need to be sold on the idea. "I like it. They'll be our closest neighbors, but you do know that means you'll be helping him build his house now, right?"

"It'll be fun. We work well together."

Lorri was amused watching Jesse try to hide the fact that he was watching for Nick to show up. He sulked all weekend. By Sunday afternoon, she gave up and finally just stuck her head out to see what was going on. Danny said, "Momma! Daddy is fixing Uncle Nick a playhouse."

Jesse corrected him, "Not a playhouse, a house place." He held up four one-inch galvanized pipes that he planned to use to mark the land that would be their gift. "Sweetie, do you have some red ribbon I can tie on these so you can really see them?"

"Let me check. You don't think you're rushing things, do you?"

"No, it's just four stakes in the ground, and it gives me something to do," he stated.

She shook her finger at him in warning. "You'd better make sure I'm there when you tell them."

It was Monday morning before Jesse finally got Nick to himself. He pushed for information, insisting, "I'm tired of waiting; are you engaged or what? Did you ask her daddy for his blessing? I'm serious, Nick, tell me what's happening."

"Sarge, I didn't know you cared one way or the other. I'm absolutely touched! The answer is yes to both questions."

"Wonderful," Jesse said. "Lorri wants you two to come over Sunday around two o'clock. We have a gift for you."

"What is it?"

"Hell if I know. Probably a cake or a peach pie. Just show up, please."

When Jesse got out of his truck Thursday evening, he noticed Kell Weeks. "What's up, Kell?"

"We've cut all the trees we can on this side of the mountain, and I wanted to check with you before we moved. Hop in and I'll show you what I'm talking about," Kell said.

"Good, I need to talk to you about some lumber for Nick's house anyway."

Confused, Kell asked, "Thought he was single. Why's he building a house?"

"He won't be for long."

As they were driving along, Kell pointed to an area that had been clear cut. "You're about to get some new neighbors. One of the men helping me at the sawmill bought that land across the road. His name is Willard Sluder and his wife is Jewell. Looks like his house is only twenty feet from a power pole. It's finally happening, you know; in a few years everybody will have electricity up here."

Jesse laughed. "About time, don't you think?"

Kell turned right onto an old road and Jesse looked around. "I didn't even know this was here."

"I think it was used by the first settlers. I had the guys cut out the sprouts and get rid of the old dead logs." Kell had picked a perfect spot; it looked like a house had been there at some point in the past. "How big a house is Nick planning on building?"

"Ah, he just got engaged. Don't think they're even talking about it yet. We'll need to give them a few weeks to figure all that out."

Kell rubbed his chin in thought. "I'll go ahead and cut some two-by-tens and some two-by-fours. Tell him I won't take all his money."

They laughed in ease.

As Nick and Marie drove up on Sunday, Jesse and Lorri pretended they were playing with the kids in the yard. Truthfully, they were dancing with excitement at their gift for the couple.

Nick got out, not sure what to expect, as Lorri was usually pretty unpredictable. Lorri yelled out, "I've got your favorite dessert, but before we eat it I want to show you something I found by our driveway." Carrying Mindy, she began to lead them. Danny was in hog heaven; he had Nick's hand on one side and Marie's on the other. He was busy chattering about school when Lorri came to an abrupt halt.

She directed, "Danny, flip that board over so we can see the other side."

Her comment got Marie and Nick's attention. When Danny turned it over, it was upside down. Frustrated, she said, "Turn it around so we can read it."

In bold letters it said, *Let it be known this is the property of Marie and Nick Turner.*

When Marie finished reading it, she sprinted to hug Lorri and then Jesse. Nick was frozen in his spot. His mouth worked helplessly as his eyes began to fill with tears. He realized Jesse and Lorri had just taught him a life's lesson—*friendship* was a much stronger word than *family*. In his entire life, he'd never experienced such generosity. Jesse was uncomfortable with the silence and started to babble. "I talked to Kell about lumber for the house. He wanted to know what kind you'd need and assured me he wouldn't charge you more than an arm and a leg. Well, you might have to throw in your first kid too."

# CHAPTER 20

Life in the mountains moved along at an easy pace until the winter of 1952. Jesse, Nick, and Billy sat around the pot-bellied stove in the store sharing stories. Jesse brought up the burning of the barracks buildings at the elementary school in Epworth. A long time ago, the school had been given a couple of army barracks to use as classrooms for all the extra students resulting from the baby boomers.

Billy asserted, "It looks like the school board and county commissioner will need to get off their fat asses and build some new schools. About time they earned their pay."

Nick was amused at Billy's passion. "Why don't you tell us how you really feel?"

"It pisses me off every time I see these little kids walking over a mile in the rain and snow to catch the bus. There's no money to buy buses, but there's always enough to give the board and commissioner a raise."

Jesse vaguely remembered Dooley warning him not to let Billy get off on politics unless he had a lot of time to waste, so he tried humor to change the subject: "They don't have it as bad as we did. Remember we had to walk five miles barefoot both ways with snow so deep we were hopping from fence post to fence post."

"Hell, Jesse. I'm serious," Billy protested.

Nick said, "Sounds like you've thought about this a lot."

The conversation was getting so serious it bothered Jesse. He blurted out, "What have you heard about the war?"

Billy corrected him. "You mean *police action*; it isn't a war! Politicians know if they call it a war it'll leave a bad taste in the mouths of most Americans. Calling it a police action makes it sound like there's no threat, but that has problems, too. Men aren't volunteering like they did for World War II. Drafting them is the solution, and boy are they starting to hit Fannin County pretty hard. That's the bad news. The good news is their families tell me most of the ones that have been drafted are staying in the States."

Nick laughed. "Billy, you know more about what's going on than those men on the radio."

"I like to listen to folks, and they like to talk. I think they know I'm not judging them—just listening," he explained. "Sometimes it's like I'm the preacher they tell all their secrets to and then ask for advice. I draw the line at that. I can't tell folks how to live."

Jesse leaned closer and asked, "Well, what do you tell them?"

"I tell them what Davy Crockett used to say: 'Be always sure you're right—then go ahead.' But his best quote is, 'Let your tongue speak what your heart thinks.' Speaking of that—you guys are both vets, what do you think?"

Nick answered first. "If this is anything like our war, the soldiers are fighting to protect each other—nothing bigger than that."

Jesse spoke up, "I agree. You know I'd never tell Lorri this, but I really miss the army and the fellowship of the men."

Nick nodded. "Me too. After I got out of the hospital for that little scratch, they made me an MP. Believe it or not, that's the best job I ever had."

Jesse shook his head. "Yeah, our job at the plant sure does pay good, but it's boring as hell and you don't have to use your brain."

"You guys want to go with me and Cathy to Florida?" Billy joked.

Jesse stood. "Nick, we'd better go home before old Billy turns us into flatlanders."

Mr. Haymore came to the changing house on Monday morning to talk to the men. "Gentlemen, Tennessee Copper Company has decided to do something about all our red hills. They've hired Bill Mercier, the Fannin County Agent, to head up the project, and basically that means we'll be planting a lot of pine trees. I need a couple of volunteers."

Nick's hand shot up. "Me and the Sarge are your men!"

Jesse looked at him questioningly as Nick said under his breath, "Didn't you say you were bored? Well, this is our chance to do something different."

Jesse shrugged his shoulders in agreement. "Oh, hell, why not?"

Haymore started writing in his notebook. "That's Barkley and Turner, right? Follow me and I'll introduce you to Mr. Mercier."

When they got to the office, he introduced them as the volunteers. Bill asked, "Jesse, are you related to Mike Barkley?"

"He's my big brother."

"Good man."

Nick asked, "What do we call you, boss or Mr. Mercier?"

"How about Bill and I'll call you Nick?"

"OK, where do we start?" Nick asked.

Bill handed them a picture and pointed to the north. "This area is just on the other side of that hill. We started the project a couple of years ago, but the pines we planted all died. There are a lot of theories on why. One is the soil is too poor to support the growth, and the other is the company lets gas escape from the smelters. It doesn't really matter either way—our mission is to turn this land green again. I've developed some tablets of fertilizer. They're about the size of a biscuit, and we'll use one of them for every seedling we plant. Our biggest change this year is we're going to move to the edge of the bare areas and plant toward the center. We'll start just north of Turtletown."

Fascinated, Nick asked, "How many seedlings are we talking about?"

"At least a million, son," Bill said.

"Are you kidding me? Sarge and I are good, sir, but I think we might need a little help," Nick said in shock.

Bill liked Nick's attitude; it reminded him of himself. "Yeah, you're right. We've got some scout troops lined up. I just need you guys to show them where and how to plant them."

Nick grinned. "Well, that's all right. We can do that. When do we start?"

"Right now. Truck's out front, and I'll show you the area we're working now," Bill said. He was eager to get started and glad it appeared he'd have competent help.

As they walked out, Bill pointed to the truck and said, "Forgot my coat, be right back."

When he was far enough away not to hear them, Jesse whispered, "Nick, what have you gotten us into?"

"Sarge, don't blame me. You're the one that was bored."

# CHAPTER 21

Lorri had noticed a change in Jesse since he'd begun work on the re-seeding program. Her curiosity made her ask, "What's changed? You seem so happy."

"It's like when I was young on the farm. At the end of the day, you can see the results. I was afraid planting a million trees would be boring after a while, but it turned out to be great watching what we've done get larger and larger. Everyone agrees. It's a really good feeling, and we're doing something that matters."

She put her arm around him and squeezed. "I like this new you. You're that happy-go-lucky sergeant at Fort Benning again. I have to admit I've kinda missed that guy."

Spring was good. They'd planted more than a million seedlings that winter, and the heifers Jesse and Nick bought had produced nine healthy calves. O'Shea had written about the rumor the soldiers would be home by Christmas.

The summer of 1952 was even better for everyone in the county. Frank had doubled the size of his cattle herd and purchased even more attachments for his tractor. His latest was a hay rake. Now he could cut hay on Wednesday and rake it up into long piles for easy loading on Friday all by himself. Jesse and Nick could pick it up and stack it on Saturday. The first cutting was the week after school closed for the summer. At the family dinner, Jesse asked Michael if he'd like to earn a little money of his own by helping them put the hay up.

Spending time with his uncle was reward enough for the child, and he quickly agreed. "Uncle Jesse, you don't have to pay me. I'll help."

It reminded Jesse of Mr. O'Neal, who had wanted to pay for the mule, but not the labor, because he'd been a little kid. "Michael, that's not the way it is. You give me a good day's work, and I give you a good day's pay. Sound OK with you?"

His nephew nodded, and Jesse stuck out his hand. "Men shake hands when they seal a deal. A man's word is the most important thing in life, and you never go back on your word once you have a deal. Do we have a deal, Michael?"

Michael beamed. He'd never felt so grown up in his life. Jesse clutched his small hand, and they shook three times with great ceremony.

Martha was sitting at the end of the table listening. She didn't like this idea at all. She couldn't believe he wanted Michael to work in a hay field, where so many dangers lurked that could snatch her child from her. It had only been a year since they'd removed the brace, and he was just now beginning to walk without a limp. She listened, and just as she began to scheme how she could put a stop to this nonsense, Jesse's lesson about a man's word being his bond stopped her in her tracks. How on earth could any self-respecting mother botch up a lesson like that? Darn that Jesse Barkley, he was a slick one!

Michael was sitting on the bench proud as a peacock when reality hit. He'd made a deal with Uncle Jesse without clearing it with his parents first. Trying to correct his mistake he turned to them and asked, "Is it OK?"

Mike saw from the look on Martha's face that she couldn't respond at that moment, so he asked, "Didn't you already give your uncle your word? I saw you shake hands. Jesse, what time do you want him in the field?"

Jesse said, "Why don't you let Michael spend the night. You could drop him off Friday afternoon so he can help Danny with the calves, and that way you can start your mail run on time Saturday morning?"

When Michael heard his dad tell Jesse OK, he felt like the luckiest boy in the entire county. Spending time with his favorite uncle and getting paid for it was as close to heaven as he'd ever get. He decided this would be the longest week in his life.

Saturday morning, Michael felt like he was living a dream. When Nick arrived, Jesse threw three pitchforks in the bed of his truck, and as the men and Michael started to leave, Danny cried. Lorri held his arm, consoling him. "They've got big men work to do today. You just need to grow a little more."

Through his tears he asked, "When I'm as big as Michael, can I go too?"

"Yes, maybe next summer." She hugged him and then started around the side of the house looking for something to distract him as she watched the others drive off.

Jesse drove down to the meadow and stopped between the two rows of hay Frank had piled the day before. Nick took one of the pitchforks and started on the row on the right side of the truck. Michael and Jesse did the same on the left. Everyone was quiet at first, putting as much hay as they could on their pitchforks and then carrying it to the truck and tossing it in. Michael quickly realized he'd made a mistake trying to lift as much hay at a time as Jesse—green hay was heavy. Noticing the problem, Jesse said, "Kid, we're going to be here all day, so slow down and pace yourself."

Embarrassed, Michael apologized. "I didn't know grass weighed so much."

"It's heavy. Take a deep breath; there's nothing that smells as good as freshly cut hay."

Like most kids, Michael felt the need to fill the space with chatter. "Did you have to cut hay in the army, Uncle Jesse?"

"Nah, we were busy fighting the war or training to fight the next one."

His questions continued like bullets. "What's it like jumping out of a plane?"

Jesse stopped and leaned on his pitchfork, staring into the sky. "At first it's scary, but after you do it a few times it's exciting, like one of those rides at the county fair."

"Do you miss it?"

"A little bit."

Nick yelled out, "Quit lollygagging around, you two. Sarge, move the truck so we don't have to carry this hay so far."

Jesse jumped in and moved the truck thirty feet down the row. As they fell into a rhythm, they constantly had to move the truck. After a couple of hours, they'd only added a few loads to the stacks, and Jesse realized they'd better to come up with a solution or they wouldn't get the job finished today. Then it hit him. "Michael, how about driving the truck and Nick and I will load it?"

Michael was flabbergasted and looked at him in horror. He didn't want to disappoint Jesse. "Uncle Jesse, I can't, I don't know how."

Nick just laughed. "Yeah you do, you just haven't tried it yet. It's easy."

Jesse put him in the truck and asked, "Can you reach the pedals?"

He tried and said, "If I sit real close to the steering wheel."

"Good, put your foot on the left one—that's the clutch. Push it all the way to the floor."

He did as directed.

"Now put your right foot on the other pedal, that's the brake. Push that one to stop."

Jesse pulled it out of gear and cranked it, easing out the throttle until it was at a fast idle. "We need you to drive down the center of those two rows. When we tell you to stop, you just push in both pedals at the same time. To make it go, take your foot off the brake and ease the left pedal out real slow until it begins to move. Let's give it a try. Push in the clutch."

After a couple of false starts, Michael finally got the hang of it and was beaming with pride. He was driving! At first they'd make him stop every twenty to thirty feet, but then their competitive nature kicked in. Nick started it; he began to pick up the hay and pitch it into the bed of the truck as it was moving.

Jesse wasn't going to let Nick outdo him, and he started to do the same. Michael ended up driving the full length of the meadow before he had to stop. He sat a little straighter behind the wheel and realized he'd done it. He couldn't wait to tell Craig.

They finished with two hay stacks well before dark. Jesse had created a monster; Michael asked every week at dinner for the rest of the summer if Frank was cutting hay again. After lots of practice, Michael was a productive part of the team.

# CHAPTER 22

Jesse was used to Nick's high energy in the mornings, but today he seemed exceptionally wired. Exasperated, Jesse finally asked, "What in the hell is up with you today?"

"Marie and I decided we weren't getting married until the house was finished. The TVA guy came by yesterday and said they'd be running power to the house today. So Saturday's the day. We want you and Lorri to stand up with us, if that's OK," Nick blurted out.

Jesse grinned. "Well, you know the answer to that. We'd be honored. We can get Momma to watch the kids. What time and where?"

"We're figuring that out after work today."

Saturday morning was hectic at the Barkley household. At sixteen months, the twins were beginning to develop their own personalities. Lorri's mother kept telling her it was time she was getting payback for being such a headstrong child. The wedding was to be at Reverend Paul Adams's house at one o'clock. When Lorri had heard the time, she'd figured she would have plenty of time to feed the kids and drop them off, but somehow babies manage to mess with the best of plans. It wasn't their fault; they were just a lot of work and had a lot of stuff. She was worried about leaving all three kids with Mrs. Barkley in case it was too much for her, but she could see no other choice.

Danny ran to Amos when they arrived, asking, "Papaw, can we go put peanuts in some Coca-Colas?"

"Yes, sir," he said, grabbing up his cap. "Me and Danny are going to the store." He didn't even wait for a reply; he just took the child's hand and headed out the door.

Momma smiled. "Good riddance. I'll have these new babies all to myself."

Lorri's worries disappeared instantly.

When they got back home, Nick and Marie were waiting on them. As they got out of the truck, Nick yelled impatiently, "Let's go. We're going to be late. I told him we'd be on time. He's got another one scheduled right after ours."

Reverend Adams met them at the door and escorted them to the parlor, asking, "Nick, do you have rings?"

Nick ceremoniously placed two plain gold rings in his hand, and the minister took his place behind a small podium. He placed the two rings on the top corner and, without saying anything, began the ceremonial words. It took less than fifteen minutes and a mere ten minutes after that the newlyweds were on the road. As Lorri got into the truck, she giggled and said, "They were as anxious as we were to be alone. Love and intimacy are great partners in a new marriage, and here we are, all alone, with absolutely nothing to do. We could go to the movies or to Harry's for a great meal or some alone time at home."

Jesse laughed. "Seeing them unable to keep their hands off each other has turned my little woman on, hasn't it?"

She smiled. "Maybe just a little bit. What would you like to do?"

"Everything, but I'm sure Momma is expecting us back soon."

"She isn't looking for us until well after dark, mister. She's the one who gave me the idea," she said smugly.

Monday morning, someone knocked on the back door. When Lorri opened it, she smiled in delight at Marie, who was carrying some freshly baked goodies. She smelled them before she even got the door open. "Is that what I think it is?"

"If you're thinking cinnamon rolls, it sure is. They're a thank you present for Saturday," Marie said.

"It was our honor, but Marie, I have a question. Don't think I'm being critical, but why was the minister was so stiff and impersonal? A justice of the peace would have been more personable."

Marie laughed out loud. "He's been expecting me to marry his younger brother since we were in school together. Jamie was a friend, but I never felt anything more for him."

Shocked, Lorri asked, "Then why in the world would you ask him to do the service?"

"Daddy insisted. Said he'd be embarrassed to attend church if I asked somebody else to marry us. Felt like I owed Daddy that much. I ask him to come but he felt it would be awkward."

"I get it. I was wondering why your father wasn't there," Lorri said. "It was a little awkward."

Marie chuckled. "You think?"

Fall was a wonderful time for the two couples, but others weren't so fortunate. Michael had been so excited the night before the first day of school. He just knew Craig would love his news. He met his friend on the trail and blurted it out: "I learned to drive Jesse's truck this summer!"

Craig didn't show any interest at all. He just scoffed and responded, "I steer Dad's car all the time. So what?"

"No, not like that. I drove it all by myself in the meadow while they loaded the hay," Michael protested.

Craig snorted in disdain. "Driving on a farm doesn't count. I've got to go. I need to talk to the principal."

Michael was heartbroken by Craig's reaction. Craig's little sister, Margaret, had overheard the conversation. As soon as her brother was out of sight, she consoled Michael by saying, "I think driving on a farm is pretty special. What does old Craig know anyway?"

Michael didn't normally pay much attention to second graders, but he liked what she'd said and was surprised that she'd taken his side against her own brother.

Another disappointment was that the servicemen were expected to be home by Christmas but it simply wasn't true; instead, the soldiers had to spend another long, cold winter in Korea. It was cold in North Georgia, too. Since Marie and Nick had moved in, Jesse and Nick had taken turns driving to work. They were still planting pines and working the bare hills of the basin. One evening, Jesse stopped at Darby's to get gas and Billy met them at the pump. "Have you heard? Tom Wilson turned the tractor over up in the pasture and crushed his chest. He's home in really bad shape. That old man shouldn't have been driving that tractor at his age."

Before Jesse thought, he asked, "Isn't he about the same age as you?"

"Yeah, but you don't see me driving no tractor. I'm going to see him tonight. I'll let you know how he's doing."

Nick didn't usually pay a lot of attention when Mr. Mercier talked to Jesse about people in Blue Ridge, but today their conversation captured his interest. Two of the sheriff's deputies had been drafted, and finding their replacements was turning out to be a problem. Apparently the sheriff was a hard man to work for since he'd returned from the war. He'd been an officer in the MPs and had gotten used to people calling him sir, but the real issue was that he'd gotten real comfortable with no one being able to question his orders.

As he listened, Nick smiled. He'd had a boss just like that in Germany, and he knew how to get along with him. A lot of *yes, sirs* and *no, sirs* went a long way, and you had to let him take all the credit. He looked over and asked, "Bill, how does one go about getting one of those deputy jobs?"

Jesse explained, "Nick was an MP in the army."

Bill shrugged and replied, "I guess the best way would be to hear it from the horse's mouth. If you're interested, you should just go ask."

It was Nick's turn to drive for the week, and he was seeking Jesse's approval on his tentative decision. "Sarge, do you think I should go see the sheriff this evening?"

"I would if it were me. It would be a shame if somebody else beat you to it. Why don't you drop me off at Billy's and I'll walk? I can find out how Mr. Wilson is doing."

Nick grinned. "Now that sounds like a plan. Where is this sheriff's office anyway?"

"It's in the rear of the courthouse. Do you know where that is?"

Nick nodded. "I'll find it."

Jesse got out of the Jeep and walked into the store. Cathy was dusting the shelves as they greeted each other. Jesse quickly asked, "How's Mr. Wilson doing?"

"Not great. Billy's over there now to see if there's anything we can do."

Jesse nodded. "Billy's a good neighbor."

"He tries to be," she said proudly as they continued to chat.

When Nick walked into the sheriff's office, he was surprised at what he saw. He'd expected a tall, skinny man like his old boss, but standing before him was a short, fat man with his stomach scrunched on the top of the desk as he slumped over. He took his seat as Nick stared at him and asked, "You got a problem, son?"

Unconsciously, Nick came to attention as if reporting to his commanding officer. When his heels clicked together, the sheriff sat up straight in his chair with interest.

"No problem, sir. I was just wondering about that deputy job I hear you have open."

"What's your name, where are you from, and what kind of experience do you have?" the sheriff asked.

"I'm Nick Turner, I live in Gravely Gap near Darby's, and I was an MP in the war, sir."

The sheriff's response was automatic. "At ease."

Nick moved to modified parade rest position and waited patiently. The sheriff opened his desk drawer and pulled out a sheet of paper. "Fill this out, and when you return it, we'll see how it goes."

Nick thanked him, did an about face, and left without saying another word. The next morning Jesse asked how things went.

Nick grinned in satisfaction, which made Jesse laugh. "What in the world did you do?"

"Mr. Mercier said he was an officer, so I just acted like a soldier."

"You're kidding me. You didn't!"

"Yep, and then he gave me an application. I need some references. Can I use you?"

Jesse nodded immediately. "Absolutely, and why don't you put down Mike and Frank Wilson? I bet Mr. Mercier wouldn't mind being on that list either."

Nodding in agreement, Nick said, "I'll ask him at lunch."

After work, Nick dropped Jesse off and continued on to the sheriff's office. He met him at the door. Nick handed him the completed application and said, "Sir, I hope this is OK."

Scanning the paper quickly, the sheriff asked, "How do you know Mike Barkley?"

"I work with his brother at the plant."

Nodding, he said, "How do you know Bill Mercier?"

"That's who I work for at the plant," he explained.

"Hmm, looks good. If this all checks out, when can you start?"

"I can be here the first of the month, sir," Nick said with enthusiasm.

"If you don't hear from me, it means you didn't get the job. I'll send you a note if you do, and you'll report here at oh-eight-hundred on the first Monday of the month."

"Thank you, sir," he called as he turned and left the office.

At the same time, Jesse walked into the store and took a cola out of the box. As he opened it, he turned to Billy and before he could even ask, Billy said, "Tom died last night. His funeral is at Barnes Chapel."

Jesse just ducked his head. "I hate to hear that. Do you know what time?"

"Two o'clock Saturday."

Jesse paid for his drink and walked home.

# CHAPTER 23

Postmaster Griffin sat at his desk munching on the cinnamon roll Mike Barkley had brought in earlier that morning. He was tickled to death that he'd chosen Mike out of the fifteen applicants he'd had for the job. It was obvious the man loved his work. He was an extremely conscientious worker who never seemed to have a bad day. In fact, he was such a good influence on the other employees that they'd begun to arrive early instead of late in order to hear Mike's daily tale and his deep belly laugh.

When he'd first become postmaster, he'd had an employee like Mike. He was so popular with the other employees that Mr. Griffin had been jealous and had fired him. His district manager had visited, and when Mr. Griffin had bragged to him about what he'd done, the manager had looked at him in disappointment and said, "That boy was the anchor of your team. When you fired him, you lost the team's respect and they fell apart." It took Mr. Griffin a while to realize the mistake he'd made by not utilizing the asset he'd had, so when he hired Mike, he knew he couldn't afford to make the same mistake. It was time to bring Mike into the office and groom him as his replacement. He knew Mike would do him proud, and a side benefit was that Martha was a great baker—the entire staff would eat well!

Sunday dinner was quieter than usual. They were discussing Tom's death and how everyone would miss him. Amos was annoyed at how serious they were, so he started telling them a story about Tom he remembered from when they were kids. "We were really close when we grew up, and believe me, if you thought my daddy was mean you should have met Tom's. He worked us boys like slaves, and one day we were laying bricks and Tom started singing "Doodah from the song Camp town Races." He sang that darn song for hours until his daddy got so mad he backhanded him and told him to quit. Tom just kept working and singing, and the old man stood up and took off his belt to give Tom the whipping of his life. Quick as a rabbit, Tom took off running with his daddy chasing him with that belt, threatening him within an inch of his life. Tom slipped into the outhouse, which was a two holer. He went through the best one, pushed the plank off the back, and crawled out. His daddy looked for him for an hour and was so mad he let us all go home. We laughed until our sides hurt. Smart old Tom saved himself from a licking."

Everyone laughed but the kids. They didn't understand what was so funny. Jesse took this opportunity to tell everyone what he'd been dying to say. "It's looking like Nick might be a deputy sheriff next month."

Amos's temper flared. "Why would that boy give up a good job at the plant to be a little deputy?"

Jesse defended his friend. "Daddy, he liked being an MP in the army and said it was the best job he'd ever had. I'm glad for him, and I know just how he feels. The plant is good, but job satisfaction just isn't there. Not like it was at Fort Benning."

Lorri looked at Jesse in surprise; he was finally confirming what she'd known in her heart ever since they'd left the army. Amos concluded the conversation with, "Still, it's a good thing you got out when you did. If you hadn't, you'd be over there in Korea. At least you're safe at home now."

Jesse sadly agreed. "I know, and it's great that Danny and the girls get to know their family."

Amos just shook his head and left the table.

On the way home, Lorri tentatively asked, "Do you want to join the army again?"

"I'm too old to play soldier, I guess," he said, brushing off the question.

The following Monday, when Mr. Griffin heard Mike's laugh, he stuck his head out the door and called, "Mike, let's talk before you start your route."

Minutes later Mike knocked on his door.

"Remember when I first hired you and you said you wanted my job one day? Well, if that's ever going to happen you need to know what goes on here. If that's still your goal, you can begin working here in the office next week. It'll also mean a small pay raise for you. What do you think?"

Mike was almost doing a happy dance and asked enthusiastically, "I think it's just great! What do I need to do?"

"You need to let Tim ride your route with you this week so he can take it over next week."

"Does Tim already know?" Mike asked.

Mr. Griffin nodded. "He's waiting at your car. You'd better get going."

Tim looked bored. He was throwing rocks into the field behind the post office. Mike yelled, "Tim, looks like it's me and you against the world. Get in and I'll show you how to do what's going to be your best job ever."

"If it's so good, why do you want to leave it?"

"I'm going after an even bigger dream," he said with his big laugh.

Mike had a talent. Some people said it was a gift. He was able to easily remember faces and numbers. This turned out to be a real asset when he worked the counter. He welcomed everyone by name and remembered their address without being prompted. It made people feel special, and they really responded to it.

After a couple weeks, Mike knew all the faces of the regulars. One lady with shoulders stooped from age who needed a cane to walk came in several times a week. Mike thought she would be perfect as the grandmother in a Norman Rockwell painting. Today when he saw her outside the main door, he turned to his coworker, Karen, and whispered, "Why does Mrs. Sullivan only ever buy one stamp? She comes in so often it would be easier on her to get more at a time."

Karen smiled. "That's Granny. Don't you know anything about her? She's part of Blue Ridge history."

"Karen, I'm from Sugar Creek; I don't know many of the city folks," he explained as he gave out one of his laughs.

She looked around and noticed an immediate reaction to the sound. It was like everyone inside just relaxed and started chatting with each other. She watched in amazement and then continued, "Granny doesn't really need stamps. She comes because she's lonely. If you pay attention, you'll notice she always comes during the busiest times."

When Karen turned to help the next customer in line, Mike was pleased to see that Granny had chosen his line. As she approached, he smiled widely and said, "Mrs. Sullivan—my, what a beautiful blue dress you have on. Is it new?"

She just snorted and responded, "This old thing? I've had it for years. I wear it on special occasions."

"Well, little lady, you should wear it more often. What's the occasion?"

"I'm getting my hair done," she explained with a smile.

"That's wonderful, and to go with that lovely dress I have the perfect stamp for you. It's blue and it honors the International Red Cross." He held it out for her inspection.

She looked it over carefully, took out her change purse, and said, "It's beautiful. I'll take two of those." She thanked him and shuffled out the door with a little wave.

# CHAPTER 24

Spring was great for everyone but Jesse. Mike got the promotion, Nick was hired as the senior deputy, Marie and Lorri wore out the trail between their houses, Michael was finishing up school with all As for the year, and even Billy was happy that the county had finally made the dirt road next to Barnes Chapel Church a school bus route. In fact, the bus turned around at Molly's house now.

Lorri realized right away what was wrong with her husband; he'd lost his best friend. She helpfully pointed this out to him. He tried to laugh it off, but deep down he knew she was right. At Sunday dinner, Michael was excited to be out of school and thrilled that he could help his uncle Jesse cut hay without shoes for the summer. "When are you going to start? Do you need me again this year?"

Jesse turned to him and said, "Boy, you're in luck. Frank is cutting it next week. Will you be able to help next Saturday?"

"I'll be there," he said, and he stuck out his hand. "Can we shake on it?"

"This is called a southern handshake. Do you remember what it means?"

"Yes, sir. You never go back on your word once you make a deal."

Jesse said very seriously, "Remember that and you will grow up to be a man your momma and daddy can always be proud of."

Looking over at them, Lorri couldn't decide who looked the happiest, Michael or Jesse.

Jesse had a routine of dropping by Darby's store and catching up on the latest gossip since Nick had changed jobs. He couldn't believe how much he missed his friend's constant chatter, even about subjects he couldn't care less about. He stopped at the pump and watched Billy slowly walk out from the store. Billy called out, "Fill her up?"

"Nah, just two dollars. That should do it for now."

Billy said, "I saw Nick today. He seems to like that new job, but he sure does still like to talk. Good news is I now have a new source for info."

"That reminds me," Jesse said. "Did I see Dooley Barnes at Tom Wilson's funeral?"

"Yeah, he was there."

"I thought he'd left to get work after closing his block factory."

Billy explained, "He did—moved his entire family to South Carolina. It's ironic; as soon as the bus started stopping at their front door, he up and moved those kids away. Funny how stuff like that happens. Bet you didn't know Tom was about to sell the farm to the county and probably would have if he hadn't turned that tractor over on himself. Guess Frank will just keep it now. I noticed he added a few cows. He's even got one of the Brahma bulls like they have down in Texas."

Jesse just nodded. "Guess he's going into the cattle business big time. Hey, at least he's still got a job."

"Speaking of that, Nick told me a lot of people are moving to Dalton to get jobs at the new carpet mill they built. I heard they want all kinds of workers, but they really need people to fix sewing machines." As usual, Billy abruptly changed the direction of the conversation without warning. "Do you think they're going to stop that war in Korea?"

"I sure hope so, but I don't know. Mike told me they drafted a couple of guys from Blue Ridge last week," Jesse said.

"That's not a good sign," Billy said as he replaced the hose. "What else can I do for you?"

"Guess you'd better check the oil. I'm afraid this old truck is on its last legs."

"You ought to get yourself one of those new ones. Can you believe it, 1953 is only half gone and they're already showing pictures of the 1954 model? Go look at them; you might find one you like."

Jesse nodded. "Might just do that."

Checking the dipstick, Billy leaned around the hood and said, "You're right. Looks like you need about a quart."

"Go ahead and put one in. That makes up my mind. I'll go check out those new cars tomorrow afternoon."

Later that evening, Jesse dropped a few hints about the possibility of getting a new vehicle, trying his best to gauge Lorri's reaction. Surprisingly, she agreed, "Now that the girls are getting bigger, we really do need a car."

Jesse was a die-hard lover of Chevys, so he went straight to the dealership in Blue Ridge. As he entered, there weren't any 1954 models on the floor. A young salesman, clad in a suit, approached him. Jesse asked about the new models.

"Sir, all we have right now are pictures, but we still have some new '53 models. The boss wants them sold before the new ones arrive. That means you'll be able to get a '53 at just above dealer's cost. Are you looking for a truck or a car?"

"I was thinking a car," Jesse said.

"Great. We still have five models for you to look at."

Jesse eyes locked on the green one on the showroom floor. "Is that one for sale?"

"Yes, sir. You have good taste. This one even comes with a radio and automatic transmission at no additional cost," the salesman said with great enthusiasm. "Normally it sells for seventeen hundred and fifty dollars, but the boss says we can let it go for sixteen hundred. Do you have a trade-in?"

"Yeah, I have a Chevy truck outside."

"OK, I'll be right back. Let me go talk to the boss." He turned and left, returning moments later. "He says we can give you a four-hundred-dollar trade-in for your truck and an easy payment plan of $50 per month for twenty-four months. How's that sound? You'll need to act fast though. When they're gone, there won't be any more. The '54 model will cost probably more than two thousand dollars."

Jesse nodded and said, "Let's do it."

When he pulled up to the house in the new car, Danny was playing outside and ran inside yelling, "Momma! Daddy's driving a new car."

She looked out the window and waited for Jesse to come in. "I thought you were just going to look. What if I don't like it?" she teased him.

Picking up Mindy, he said, "Come out and look at it. It even has a radio."

She didn't show it, but she loved his choice. "How does it ride?"

"Get in and I'll show you," he said. Feeling like he needed to sell her on the purchase he said, "You can drive. It has an automatic transmission, so you don't even have to change gears."

After a few miles, she could see he was still anxious, so she put him out of his misery, "I love it. It drives like a dream."

Jesse just grinned in satisfaction.

Jesse inhaled the distinctive smell of his new car and turned on the radio as he left work. On one of their drives, Michael had moved the dial to a station out of Chattanooga, and Jesse loved it. Michael called it rock and roll. They'd play several songs and then break for news. He was almost home when they announced that South Korea and North Korea had agreed to a truce but the country would still be divided. They'd create an area between them called a demilitarized zone. Jesse couldn't help but wonder how O'Shea would be affected by this change and decided to write him that evening.

Later that summer, Jesse was passing through McCaysville and starting up Harpertown Hill when he was suddenly halted by cars slowing down and then stopping. Leaning out his window, he asked the closest person, "What's happening?"

"McCaysville High School burned down," he said. "Thank God no one got hurt! Wonder where the kids will go to school this fall."

Jesse reassured him, "I'm sure they'll figure it out." He then turned down a side street to bypass the congestion. When he was almost home, he decided to stop at Darby's and tell Billy the news. It would be a first—he actually knew something before Billy. He pulled up at the pump, and Billy rushed out to meet him.

"Jesse! Did you hear? The high school burned today."

Amazed at Billy's ability to get the news, Jesse shook his head. "How in the world did you know that?"

Billy chuckled in delight. "I have my ways."

"Where do you think they'll go for school this fall?"

Billy said, "That's easy, Epworth."

Jesse decided to just listen, as Billy was more informed than any newsman.

The next Saturday, Jesse and Nick were giving shots to the new calves, and Jesse told Nick about the fire. Nick just said, "Boy, when it rains, it pours."

Jesse asked, "What do you mean?"

"The county doesn't have any money for new schools, and I heard all the farmers are going broke soon. If you haven't heard, the price of beef hit rock bottom. They say they almost have to give the cows away. Everyone is getting out of the business, and that makes things even worse."

Jesse put his hand on Nick's shoulder to get his attention and said, "Are you saying we need to get out too?"

Nick nodded. "The sooner the better."

"What about the hay we're putting up in two weeks?"

Nick said, "I think the best thing to do would be to give it to Frank. That way the meadow will get cut."

Thinking more like military men than farmer's a plan was hatched. Rubbing his head as he thought, Jesse said, "Can you get some days off next week? I have a little vacation time, and if we're going to do this, let's get it done. What do you think?"

"Sarge, welcome back. That's a great plan. How many do you think we should sell?"

"All but the two milk cows," said Jesse.

The next ten days were hectic, but they accomplished the mission of selling the cattle. Unfortunately, they only got half of what they thought they should. Jesse's share was enough to pay off his mortgage, with enough left over to pay ahead several months on his new car.

They drove out to see Frank about the hay on Saturday. Stopping next to the farmhouse, they could see Opal and another woman on the front porch. Opal yelled out to greet them, "Come on in the house and meet Thelma, Frank's wife!"

They were so surprised they couldn't think of anything to say. Jesse nudged Nick and said under his breath, "I didn't even know Frank had a girlfriend, much less a wife."

Opal smiled and explained, "Frank and Thelma met at church years ago. When we went to the revival at Damascus, I recognized her and reminded him who she was, and the rest is history."

Jesse held out his hand. "Welcome, neighbor. Frank's a lucky man."

"Thank you, but I'm the lucky one." She smiled shyly.

"Where is Frank?" Jesse said.

"Downstairs taking a bath," Opal said. She went inside and they could hear her yelling, "Frank, you've got company!"

When he appeared moments later, Thelma slid her arm around him and kissed him on the cheek. Nick and Jesse could see he was embarrassed. They explained how they'd sold the cattle and why. Familiar with the slump in prices, Frank said he'd decided to hold off selling for now and wait for the demand to be higher with fewer cows to sell. When Jesse offered to exchange the hay for keeping the meadow cut, Frank didn't hesitate to agree. It was a win-win situation, as Frank had just purchased a new bailer. He even offered to leave enough hay to keep Jesse's milk cows fed.

Later that evening, Jesse told Lorri about meeting Thelma and she smiled. He recognized the look. "You already knew about her, didn't you?"

"Yeah, Marie and Thelma are close friends. She kept me up to date on their courtship."

"Why didn't you tell me?" Jesse complained. He hated being kept in the dark.

Lorri placed her hands on her hips and calmly said, "Now aren't you the one always complaining about Billy being a gossip?"

He just said, "I'm digging myself a hole, aren't I?"

"A pretty good sized one, I'd say."

Later that night, Jesse was unable to fall asleep. He admitted to himself that he really wasn't all that disappointed about being out of the cattle business. When he was younger, he had thought owning a farm of his own would be a perfect life; however, the last few years he'd felt like something was missing. He just couldn't put his finger on why he was feeling this way. He had his own home that was fully paid for, he had a wife and three beautiful kids, and he had a great job. He felt guilty for feeling that it wasn't enough, but he knew sooner or later it would come to him.

# CHAPTER 25

In late October, Lorri learned that her parents needed to move to Marietta in order to be closer to her dad's new job. Every time she brought it up to Jesse, she would cry. She said, "We moved back here so Danny and the girls could be close to their grandparents, and now they're moving away."

"Look on the bright side, honey," Jesse said to try to comfort her, "when your dad got hurt and couldn't do the steel rigging anymore, he was lucky to get a better paying job with Lockheed. But what I want to know is why did they decide to move now? He's been working there for six months."

"The stretch of Highway 5 just before you get to Talking Rock is always getting flooded out, and he's missed two days of work already. He says with winter coming, he can't afford to miss more time or he might lose his job," she said as she sobbed.

He just hugged her. "You know they've made the right decision, don't you?"

"I guess you're right," she admitted reluctantly, wiping away her tears.

"Maybe you should tell them you're happy for them and we'll just have to drive down to see the new house." He was relieved to see she was nodding.

When she told Momma Barkley and Martha on Sunday, it seemed to upset Martha. She brooded over it the entire week, and the following Sunday she told them all she was doing her usual Thanksgiving dinner and expected everyone to be in attendance. Jesse could see Lorri's face light up, and he appreciated what his sister-in-law was trying to do. He threw out,

"Guys, we can go rabbit hunting in the morning like we used to when we were kids."

Michael started bouncing in his seat. "Can I go this year?"

Before anyone could respond, Amos got up and went to his bedroom. He came back holding his shotgun and a box of shells. "Here, take my old .410. It's killed many a rabbit and squirrel, but you'll need to shoot it a few times before you go hunting. It shoots like a rifle with a really small shot group."

Jesse jumped in and offered, "Why don't you spend the night with us next Friday and I'll take you and Danny squirrel hunting?"

Michael turned and looked at his parents with his heart in his eyes. Mike knew there was no way to disappoint him. It had been one of his own favorite activities as a child.

Saturday morning, Jesse, Danny, and Michael walked down to the meadow where Jesse had set up some boards with large black Xs in the middle. He showed Michael how to load the .410, then he demonstrated how to hold it. "Aim it at the center of the X, and gently squeeze the trigger."

Michael jerked in surprise when the gun went off. All three walked over to check the target. Jesse took off his cap and covered the shot group. "See how little it spreads? That's what Papaw meant about aiming it like a rifle."

The next target was twice as far away. The shot group was larger this time. Jesse pointed it out. "That's the perfect distance for a squirrel or rabbit. Always wait until you can get this close before you shoot."

Danny had run out of patience by this time and jumped up and down insisting, "Let me shoot one."

Jesse loaded the gun, cocked it, and placed it in Danny's hands. He paused for a moment to capture the beauty of this moment—a father teaching his son to shoot for the first time. Smiling, he said, "Now hold it tight against your shoulder when you shoot." He noticed Danny moved the gun away from his shoulder just before he fired. The recoil of the weapon rocked him on his feet, almost causing him to drop it. Instantly Danny teared up. It was obvious he was hurt, but he was doing his best to be brave. He shook his head no when Jesse asked if he wanted to try again. Jesse just picked up the .22 he'd bought when he was a teenager and said, "Let's go find us some squirrels. Guys, you need to be really quiet and sneak into the woods like an Indian." He led the way to a large hickory nut tree he'd scouted out the day before. Several squirrels were eating nuts at the top, and the falling shells sounded like rain as they struck the leaves on the ground. He had Michael sit at the base of a large oak, and he and Danny moved down to another site. Everyone sat perfectly still for about twenty minutes until Danny saw one in the tree.

"There's one!" he yelled.

The squirrel slid around to the backside of the tree so he couldn't be seen. Jesse frowned and shook his head. Danny realized he'd made a mistake and quieted. A few moments later, Jesse saw one, but he decided to wait and let Michael find one of his own. He sat, ready to shoot. When he heard Michael's gun go off, the squirrel Jesse had been watching raised his head to see what had happened. Jesse made a perfect head shot. Michael came running, holding his squirrel by the tail.

"I got one, and he's really big, too!"

Jesse picked up his and said, "Now you need to learn how to skin it."

Thanksgiving morning finally arrived. Michael hadn't slept well since he'd killed and skinned his first squirrel. His daddy had told him he needed to clean the .410 every time he used it, so he'd cleaned it every day after school. He didn't want any dust to build up inside the weapon. When he and his dad arrived at Jesse's, they were surprised to see Nick.

"Uncle Nick, I didn't know you were coming," Michael said with pleasure.

"Do you think I'd let your uncle hunt our dogs without me?" Nick teased. "He doesn't know much about rabbit dogs."

"I heard that," said Jesse. "You're not planning on hunting them with that pistol, are you?"

Nick just grinned at his friend, then he took off his pistol, gun belt, and badge and placed them on the front seat of his car. "Don't you worry about me, buddy."

As they walked toward the meadow, the dogs jumped the first rabbit of the day. It was too far away for anyone to get a shot, but the dogs were hot on its trail. Nick stood still and listened to the dogs, then he followed their howls. When he determined they were going to the right, he told Michael to move to the right about twenty feet, stand in the tall weeds, and watch the edge of the meadow. About the time Michael began to get impatient, he noticed movement coming toward him; it was the rabbit slipping down the edge of the garden. He picked a spot about twenty feet away and waited for it to get to him. When it did, he fired, and the rabbit took one more hop.

Everyone started yelling and congratulating him. At that moment, he was on top of the world, and then reality hit. Jesse tied the rabbit to Michael's belt. The reward for killing it meant you had to carry it for the rest of the hunt. Oh joy...

Amos and Mother Barkley were there waiting when Michael got home. He ran to Amos, "Papaw, I killed a squirrel last Saturday and a rabbit today with your .410."

Looking as stern as he could manage while smiling inside, Amos asked, "Did you clean the gun after you shot it?"

Mike piped up, "Are you kidding me? He cleaned it every night last week and wouldn't even get in the car until he'd cleaned that rabbit and the old gun."

Amos was proud. "That's my boy. I tell you what, if it's OK with your momma and daddy, that old gun can be your Christmas present."

Michael quickly turned and gave his parents a look that would have melted an iceberg. Martha immediately surrendered. "It'll be OK with me if you promise not to touch it unless an adult is with you. Do you promise?"

"Cross my heart, Momma, and hope to die."

"Then go get cleaned up for Thanksgiving dinner."

Mike came back into the dining room just as Martha's parents were arriving. He knew Mr. Burke had been sick recently, but he was surprised to see a mere shadow of the big man he'd first met at the gristmill. He'd lost a minimum of twenty pounds since Mike had last seen him. As his momma would say, he looked like death warmed over. Mrs. Burke helped him to the nearest chair as young Michael came running, excited to tell Mr. Burke all about his hunting adventures. As badly as he obviously felt, he kept encouraging Michael to tell him all about it.

What really floored Mike was that Mrs. Burke was almost being friendly to him. He had no idea how to respond to this suspicious overture. He'd learned at age ten to be wary of that woman, and things really hadn't changed much since, even though they both always made an effort for Martha. They were the last to arrive, and Martha directed them to be seated. Over the years, she'd finally taught Amos that at her table he had to wait until after the blessing before he could start eating, but he continued to act like he was in charge. He approached the table slowly so that he would be the last person seated. As he did, Martha inventoried the spread. Everyone sat in silence as they gave her that moment of pride in the huge feast she had so lovingly prepared. She nodded to Mike to say the blessing.

Instead, he turned to his father-in-law and asked, "Mr. Burke, would you honor our tradition and say the blessing this year, please?"

As he spoke, his voice was so weak it was hard to hear until he reached the end. In a loud, clear voice he said, "Dear Lord, please let this food taste as good as it smells."

Everyone laughed, as these words had been the heart of the meal for the last decade.

In February, after a lifetime of poor health from the scarlet fever he'd contracted as a teen, Mr. Burke passed away. He was two weeks shy of his fifty-eighth birthday.

# CHAPTER 26

With spring coming early, Nick and Marie decided it was time to plant their own garden. Northeast of the house was a perfect opening; Nick figured it must have been a pasture at some point in time. That meant there weren't any stumps to be dug out before they could plant. Frank and his tractor were called and made quick work of plowing the field. Nick laid off the rows with his garden hoe, and since Marie had years of experience, she had them fertilized and planted as fast as Nick could lay them out. He was proud of it when they finished. Crime in the county was really low, so he reasoned he would be able to spend a lot of time cultivating it and his little family.

He couldn't help himself, he had to show off his labors to his friend. It was twice the size of the garden Jesse usually planted, so he told him he and Marie should be able to share their harvest with them for a change. Jesse just looked it over and drawled, "It sure is big. Remember telling me how little I knew about training rabbit dogs? Well, I hate to tell you, but that's about how much you must know about having a garden."

"What do you mean? The rows are straight, aren't they?" Nick questioned indignantly. "Marie put down fertilizer before she planted everything. The good Lord will take care of the rain; what else is there?"

"The most important thing, buddy. The sun. Look at your garden. At least two-thirds of it is in the shade. Only a couple of the rows get sunshine all day. Beans, tomatoes, and potatoes need lots of sun."

Nick just stood there in shock. He could see exactly what Jesse meant. "How do I fix it, Sarge?"

"That's easy. We cut down all the trees causing the shade. The bonus is you get your year's firewood at the same time. Let me go eat supper, and we'll cut the first one tonight."

Nick knew some strings had been pulled for him to have gotten the first telephone in Gravely Gap. He was on a party line with two other families and had a simple number, 3993. Four short rings identified the call as his. Just as he was leaving for work on Monday morning, he heard his ring tone. It was the office telling him to go by the sheriff's house on the way to work. Evidently, his boss had pneumonia and needed to talk to Nick directly in order to brief him on what was happening in the county.

A woman answered when he knocked. She introduced herself as his nurse, Mrs. Panter. "Come on back, sir; the sheriff wants to see you."

"How on earth did he catch pneumonia?" Nick quizzed.

"He'll explain," she said.

The bedroom looked just like a hospital room, with all the tubes and oxygen going. Instantly, he knew his boss didn't have pneumonia.

The sheriff gave him a weak smile. "Come in, buddy, we've got a lot to talk about."

Shocked, Nick just responded, "What's going on?"

"It's my ticker. I've had a couple of heart attacks before, but this last one was bigger. I'm going to need you to step up and act as sheriff until I can get back to work. It could be as long as a few months. Are you up for it?"

"Whatever you need me to do, sir."

"That's what I thought. Once a soldier, always a soldier. I'm going to be very candid with you, son. We have positive control on the crime, but it's the other things that can slip up on you. I have a gentlemen's agreement with the two guys in Blue Ridge who sell moonshine. I leave them alone as long as they don't sell to minors. Fannin County is as poor as any in the state, and because it's Republican, the guys in Atlanta don't care about us. A lot of our farmers actually make their living by selling moonshine. It's not my job to make their life harder, and I try to leave that up to the revenuers. A list of all the shiners in the county is in my desk. Some of them will try to test you; if they break our agreement, make examples of them. Give the top ten names to the revenuers. Are you clear on that?"

"I understand completely, sir."

The sheriff craned his neck to see if his nurse would be able to hear their conversation, and when he felt comfortable, he whispered, "Your real problem is the men in town who think Fannin County is their sandbox. As soon as they hear you're acting sheriff, they'll start pushing you." He handed Nick a piece of paper and said, "Here's a list of the ones to watch out for. One name not on the list is Bobby Foster, but you really need to watch out for him. He has his finger in everything and every business in Blue Ridge. He's a slick talker, but he'll stab you in the back in a heartbeat. Watch out for him and his nephew, Randall. Nick, it sounds complicated, I know, but just have fun. It's the best job in the county." He relaxed his head back onto his pillow. He looked relieved he'd gotten through the conversation. "Take this note back to the office and read it to the rest of them. It tells them you have my approval and you're in charge until I'm well enough to come back from this pneumonia." He winked as he handed him another piece of paper.

The nurse followed Nick outside as he left and used her hand to stop him. "Mr. Turner, you need to know I don't think he'll get better."

Uncomfortable, Nick said, "I'll try to stop by as often as I can."

She nodded. "I'll update you if there are any changes. You know he doesn't have any family and he talks about you like you're his son. I think you really mean a lot to him."

Nick's first experience as acting sheriff began smoothly, but as soon as he relaxed enough to feel confident in his abilities, his world fell apart. The first disaster was a prisoner just walking out of the jail, and of course, no one seemed to know how it happened. Before he could rectify that situation, one of the deputies wrecked his patrol car in his own garage. When Nick reported all of this to the sheriff, he expected a good old military ass-chewing. Instead he received a weak smile and a sympathetic murmur: "Nothing like learning the job under fire. I'd been worried the boys were protecting you these last few weeks. Tell me how you handled each event."

Nick explained as best he could what he'd done and why. The sheriff nodded in approval. "Hell, boy, I couldn't have done any better myself."

Nurse Panter moved to where the sheriff couldn't see her and motioned for Nick to follow her outside. He took the hint and said his goodbyes. When he got outside, she whispered, "Mr. Turner, I don't think he has much time left. He is still in denial, but if you have any questions you need answered, I suggest you do it quickly."

Nick had noticed the decline, but with her words, he began to panic. He racked his brain as to which questions needed to be asked. Later, he told Marie and said in defeat, "I just don't know what to do."

She gave him a big hug. "Nick, ask for help. You keep telling me the men are a well-oiled team, so use them and ask for their opinions on what to do."

He kissed her on the forehead. "How did such a smart lady like you ever get stuck with the likes of me?"

She reached up and smoothed his frown lines. "It took a lot of work and planning. Now sit down and eat your supper before it gets cold."

Nick couldn't believe how the office responded to his plea for help. He was looking for problems and questions that he should ask of the sheriff, but with that he got great solutions from the administrative staff to some of those very problems. It was obvious this was a completely new approach for them, and boy did they like it. The sheriff had always just told them what to do and expected them to do it. The meeting was so successful that Nick decided they would have one every month until he no longer had the job of acting sheriff. He felt unexpected feelings of relief. It was as if a heavy load had been lifted from his shoulders.

Two months later, the sheriff failed to wake up one morning. The strange part for Nick was that the department continued to run normally. The powers that be in the county didn't see the need to run a special election to fill the position. They felt it was a waste of money; their plan was for him to remain as acting sheriff until the next regular election. When they asked which party he belonged to, it caught Nick off guard. "I don't know. I think I'm just an old soldier."

One man in the group suggested, "Then your answer should be you're a Republican. This is a Republican county and always has been. If you run on that ticket and continue to do the job you've been doing, I'm guessing you'll run unopposed."

The man knew what he was talking about. Nick received nearly fifteen hundred votes versus ten write-in votes against him. The next Monday, the office held an impromptu celebration with cake and a selection of pastries.

Nick thanked everyone and announced that their planning meetings would be held on the first and third Wednesdays of each month. That would be the only change until their first meeting. He closed with, "Now get to work!"

The office cheered in response.

# CHAPTER 27

The second Thursday in June, Bill Mercier was reading the *Copper City Advance* when Jesse arrived at work. He read the headline Etowah Firm Is Awarded Contract to Build Six Fannin Schools. When Bill put the paper down, Jesse asked if he could look at the front page.

"Sure, I've already read it. It's a good one, since there's no bad news about the plant."

Jesse cut out the article about the schools and laughed to himself that he finally had some news before Billy. He could hardly wait to show him the article. He stopped at the pump and Billy walked out to greet him. Jesse handed him the article and said, "Looks like the county is going to get some new schools."

Almost before he finished reading, Billy launched into a tirade. "Now why in the hell would they give the contract to a Tennessee company?

Look! It's almost a million dollars. I'll say it again: those boys in Atlanta only use their heads for hat racks. How much gas do you want?"

"A dollar's worth should do it." Jesse just shook his head—he'd never get the best of Billy when it came to politics or news.

As he sat down for supper, he asked, "Where's Danny?"

Lorri frowned in annoyance. "If I had to guess, I'd say he's at the Stewarts' house. He's helping with their garden. Would you believe how they're paying our son?"

"Fried apple pies?" Jesse guessed with a secret grin.

"That's right! How in the world did you know that?"

"That's what they paid Mike and me. Those two ladies are too old to change now."

Danny came running in as they were getting up from the table. He slammed the back door, yelling, "Daddy! Mr. and Mrs. Sluder got a television set! They say they can see the people talking on the radio. They said if I'd come over Friday night, I can see a red skeleton. Can I go? I've never seen one!"

Jesse tried his best not to laugh out loud at his son as he explained to him that *Red Skelton* was a man who told jokes for a living. The news didn't seem to damper Danny's enthusiasm. "Can we go? Can we, please?"

"We'll see," Jesse said as he went into the living room to read his latest letter from O'Shea.

Hi, Mountain Boy,

Bet you won't believe me when I tell you I'm back at Ft. Benning in my old job. I miss your old ugly mug. Top says we have a class of West Pointers next week. Remember how easy it was to work with them last time? We'd laugh every time we thought about the fact it was the last time they'd ever be afraid of NCOs. You wouldn't believe how many people they're kicking out of the army now that everything has settled down in Korea. I'll bet my next paycheck they'll regret that. You take care and don't forget your old army buddy.

O'Shea

Michael had great news he needed to share with his daddy. He was hoping he'd be really proud of his accomplishment. As soon as Mike walked through the front door, Michael burst out with it: "Daddy, I've got a paper route. I'm selling *Grits*."

Mike was preoccupied and just nodded absently. "That's fine, son." Then he wandered into the kitchen. "What's for supper? I'm starving."

Martha had overheard their exchange and was not pleased, but she decided to wait until they were alone to let Mike know his mistake and how she felt about it.

Friday afternoon, Michael received his first order of twenty copies. When he opened them, he found a white canvas bag with *Grits* printed on the side. He couldn't wait to sell them. Seeing how excited he was, Martha told him to go ahead and she'd save supper. His first sales were to the houses along his route to school. He sold until almost dark. When he got home, he counted the copies left and discovered he'd already sold twelve, with only eight more to go. He couldn't sleep that night thinking about where he'd go tomorrow. After midnight, he decided he'd go up Highway 5 toward Sugar Creek Groceries, then he dropped off to sleep.

Martha put her foot down when he came in the kitchen so eager to sell his papers that he declined breakfast. She could see Mike in her son—he wanted to get the job done right now. She was disappointed Mike was missing out on his first real act of independence.

Michael got home just before noon and laid out his money on the table. He multiplied twenty times ten and realized he should have a total of two dollars. He counted the money and realized he had $2.02, but he couldn't figure out where the extra two cents had come from. His profit on the ten cents per copy was four cents. That meant the company would receive $1.20, so he placed that amount in the envelope. Martha suggested he exchange ten dimes for a dollar bill from his daddy, as it would be easier to keep track of. Michael liked the idea, but he wasn't too keen on asking his daddy for it. After thinking about the problem for a moment, he picked up ten dimes and put them in his pocket. Without saying a word he ran out, slamming the screened door behind him. As usual, Martha yelled, "Don't slam that door!" about two seconds too late.

He ran to the small patch of woods on the southeast side of the house. He'd worn a trail to Highway 5 and Tommy Elliott's gas station. He'd started a friendship with the owner months before, and it had been solidified when Mr. Elliott didn't laugh when Michael confided he wanted to be a soldier. Very few adults took his dream seriously, and when one did he considered them his friend for life.

As their relationship progressed, Mr. Elliott told Michael he'd been a sergeant in the army air corps and shared his own secret—he wished he'd never gotten out of the army. Michael had been surprised and commented, "But you've got a great job here at the station."

Mr. Elliott considered that for a moment. He wanted to be honest with his new friend, so he said, "It puts food on the table, son, but it's just a job to me. In the army I always felt like I was serving a higher purpose."

When Mr. Elliott saw Michael cross the highway, he opened two Cokes and handed one to his friend as he came in the store. "What a pleasant surprise. I think I've told you all my war stories at least twice."

Michael dug out the coins and hesitantly asked, "I need to exchange these for a dollar bill if that's OK."

"My my, son. Where on earth did you get so much money?"

"Selling *Grits.*"

"Did you bring me a copy?" Mr. Elliott asked with a smile.

Ashamed, Michael admitted, "No, I sold them all already."

Mr. Elliott pulled a dollar from his pocket and held it out. "That's OK this time, but I expect to be your number-one customer from here on out."

Michael handed him the coins and gulped down the Coke, which gave him the hiccups. They both laughed as Michael tried to thank him.

At home, he placed the money in the envelope and sealed it. He noticed his momma had already put two stamps on it for him. He ran to the mailbox and placed it inside as he raised the flag. Walking back, he realized he was really proud of himself. He had done something on his own for the first time, and done it well. It was a nice feeling. He knew Craig hadn't ever done anything like this, and he couldn't wait to brag. Looking up, he saw his momma watching him out the window. In that moment he decided he wasn't going to mention any of this to his daddy.

# CHAPTER 28

The new schools were a catalyst for growth in Fannin County. Along with the money to build them, the state allocated funds to build a new Highway 5 from Blue Ridge to McCaysville. Blue Ridge continued to grow and even got a new drive-in theater and Tastee Freeze. Not to be outdone, McCaysville quickly built the same. The teenagers in the area reaped the benefits. When Lance's Drive-In was built, they began to cruise back and forth from there to the Tastee Freeze. McCaysville only had one drive-in, but they had an ace in the hole—Ralph and Grady's Pool Hall, just across the bridge in Copperhill. They also had the larger walk-in theater. In just a few years, the teens in the area had more entertainment at their disposal than their parents had ever had.

Craig Foster became very popular because he had a car and could cruise from one hangout to another. The carhops at both locations got used to delivering hamburgers and Cokes to his driver's window without a tip or even a thank you. He was comfortable with his status in the town and would test the limits of the local police by filling his trunk with kids and sneaking them into the drive-in. Once in a parking spot, he'd open the trunk and they'd all pile out and enjoy the movie for free. He liked the attention from the kids, and his adventures went on until some of the kids began to brag about them. Mike overheard what was happening one day at the post office, and that evening he confronted Michael. Even though he denied it, Martha could see he was simply trying to cover up for his idol, Craig Foster.

Craig's first encounter with the Fannin County Sheriff's Department occurred about ten months after he got his license. He was extremely proud to be driving around in the biggest, most expensive car in the entire county—his daddy's Cadillac. He would drive through town with a carload of teenage girls eager to impress him. There were three red lights on the main street in Blue Ridge, and Craig ignored every single one of them. He assumed no one would have the nerve to even come close to hitting Bobby Foster's car. One Saturday, he ran the center red light, and the newest deputy in town spotted him. He'd only recently moved to Blue Ridge after inheriting land from his grandfather. To the deputy, there was no question about it, he'd witnessed a straightforward violation. He approached the vehicle with the intention of issuing a warning until the young driver began to mouth off. "Do you know who I am? Don't you recognize this Cadillac? I dare you to write me a ticket. My daddy will have your badge before dark."

Irritated and determined, the deputy pulled out his summons book and began to write the ticket. He silently handed it to Craig. "Does your daddy know where the sheriff's office is? Tell him I'm Deputy Weaver and he can come by and pay the fine whenever it's convenient. Now you watch out for those other red lights. Have a good day, sir."

Craig's face was as red as his hair. He sat and fumed for a moment, then he gunned the car as he went to find his father.

The deputy went straight to the sheriff's office to report the incident. Nick listened and reassured his employee, "Weaver, you did your job. Now get back on patrol. It sounds like a rich kid's rant to me. They always think they're special and the law doesn't apply to them. Don't worry about it. I'll handle it from here."

Just before noon on Monday, a gentleman strutted into headquarters in a three-piece suit and loudly announced, "Tell Sheriff Turner that Mr. Foster is here to see him."

Before the secretary could say anything, Nick walked out of his office. "Mary, I'm off to McKinney's Café for lunch and should be back by one o'clock."

Foster stuck out his arm to stop Nick and said, "Excuse me, Sheriff, I'd like to talk to you."

Nick said, "I'm going to lunch, and can see you when I get back." He walked quickly away, trying not to laugh at the expression on Foster's face. The man was absolutely furious and was obviously not used to being handled.

"Now wait just a minute," said Foster. "You obviously don't know who I am. I'll go with you to the café and we can get ourselves acquainted. There are some things you need to know if you intend to stay sheriff in this county."

"That'll be fine with me as long as we each pay our way. As sheriff, I can't be seen as taking bribes. You're right, I haven't been in Blue Ridge very long."

Bobby looked around the café with interest and mumbled, "Nice location across from Western Auto."

Mrs. McKinney walked up to Nick with a smile and said, "Well hello, sheriff. Let me guess—the Monday special?"

"Yes, ma'am, with coffee. Mr. Foster, this is Lucille McKinney. She's the best cook in Blue Ridge."

She laughed. "I notice you didn't mention Gravely Gap. Guess you can't compare me with your wife, can you?"

Foster rudely interrupted, "What is the special?"

"Green beans, new potatoes, and meat loaf with sweet tea or coffee," she answered.

"I'll take it with sweet tea," Foster said.

She yelled back to the cook with their orders. Nick looked around to see if his normal table near the window was open, as the café was packed with happy customers. Seeing it was, he slid into his usual chair. He was a little puzzled that Foster didn't appear to be at all familiar with the café or its occupants. He asked Nick, "How long has this place been here, and where are the McKinneys from?"

Nick didn't know the answers and little surprised at the questions. He had been warned by the previous sheriff that Foster had a finger in all the businesses in town, so he was pleased to see that this one had escaped his grasp. Foster noticed the expression on Nick's face. "What's so amusing?"

"I was just appreciating the family atmosphere of this place. What did you want to talk to me about?"

"I'm hoping you'll be more cooperative than your predecessor. My sources tell me you're not from here. You lived in Ducktown and worked for Tennessee Copper Company, then you spent some time as an MP. You moved to Gravely Gap after marrying a woman from Epworth. I know all about you. The commissioner tells me your department needs another patrol car. In case you aren't aware of it, son, I have a lot of pull in this county, and I'm someone you definitely want on your side."

Nick drew in a deep breath, chose his words carefully, and said, "Your source is correct. Mr. Foster, I owe you an apology. I thought you were one of those people the sheriff warned me about—you know, the kind that feel they're above the law. I had one of them come in last week demanding I tear up his son's DUI. I'm truly sorry I put you in that box when all you want to do is help. I really appreciate it. I promise you, when I have a problem I can't solve, you'll be the first person I call. Let me ask you, are you from here?"

Foster was flabbergasted. "I was born and raised here."

Nick asked, "How about your daddy?"

"Ah, he moved here in the latter part of the twenties and started up the sawmill."

Nick smiled. "That means we have something in common. We're outsiders. Now you'd better eat those beans and potatoes before they get cold."

The rest of the meal was eaten in silence. Nick knew he'd just made an enemy, but he really didn't care. Inside he was chuckling; now he knew why Mike Barkley despised this man so much. As the weeks passed, Michael continued to enjoy selling his papers. By the time school started, he'd increased his sales to thirty a week. He'd walk past the Fosters' house all the way up Highway 5 to Mercier's apple stand. He'd broken it down into two routes—Friday afternoons in Blue Ridge and Saturdays up Highway 5 and back to Tommy Elliott's service station. After that initial conversation with his daddy, he'd never brought the subject up again. He always updated his mother and Mr. Elliott, because they gave him positive feedback. Their praise was nice, but the words he valued the most were from his uncle Jesse.

In the fall, West Fannin High School opened and students from Blue Ridge, Epworth, and McCaysville were bused to the new school. One night, Michael asked his momma, "Why do you think Craig wants to quit school?"

Martha sat at the table peeling apples to make a pie for Mike. "Where did you hear that?"

"Margaret told me at school today." He shrugged. "He rides the bus now, and boy does he hate that."

"Oh, is that all? Don't worry, he'll get used to that. Some people don't like change. You know Craig," Martha reassured him.

"But that's not all she said. He told her the teachers and most of the kids don't even know who he is."

Martha laughed out loud. "That explains it. He's not the center of attention any more. I'll let Amy Jo know Craig's having a tough time if you don't mind."

The next day she talked to her friend about Craig. Amy Jo said, "So that's what's been bothering him. He keeps telling me he hates school and thinks he should quit."

Concerned because her friend looked so worried, Martha asked, "And what does Bobby say?"

"Ah, he doesn't know. Craig knows better than to tell him something like that. Bobby would go through the roof. He has plans for Craig, and no one better get in the way of them."

Martha asked, "Is there anything I can do?"

"Not really. This is the first time he hasn't been the center of attention and has to ride the bus with everyone else. I'll drop a hint to his daddy that Craig wants a car so he can drive to school like the seniors."

"Leave it to a mother to identify the solution to an earth-shattering teenage problem," Martha laughed.

"We do, don't we? That calls for a batch of sugar cookies. You ready to cook?"

Bobby was very receptive to Amy Jo's suggestion. "You're right. My son's not riding the bus with the poor kids."

She had mixed feelings about his response. It was good that he'd accepted that the kid needed a car, but she didn't like his reason for why. Later that evening, Bobby was waiting at the bus stop for Craig after checking out some used cars at the lot across from the Tastee Freeze. He showed them to Craig, who made his choice before they could even get out of the car. "That white Ford is perfect. How'd you know what I'd like?"

Bobby puffed up with pride. "'Cause I'm your daddy and I'll always know what's best for my boy. I convinced your momma this is your Christmas present."

Surprised, Craig asked, "Momma knows about this?"

"Yeah, I told her what I was doing. It's men's business."

"But Daddy, there are three more months 'til Christmas," Craig whined. "Is this all I'll get?"

"Well, if you want more presents, I guess you better hug your momma when we get home."

As the salesman handed the keys to Craig, he said, "The brakes are a little soft on it. You might need to pump them occasionally."

Craig was furious that a salesman was telling him what to do and snapped, "I know that."

# CHAPTER 29

Jesse whipped into Darby's store for his weekly update. Billy met him at the pump. "Fill her up?"

"Two dollars should do it."

"You know, I've asked people that question at least a thousand times, and no one ever says yes."

"Billy, it would cost more than five dollars to fill up, and who around here can afford that?"

"Guess you're right. Say, have you noticed that with all the rain we've gotten, that new road is one big mud hole? Have you seen the culvert they built on Frank Wilson's farm?"

Jesse answered, "Haven't seen it yet, but I've sure heard about it."

"I haven't seen it either, but you know the road cuts right through the middle of his pasture. I've heard they built a culvert big enough that the cattle can go from one pasture to another right under that new highway," Billy said in amazement.

Jesse asked, "You think Frank asked them to do that?"

"He had to; why else would they do something like that?"

"Well, it's a great idea. I'll have to check it out the next time I'm around there."

Billy said, "Let me know and I'll go with you. I've never seen anything like that. That reminds me, have you seen Willard and Jewell Sluter's new television? They asked me to come over and see it."

Jesse said, "I took Danny over to see Red Skelton. He was bored in about ten minutes. Guess it's just for adults."

"Can't see it ever taking the place of radio. The cost will keep most from buying it."

Jesse said, "I heard the guys talking in the mines and they love the Friday night fights it shows."

Smiling, Billy said, "Well that might keep it going for a few years, but it'll never work up here in the mountains. Hear it's really snowy. Kids will go blind watching that thing. Did you say the mines?"

"Yeah, After Nick left I ask to go back to the labor gang and they offered me the mines. It's better pay but I'm not sure I'm ever going to get used to it."

"You would be surprised what you can get used to." Billy said with a grin.

"Well, Billy, I've got to go. See you later. Nick and Marie are coming for supper, and I've got marching orders."

"Tell that new sheriff hello for me. Tell him I voted for him so he ought to come by once in a while," Billy said as he waved goodbye. As Michael walked down Highway 5 headed to the service station Saturday morning, a car stopped and blew the horn. It was Craig in his new white Ford. He rolled down the window and called out, "Get in, I'll give you a ride. Where are you going?"

"Elliot's. He always buys my last paper," Michael explained.

"That why you like him so much?" asked Craig.

"Nah, he's a friend like you. He doesn't think being a soldier is a stupid idea."

"Do you tell him all your secrets?" asked Craig slyly.

"Yeah, we share. He tells me stuff, too."

"I can't believe a grownup would waste time with a kid."

Puzzled at Craig's attitude, Michael said, "Well, he does." They rode the rest of the way in silence.

Craig realized he'd hurt Michael's feelings and offered, "You know what you need? A bicycle. I have an old one I put in the pile for a yard sale for three dollars. You want it?"

"For three dollars? Yeah I want it. You're not kidding, are you?"

"No. Sell your paper to Elliott and we'll go get it," Craig said.

"Let's go get it now and I can ride it back and show him," Michael coaxed.

"Do you even have three dollars?" Craig asked skeptically.

"Drive me to the house first and I'll get it."

Craig waited in the car while Michael robbed his bank. When they got to Craig's house, Michael looked around but didn't see a bike. Craig took him out to the garage and began to move piles of boxes and other stuff until he finally uncovered it against the back wall. It was painted solid white and had both fenders and sprocket guard missing. Michael didn't care. He wouldn't have been any happier with a brand new bright red *Western Flyer* from the showroom floor at the Western Auto.

At the station, Tommy could see from Michael's smile that he was one happy lad. "I see you got yourself a bike. I always liked mine stripped down because they go so much faster. I really like it."

His remarks added to Michael's joy and excitement over his new purchase. After selling Tommy the paper and exchanging his change for dollars, Michael headed home to show his mother. Like Tommy, she expressed her approval. He parked the bike next to the well house. His plan was to show it to his daddy and grandparents after Sunday dinner.

The next day when Mike stopped the car, Michael ran around and wheeled out his prized possession. When Mike saw it, his expression was not pleased. He frowned, "Where'd you get that thing?"

Proudly Michael said, "I bought it for three dollars from Craig."

"Young man, take it back."

Horrified and beginning to get angry, Michael asked, "Daddy, why?"

"You'll get hurt on that thing. You're going to ride it on Highway 5, aren't you? Take it back, and that's final."

Michael sucked it up and refused to let his daddy see him cry. He just turned and started pushing the bike toward Craig's house. When Craig saw him, he asked, "What's wrong?"

"Daddy told me I can't have it and to bring it back."

Craig shrugged his shoulders. "Well, that's too bad, I've already spent most of your money."

"How much is left?" asked Michael.

Craig emptied his pocket into his hand. "A dollar and fifty-seven cents."

"That's OK. I'll take that," Michael said, hiding his disappointment. He put the money into his pocket, turned, and began the long walk home.

Martha had waited until Michael was out of sight before she jumped on Mike with both feet. "Why did you do that? Is it because he bought it from Craig?"

"No. He needs to learn he has to ask permission before he does things," Mike protested.

"What you're teaching him is not to seek out your love, respect, or approval," Martha stated quietly. "Mike, he wants so much for you to be proud of him. You just broke that child's heart. You do that all the time, and what scares me the most is this just might be the last time he even tries."

Mike's face turned pale, and he immediately tried to defend his actions. "He's a smart boy. He understands why that bike has to go back."

"Oh, really? Mike Barkley, *I* don't even understand why. He earned the money himself. Let's just hope you don't regret this decision," Martha cautioned, as she stomped off, shaking her head and muttering to herself.

# CHAPTER 30

Amy Jo met Craig at the door as he got home from school. "I need you to run up to Mercier's and get me some apples so I can make the pies for Thanksgiving."

"Momma, don't make me go. I don't know what kind you want, and if I get the wrong ones, you'll send me right back. Why don't you just go? I've got a full tank of gas."

Giving in to the men in her house was second nature to her. She'd learned long ago it just wasn't worth the fight. "Fine, but you'll have to watch Margaret when she gets home."

Craig and Margaret didn't notice how long their mother had been gone until their father got home looking for his supper. He stormed in, demanding, "Where in the hell is your momma? Why isn't there any food on the table? She knows I've got a meeting tonight."

Just before dark, Sheriff Turner pulled up to the rear of the Foster home. He got out of the car, steadied himself, and started walking around front. He rehearsed in his mind what he would say, as this was his first death notification and he couldn't think of anyone he dreaded more to have to tell this news. He knocked on the front door, and when Bobby answered, Nick noticed he looked annoyed, so he asked, "Could you come outside? I'm afraid I have some bad news."

Bobby pulled the front door shut and demanded, "What the hell is it now?"

"It's your wife. She's been involved in a car accident."

"Where, when?" Bobby asked impatiently.

"The S-curve on Highway 5, next to the city limit sign. I'm afraid she didn't make the first curve, and her car went over the edge and dropped almost fifty feet. I'm not sure when it happened, but we just found her. It looks like she might have been going too fast, but what's strange is it doesn't look like she even used her brakes."

Bobby just glared at him. "Did you take her to Copper Basin?"

Nick began to squirm. The moment to deliver the bad news was here, and he just hoped he could handle it well. "Mr. Foster, I'm sorry, but your wife didn't make it," Nick said sympathetically.

Craig opened the door and came outside. "What's wrong?"

Bobby answered, "Your momma's been in an accident."

Furious, Craig complained, "She wrecked my car, didn't she?"

"It looks like she lost control of the car at that steep curve at the city limit sign," Nick explained.

Craig was really annoyed—he'd have to ride the bus again. "Didn't she know she had to pump those brakes to get them to work? Guess I'll show her how to do it when she gets home. Daddy, you're going to pay to fix my car, aren't you?"

Realizing the boy hadn't comprehended his mother had passed away, Nick quietly excused himself. "Mr. Foster, I'll let you have some time with your children."

Bad news traveled faster than a wildfire in a windstorm in most small towns, and Blue Ridge was no exception. When Mike heard about Amy Jo at the post office, he rushed home. He didn't want Martha to hear that her best friend was gone through gossip. He walked into the house and she instantly sensed something was wrong. Fearing the absolute worst, she demanded, "Mike? What is it—is Michael OK?"

"I'm afraid it's bad news, sweetie. Amy Jo was killed in a car accident last night."

She collapsed onto the kitchen floor, and Mike rushed to hold her. As she processed the news, she couldn't help but remember the day her daughter, Betsy, had died. Margaret immediately came to mind. "Oh my God. Where's Margaret? She shouldn't be alone right now. Will you take me to the Fosters'?"

Mike was filled with love for the warm, compassionate woman he'd been lucky enough to marry. Southern women always show strength in time of crisis, and his woman was no shrinking violet. She rushed to the back door. "Well, come on. That little girl needs somebody."

When they arrived, even though he dreaded it, Mike insisted he accompany her inside. Helen opened the door and greeted them. "Hi, Mrs. Barkley. Thank goodness you're here. Mr. Foster and Craig have gone to Akins to make the arrangements. Margaret is in her room and won't talk to a soul."

Martha turned to Mike and said, "You go back to work. I can walk home."

He gave her a kiss on her forehead and murmured, "Yes, boss."

She knocked quietly on Margaret's bedroom door but didn't get a response. She said, "Margaret, it's me."

The door flew open, and the devastated child flung herself into Martha's arms, sobbing. "Aunt Martha, my momma's dead."

Martha just held her tightly and let her cry herself out. Most people felt uncomfortable when people cried, but Martha knew it was what Margaret needed in order to prepare herself for the events to follow. When Betsy had died, Martha had held all those emotions in check, and it had turned out to be a disaster. She wanted Margaret to feel free to express her sadness where she felt safe, so she just hugged her tighter until she had cried herself to sleep, exhausted.

# CHAPTER 31

Being a freshman in high school wasn't at all what Michael had expected. There were twice the number of students, for one thing, but his biggest problem was with his friend, Craig, who was a junior. He had no desire to be seen with a lowly freshman like Michael, and he even began to ridicule him for selling *Grits.*

Michael desperately wanted to talk to his uncle Jesse about what to do, but since taking the job in the mine he hadn't been able to attend Sunday dinners. It was five miles from Blue Ridge to Jesse's place in Gravely Gap, and that was just too far for him to walk. If only he still owned that bike...

One Saturday morning, Michael decided to confide in the adult he trusted the most after his uncle Jesse, Tommy Elliott. He was sitting in his metal chair in front of the service station when Michael approached. "Well, it's about time I got my newspaper!" They did their usual exchange of papers and change for dollar bills.

Just as Michael was ready to unload his problem, Tommy jumped up and rushed to the edge of the highway to meet an old woman. Michael had seen her before, but he had no idea who she was. Tommy sure seemed to know her, though. She was carrying a small kerosene can, which Tommy took from her. He looped his arm in hers and assisted her to the station. "Boy, does time fly. Do you need kerosene already?"

She responded in a soft voice. "I'm afraid so. I had to use a lot to clean Paw's old tools. I was putting wood in the shed and noticed they'd gotten so rusty. I hate to admit it, but the last time they were even looked at was before Irving went to war."

Tommy sat her in his chair and started walking toward the corner of the store. He turned and called out, "Michael, why don't you come with me and I'll show you how it works?"

Michael followed and asked, "Who's that lady?"

"That's Karen Farmer. Her son was killed at Normandy, and her husband died about ten years ago. She doesn't have electricity, and she uses the kerosene for her lamps. You'll never find a sweeter woman. All she has is a small pension from the government because her son got killed in the war."

Michael realized his problems weren't anywhere near as huge as he'd thought. When they came back out front, Tommy asked, "Mrs. Farmer, do you have time for a cup of coffee?"

Her eyes lit up and she smiled in delight. "I always have time for a friend. Who's this young man you're training?"

Tommy was mortified at his bad manners. "Oh, I'm sorry. I figured you two knew each other. This is Michael Barkley. Michael, this is Karen Farmer."

She stuck out a trembling hand. "Nice to meet you son. Are you any relation to our postmaster?"

"Yes, ma'am. That's my daddy."

"Well he's a fine man and I bet he's proud of you. Does that *Grits* bag belong to you?"

"Yes, ma'am, it does."

"I'd really like one, but you'll have to follow me home to get the money. I don't have any extra on me."

Tommy wanted to offer the dime, but he knew she'd perceive it as charity and be offended. He'd rather die than hurt her, so he offered, "I'll bet Michael wouldn't mind carrying your kerosene."

She agreed, "That'd be nice. That can gets heavier every trip."

She only lived a couple hundred yards from the station, and Michael noticed a pile of stove wood that looked like it had been just dumped off. He asked, "Is that the wood you were putting in the shed?"

"Yeah, the Davenport boys brought it by a couple of weeks ago."

Michael remembered how his daddy and Jesse had stacked firewood for the Stewart sisters when they were younger and knew immediately what he should do. "Mrs. Farmer, where would you like for me to stack that stove wood?"

Her eyes watered. "Oh, son, I can't let you do that. Surely you have more important things to do."

"Mrs. Farmer, please let me. I always stack Mamaw Barkley's stove wood. It's fun; you just tell me where to put it."

She pointed to her back porch, and he took off his canvas bag and picked up an armful of wood. It took him almost an hour to finish, and when he got to the bottom of the pile, he noticed it was dry, so he grabbed an armful and took it in the house, placing it in the wood box next to the stove. When she noticed, she said, "Buck, you're a good worker. You remind me of my son, Irving. You know, he was a soldier."

Michael nodded. "I'm going to be a soldier someday, just like my uncle Jesse."

"You'll make a fine one. Here's your dime for the paper, and if you'll sit down I have a fresh jar of apple butter. It tastes best on hot biscuits, and they should just about be ready." She opened the oven, and the smell of fresh biscuits wafted through the kitchen.

She sat next to him and sipped her coffee, handing him a glass of milk. For the next hour or so, a lonely old woman and a young future soldier became friends.

The next Saturday, Tommy asked, "Have you been to Mrs. Farmer's house yet?"

"No," he said grinning. "That's my next stop."

"Why not go there now and get her kerosene can? That way she won't need to get out in this cold weather." Tommy suggested.

As he walked over, he began to anticipate the visit. He climbed up on the porch and knocked softly, calling out, "Your paper boy is here."

She pretended to scold him. "Well, it's about time! I've been waiting for you all morning." She smiled as she handed him his dime.

"You know, it's really cold out here today. Why don't you let me get your kerosene for you? I'm already dressed for this weather."

"Buck, are you sure it wouldn't be any trouble?" she asked hopefully.

"No, ma'am. It'll only take me a few minutes."

"Well, here's the can and the money. Now you just get a quarter's worth, you hear?" She closed the door behind him, touched that he'd want to spend time with a lonely old widow.

When he got back to Tommy's, all he could do was grin. Tommy asked, "Well, what's up?"

"She wants a quarter's worth."

"Well, boy, you know where the tank is. Go fill it up."

"Is that a quarter's worth?" he asked.

"It is for her," Tommy said with a wink.

"Mr. Elliott, she calls me Buck. Do you have any idea why?"

"Does it bother you?" Tommy asked.

"No, sir."

"Then it doesn't matter, does it?" He handed Michael a dime and a dollar bill and said, "Now get out of here. She's waiting on you. You be sure and take whatever she offers. It won't be money, but she'll feel obligated to share some of whatever she's got because you got her kerosene."

When Michael knocked on the door, she called out, "Put it on the back porch and come on in."

He did as she said, and when he entered the room, she was sitting at the table sipping her coffee. A plate with two biscuits, a jar of apple butter, and a glass of milk was waiting for him. He remembered Tommy's guidance and sat down with a grateful smile.

This was the routine all winter. Michael's personality began to change, and his mother couldn't help but notice. She was pleased his attitude had gotten so much better; his grades had even improved recently. When she complimented him, he responded, "You have to be smart to be a good soldier."

What still bothered Martha was the relationship he now had with Mike. If they spoke at all, it was to snap at each other. Mike was so preoccupied with the post office that he no longer laughed and told stories with the employees, and diffidently had no clue what was happening with his son. But what really worried Martha was that Michael no longer seemed to care.

Michael was halfway between Sugar Creek Grocery and Mercier's on Saturday morning, crossing the stream, when he heard a strange noise. He listened, trying to figure out what he'd heard, but he finally just gave up and continued on his route. He had two papers left when he began the long walk to Mrs. Farmer's house. As he went to cross the stream, he heard it again. This time he investigated. He went down the bank of the highway into the thick underbrush. The noise got louder, and he finally realized it was an animal of some kind whimpering in pain. After twenty feet, he found it. The dog was so deep in a muddy sinkhole that Michael couldn't even tell its color. As he approached, the animal became very still and quiet. Cautiously, Michael began to creep closer, afraid it would become aggressive, but after looking it in the eye he determined it was no threat. He took off one of his gloves and eased the back of his hand close to the dog's nose, reassuring him in a calm, soothing tone. When he was an inch away, the dog licked his fingers. Michael could tell the animal had been trapped in the hole for a long time, because he'd dug off the sides trying to work his way out to freedom. Michael looked closer. It wasn't very deep, and he couldn't figure out why the animal hadn't been able to free itself. He put his glove back on, put both of his hands on the dog behind its front legs, and pulled. The dog yelped, and Michael immediately stopped and looked closer. There was a steel trap on its hind leg. The chain was tangled in the brush at the bottom of the hole. He looked around and saw a drag trail through the underbrush that led deeper into the woods. He wondered how far the poor dog had gone before he'd fallen into the hole. He placed the dog on flat ground and pushed the springs of the trap down to release the leg. It was too weak to walk and just thumped its tail weakly. Michael took the last two papers out of his bag and carefully placed the dog inside. He carried him to the stream and let him take a drink. He had to laugh at how greedily he drank. It was hard to imagine such a small animal could consume so much water. Once the animal satisfied his thirst, he collapsed in exhaustion. Michael carefully placed him in the bag again and began the long walk home, cooing to the animal to reassure him.

With every step he took, he contemplated solutions to his problem. He knew instinctively that if he took the dog home with him, his daddy wouldn't like it one bit. As he passed Mrs. Farmer's house, he could see her get up out of her chair and come to the front door. She called out, "Buck, get in here and warm up before you go get that kerosene. It's freezing out there and you'll catch your death."

As he started up the porch, she noticed the dog. "I see you found a friend."

"Yes, ma'am. Found him just past Sugar Creek Grocery with his leg in a steel trap. I don't know how long he was there, and I don't know what to do. I'm afraid to take him home and tell daddy. He'll make me put him down."

"Don't worry, Buck. No one is killing this little dog!" she protested. "Go on the back porch and get my tub. We need to clean him up and bandage that leg."

Relief flooded Michael. He retrieved the tub and looked to his friend for guidance. "What do we do now?"

"Go over to the cook stove and get some hot water out of the reservoir, then pour it in the tub."

He couldn't believe how quickly she dropped to her knees and began to tend to the animal. While she worked, she began to give him orders. "Empty that wood box and put that blanket that's on the couch in the box. We'll make him a nice bed." She dried the dog off with a worn old towel, and Michael chuckled as the dog's tail kept whacking her every time it wagged. She carefully placed him in the bed and washed her hands in the sink. Then she dried them and opened the oven door. The aroma of fresh biscuits hit his nose. As soon as the dog smelled them, he became alert and whined softly. She immediately tossed a hot biscuit within reach. He caught it in midair and quickly devoured it. She laughed. "Like that, huh?" She tossed him another. "I guess we'll just have to call you Biscuit."

Michael didn't know what to say. What a perfect name. It looked like Biscuit had a new home.

# CHAPTER 32

With Jesse's new job in the mine and Nick's as sheriff, they didn't get much time together. Any side projects were completely out of the question due to their strange hours, but they refused to give up the occasional rabbit hunt. Danny was finally old enough to hunt with them, and he used the .410 Michael stored at Jesse's house. Of course, along with fun came work, and Danny now had the chore of keeping the beagles fed. Jesse had been taught never to pet or play with hunting dogs, but he refused to enforce that with Danny. Every little boy needed a dog.

Marie and Lorri didn't let the men's work schedules impact their friendship. The trail between the two houses was well worn. With the twins old enough to wander to Marie's on their own, it became paradise to them. Marie made it her mission in life to spoil those two little girls rotten, and she couldn't wait to see them toddling down the trail into her waiting arms. Lorri would threaten her, "Just you wait. One day when you have your own, I'm going to make your life miserable and spoil them just like you have mine."

When Marie discovered she was pregnant, it was hard to determine which of the two women was the most excited. One thing was for certain, Poppa Nick was over the moon and decided it would definitely be a boy. He began to collect every toy he thought a little boy would like, and age had no impact. If he saw it and thought his child would love it, he bought it. It might be a bicycle or a rocking horse, a bunk bed or a cradle. Marie would just shake her head as she confided in Lorri, "I believe he's as big a kid as Danny. What on earth am I going to do raising two kids instead of one?"

Lorri just laughed. "See, I told you. It's called payback, girl."

When Jesse got home from work, Lorri began to talk to him about how Nick was acting. "It's like he's a kid again. Marie complains, but I know she really loves how happy he is. It reminds me of how you acted at Fort Benning when I told you I was pregnant with Danny."

Looking around, he asked, "Where is he?"

"He's probably over with the Stewart sisters."

Jesse grumbled. "How many times have you told him to be home for supper? I'll go get him, and when he feels my belt, he'll remember next time."

"Jesse Barkley, what on earth is wrong with you? You're starting to sound like your daddy, and I don't like it one little bit," Lorri scolded him. "Just a couple of months ago you thought it was funny he enjoyed spending so much time with them. What's caused you to change? Whatever it is, you'd better get over it. Go spend some time with those women and try to remember how much you loved them when you were his age. Now go; supper can wait."

Instinctively he wanted to bite back and say, "Yes, boss," like Mike did to Martha, but he realized he'd hadn't seen her so mad in quite a while. He couldn't believe how badly he'd been acting. He really didn't understand why he was so grumpy; he just felt so unhappy. Why on earth was he feeling this way? He had a beautiful wife who loved him, three healthy kids, and a job that paid better than any in the county. He should be on top of the world, but instead he felt like kicking rocks.

When he saw Danny sitting on the front porch with a fried pie clutched in his hand, laughing and talking with the sisters, his depression melted away. That kid wouldn't want a bite of supper, and he should be mad, but all he could think about was how loved those two old women had made him feel when he was a kid. So he just smiled and stepped up onto the porch. He'd been feeling guilty about how he'd acted with Lorri, and as she'd predicted, the visit with the Stewart sisters was exactly what he'd needed. He and Danny began the long walk home an hour later.

"Danny, boy, I've really messed up this time. I've got your momma all mad at me."

Worried, Danny just looked up at him. "Oh no! That's bad, Daddy. Is she mad at me too?"

"You know, when your momma's not happy, nobody's happy. I don't know what to do."

Danny stopped in the middle of the road. With wide eyes, he began to think frantically, sticking his tongue out the side of his mouth like he did when he was solving problems. After a minute, he helpfully suggested, "She likes hugs, you know."

Jesse bit back a laugh. "I'm not sure that'll work this time, son."

Danny continued to brainstorm. "We could go to Mr. Darby's and buy her a box of chocolate covered cherries."

Jesse sent Danny in the house ahead of him to soften the way. Danny handed the candy to his momma and said, "Daddy and I got you a present."

She bit back a grin and gave him a stern look. "Go tell your daddy supper's in the oven."

He hurried to do what he'd been told, then went to wash up before being told. As Jesse came through the kitchen door, Lorri stuck out her hand to impede his progress and whispered, "Coward. Shame on you getting a little boy to fight your battles for you. What do you think O'Shea will have to say when I tell him about that?"

"He'd ask, 'Did you win?'" he said with a saucy grin.

She gave him a big hug and said, "I love you, but don't think for a minute I'm sharing those chocolate covered cherries."

# CHAPTER 33

Since his mother's death, Craig had used Bobby's guilt about the bad brakes on the car to every advantage. He'd gotten another car out of the deal, and then a small cabin on Lake Blue Ridge. He'd also managed to convince his daddy he needed a small speedboat for skiing. In return, he had agreed to attend Young Harris College in the fall. Bobby bragged at the café that his boy had grown up and would be attending college when he graduated. What he didn't realize was that no one in the room cared. Every single one of them thought he was a spoiled rich brat, just like his father.

Craig enjoyed sharing his place on the lake with what few friends he had and all of the hangers-on. He could always count on Michael Barkley to be at his parties, but since Michael still had his *Grits* route, he could only attend on Sundays. That would change the Fourth of July weekend.

Craig's cabin was in a cove with five others, and all had private boat docks. The teens who spent every summer on the lake usually stayed on their own, but since the McFarland dock had the best view of the marina, they all congregated there to watch the fireworks on the fourth. The crowd of teens was laughing and talking, but when Michael arrived, he only had eyes for one girl. Her name was Susan, and with her golden tan, blond hair, and bright blue eyes, he was convinced she was an angel on earth. She was very popular, and he couldn't believe he'd never seen her before. It seemed everyone was calling out to her in an effort to get her attention. Michael decided some way or somehow he was going to get to know her, and at that moment he knew he had a new goal to write in the *dream book* his mother had given him when he was ten so he would never forget the things that would be important to him in life to achieve.

The fourth had been on a Thursday this year, so Michael could sell all of his *Grits* on Friday, which enabled him to spend the entire weekend at the cottage with Craig. He hurried through his route and decided that this month would be his last time. He dreaded having to tell Mrs. Farmer about his decision.

Michael could hear Biscuit barking in greeting before he even got into the yard. He heard Mrs. Farmer scold him, "Biscuit, be quiet. That's not Buck. It's just Friday." She opened the door and gave him a welcoming grin when she saw him. The dog dashed between her legs before she could grab him. He jumped off the porch and hit Michael in the middle of his chest, confident he would catch him. Michael grabbed him tightly and they rolled to the ground laughing and barking. Mrs. Farmer watched them for a minute and then said, "You two come on inside. I'm not sure if I have any biscuits left, but I'll check. It's pretty darn suspicious how those little things just disappear around here since Biscuit showed up." She opened the oven door and smiled. "You're in luck; looks like there are a few of them after all."

Michael was already seated at the table with Biscuit jumping at his feet in excitement. She tossed one to the dog and handed a few to the boy. Michael filled his with a heaping tablespoon of apple butter. He swallowed the first bite and blurted out the bad news. "Mrs. Farmer, this is my last week selling *Grits*. I'm going to try to find me a better job."

Shocked and saddened at the thought of losing her young friend, she quietly asked, "Do you know what you're going to do, son?"

"Not yet, but I'm sure my Uncle Jesse will let me put up his hay. I've got a friend who lives on the lake, and I'm trying to learn how to swim this summer."

"Buck, I bet there's a girl at that lake that's caught your fancy, right?"

Michael blushed. "Yes, ma'am."

"Well what's her name? Does she like you too?"

"Her name is Susan," he said. "And she doesn't even know I'm alive yet."

"I bet she knows more than you think," she said, trying to encourage him. "Buck, let me let you in on a secret. I discovered a long time ago there ain't no gold in those golden years. Don't waste your life putting it off for the future. Let Susan know you like her. But I do have one request. Will you come by and see me and Biscuit once in a while and let us know how you're doing? I'd like to meet this Susan one day."

Michael loved the way the old lady made him feel. She treated him as an equal, and after talking with her he always felt like there wasn't anything he couldn't accomplish. He wondered what she would think of Susan and realized that Mrs. Farmer's approval was important to him. He was so glad she now had Biscuit to keep her company.

There was laughter coming from the kitchen as Michael entered the house. Curiosity got the best of him, and he stuck his head in the door. Immediately he saw Margaret Foster, his mother, and three other girls. They were making cookies, so he headed straight for the plate. His mother slapped his hand as he reached out to grab one. "Those aren't for you! They belong to Margaret."

Sweet as always, Margaret searched for a compromise and held up two cookies. "Mother Barkley, he can have two of them."

Martha was speechless; it was the first time anyone had called her that, and she liked it. Michael grabbed the cookies and rolled his eyes. He saw that his mother was getting ready to cry at Margaret's comment, and he rushed to defuse the situation: "Ah, Momma, I thought sure you'd made them for your little boy."

She hugged him and fussed, "Take those cookies and get out of here. This party is for girls. Now shoo before I get a switch."

He chuckled and went to his room. He sat down and wrote a note to the *Grits* company terminating his standing order. He placed the money and note in an envelope and then put a stamp on it, and then he walked down to a neighbor's mailbox. He raised the flag for the mailman. His daddy had removed their mailbox when he started working at the post office. With all the girls at his house, he decided to visit Tommy. It was pretty obvious a slumber party was in the works. Since Amy Jo had died, the only place the parents would allow their daughters a sleepover was at the Barkley house. Michael was happy for his momma. She finally had the daughter she'd missed out on.

That night, he set his alarm early so he could get up before the girls. He quickly got dressed and ran over to Craig's so he could catch a ride to the lake. Craig was surprised to see him. "Thought you sold papers on Saturday mornings."

The car was already full, with two guys and three girls in swimsuits. Craig bent down and said to them, "You guys make room for one more back there."

They put Michael in the middle of the backseat. The girls were at least three years older and felt safe practicing their flirting on a kid. He didn't care; he was going to see Susan.

At the lake, everyone crowded out and ran to the dock. The guys went right into the lake for a swim while the girls carefully laid out their towels to sunbathe, not wanting to get their hair wet after having spent hours getting it exactly right. Michael stood next to the car and watched them. He walked down to the edge of the lake and checked out all the neighboring docks. It was too early for anyone to be out yet. He tried not to be disappointed and decided to walk the dirt road that ran around the cove behind all the cabins. That way he just might run into Susan. After two trips around the mile-long road with no success, he needed to come up with another plan. He saw an old man fishing the point between the two coves and followed the little path down to him.

"Son, it's a great day for fishing, but you forgot your rod and reel," the old man said.

Caught off guard, Michael blurted out, "I don't have one. I've never fished in the lake before."

"That's hard to believe. You're missing out on one of life's greatest pleasures."

Insulted, Michael explained, "I've fished a lot on Sugar Creek and the river, but we use cane poles there."

The old man realized he'd hurt the boy's feelings. "A cane pole is great on the lake if you go back into the cove where the creeks come in. You can catch a mess of brim or crappies in no time. Grab your pole and I'll show you where I'm talking about," he offered.

Obviously, this man had never had met a stranger. Michael blushed and admitted, "I left it at home. Maybe I can just watch you, if you don't mind."

"That's fair enough."

The lake was down in depth about ten feet from being full. Michael sat on a big rock next to the man and watched him cast out as far as he could and reel it in quickly. "This is a white bomber. It works better when you're trolling."

Michael asked, "What's trolling?"

He explained, "You use a small boat at a slow speed and pull this bomber about fifty feet behind it. You usually get a hit about every time you cross a point like the one we're on."

"Why aren't you in a boat, then?" asked Michael.

"I'm getting too old to be out on this lake by myself," he explained as he put his hand up to his mouth and winked. "Truth is my wife won't let me."

Not knowing what to say, Michael just grinned in sympathy. All of a sudden the old man yelled out, "Look at that! We're getting a bite." He pointed to a rod on the ground Michael hadn't even noticed. "Watch the line; see he's picking it up. He'll drop it and the next time he picks it up, he'll run with it."

Michael was amazed, because that was exactly what the fish did. The old man picked up the rod. "We'll let him run about ten feet and then we'll set the hook." As he spoke, he snapped the rod back over his head in a quick fluid motion. The fish came flying out of the water about a foot and a half high. Michael had never been more excited in his life and started jumping up and down and shouting, "You've got him! You've got him!"

The old man went on with his lesson. "Now you've got to keep the line real tight or he'll get off." He pulled the fish up on the bank and smiled in satisfaction. "It's perfect. Just the right size for supper for Liz and me. He's the one I've been looking for all day." He began to gather all of his equipment and asked, "Son, what's your name?"

"Michael."

He handed him the rod and reel he'd just used to catch the fish and suggested, "Why don't you use this for a while? Let me show you how to put on a spring lizard."

Once it was on, he pushed the black button on the back of the reel and threw the bait about sixty feet away from the bank. The old man turned and winked. "Now comes the best part of fishing: the waiting. When you catch all you want, just put the rod and reel on the back porch over there. It'll be there anytime you want to use it. Good luck, son."

As he walked away, Michael yelled, "Thank you, sir!"

Michael had learned a long time ago that old people never tell you their name. They just seem to think you already know it. He sat on the big rock in the sun, and after a while he began to get sleepy. He wrapped the line around his hand and laid back. Just about the time he began to doze off, the line got tight and then loose again. He grabbed the rod and got ready. It seemed like an eternity before the line began to move toward deeper water. He began to count the feet: "Three...four...five." By the time he got to six he was counting out loud. "Seven...eight...nine...ten." Then he set the hook.

From behind him he heard a small voice. "He's got one."

He was afraid to turn around and look because he remembered the old man had told him to keep the line tight or the fish would get off. Seconds later, when he pulled it up on the bank the kid yelled, "It's a big one, too!"

Michael turned to talk to the kid and was looking right into the sun. All he could see was the outline of two people. He asked, "You think so? What's your name, buddy?"

"My name is James Edward and I'm five years old," he said holding up five fingers.

"Is that your momma?"

"Nah, silly. She's just an old girl. She's mean one, too."

Michael burst out laughing. "Now how can she be mean to you?"

Scrunching up his face, the little boy stomped his foot and complained, "She won't even let me get in the water."

"Boy, that's serious," Michael commiserated. He held up the bass and smiled. "This is the biggest fish I've ever caught." Then he realized he didn't have anywhere to keep it all day, so he asked, "James Edward, what do you think we should do with this big old fish?"

The girl answered for him. "Do what Mr. Harper does. Throw it back and catch it again another day. He only keeps what he eats."

The little boy said, "Yeah, let it go so it can grow up!"

Without thinking, Michael just tossed it back into the lake. He felt good about the act. He turned around grinning, and his heart almost stopped. He was face to face with the woman of his dreams, Susan. He just stood there with a stupid grin on his face and not a thought in his head. Sensing how uncomfortable he was, she stuck out her hand and said, "Michael, I'm Susan. Nice to meet you."

"Nice to meet you. How'd you know my name?"

"Mr. Harper told us there was a nice boy named Michael on the point and he might help us find some old lures."

He stood still while processing what she'd said, and then he asked about the one thing he didn't understand. "Old lures? Where do we look?"

Susan liked this Michael. He wasn't acting like most guys—thinking they are God's gift to women. She sent up a silent prayer that he wouldn't change. Then she answered him, "A lot of fishermen lose their lures here early in the spring while trolling. Now that the lake is so low, James and I make a game of trying to see how many we can find."

James Edward said, "It's a treasure hunt. Mr. Harper, Mr. Middleton, and Mr. Branch give me a whole quarter for some of the good ones I find."

"Sounds like fun," Michael agreed. "Let me take this rod and bait bucket back up on the porch and I'll be right back."

As he ran to the porch, he looked up to the sky and said a quiet prayer: "Thank you, Lord. I promise I'll never use another curse word."

By the time he returned, they'd already found one lure. It was stuck in a small stump that had turned black from years of being submerged. Susan looked up in relief when she saw him. "Great, you're back. We can't get it loose."

Michael put his hand in his pocket and pulled out his knife. He stuck the point in the wood near the hook and twisted it back and forth until the plug popped loose. James Edward picked it up and examined it. "It's pretty. Mr. Branch really likes this color."

He dropped it into the little bucket Susan was carrying and headed off to search for more. This was the first time Michael had even noticed her carrying it, and he couldn't help but smile. She noticed and asked, "And why exactly are you smiling?"

"Oh, nothing. You know this is kind of fun."

She just nodded and sized him up. "Yeah, it is, isn't it?"

As they wandered around the point, they eventually entered the cove where Craig and his friends were. One of the boys was pulling Craig on skis. The wakes were causing the waves to go up four to five feet on the bank. As Michael and Susan watched Craig, James Edward called out, "There's one! It's on that old board next to the water."

Susan warned him, "What's the rule about water?"

He whirled around and stuck out his tongue at her, then turned to Michael. "See? I told you she was mean. It's just a little wet and I'm no baby!"

Michael sat on the large rock, took off his shoes and socks, and rolled up his pants legs to his knees. He waded through the soupy mud and retrieved the bright green lure. He tossed it over to the boy and said, "Here you go, buddy."

He pulled the board out of the mud and discovered two more lures. They walked around the cove with Michael carrying his shoes and socks in his hand. He quickly figured out it was easier to use a conversation with James Edward to get the information he needed. "Buddy, do you live here?"

"Nah, I live in Jasper. I come up and stay with Mamaw and Papaw sometimes though."

Susan chimed in, "I go to church with them, and they let me babysit him when he's here."

Hearing her, the indignant child quickly turned around. He couldn't believe she had embarrassed him in front of Michael. He wanted him for a friend more than anything. "I told you I ain't no baby! I'm almost five. You are so mean!"

They both laughed as James stomped off toward Craig's dock, mumbling to himself.

As they got near, Craig dropped into the water next to the dock and called out, "Hey, I see you found Michael."

Startled, Michael looked at her curiously and said, "Yeah, I guess she did."

James Edward didn't like it that the adults were ignoring him. "Look, we found four lures."

Craig dismissed him. "Yeah, they're all rusty though."

Michael didn't like seeing the hurt in the kid's eyes at Craig's thoughtlessness, so he turned and suggested, "Let's go see if we can find some more."

As they walked away, he looked at Susan and said, "I thought you said Mr. Harper told you where to find me."

"He did; I knew then it was the right thing to do. I was a little apprehensive when Craig told me about you."

"How do you know Craig?"

"I see him at the teen canteen in Blue Ridge all the time," she explained.

"Where do you live?" Michael asked.

"Lakewood, where do you live?"

"Blue Ridge."

Surprised, she just looked at him. "And you don't go to the canteen?"

He dropped his voice and confessed, "I can't dance."

She couldn't believe this gorgeous boy didn't know how to dance. "I'll teach you."

Afraid to get his hopes too high, he said, "Are you sure? You have no idea what you're getting yourself into. I've tried and tried, and believe me when I tell you I have two left feet."

She sighed in relief. "Everyone can dance, silly. You just have to let yourself go and listen to the music."

Suddenly everything clicked in his mind and he blurted out, "You go to East Fannin, don't you? That's why I don't know you."

She put her hands on her hips and glared at him. "And is that going to be a problem?"

"It might be a little harder, but nothing that can't be fixed. Are you going to the canteen tonight?"

"No, I promised to watch James Edward until at least nine o'clock," she said with disappointment. Then she looked worried. They'd been so wrapped up in each other that they'd forgotten all about James Edward. They both looked around frantically as they heard him yell out, "Look! There's another one in that bush." They'd moved around the cove until they were next to a small stream that ran into the lake. Both sides had bushes about ten feet tall, and Michael could easily see the plug the kid was talking about. It was right above the small stream, which was only a couple of inches deep. He didn't ask Susan, but just dropped his shoes and got on his knees and held out his hand to the kid "Buddy, climb up on my back."

James Edward eagerly hopped on and clutched his arms around Michael's neck. He waded through the mud until he was in the middle of the stream, which turned out to be solid ground. He quickly moved to the bush that held the plug. When they were back on dry ground next to Susan, James Edward gave her the stink eye, stuck out his tongue and boasted, "See there, I didn't get wet at all. You think you're so smart, but you don't know nothing."

Susan turned away so he couldn't see her laughter. When she got it under control she turned and said, "Yeah, I see that. I guess it's time we get you back home so your grandparents won't worry about you."

He jumped down, stuck both hands on his hips, and decided to press his luck since he had Michael on his side. "Do I have to? Why do you have to be so mean?"

Michael decided he needed to nip this bit of defiance in the bud before Susan lost her temper. "You'd better do what she says, boy. That way they won't be mad at me for keeping you away so long and will let us hang out again."

James Edward hung his head and kicked a rock. "Well, OK. But I'm only doing it for you—not that mean old girl."

Michael snickered and looked over at Susan. "Will you be here again tomorrow?"

"No, it's decoration day at the church. I hope to see you at the canteen next Saturday, though."

When Michael got back to the cabin, Craig called out, "I'm making a party run. You want to go with me?"

"To Blue Ridge?" Michael called back.

"Yep, through town to the supper club."

"OK, then," Michael agreed. "Just drop me off at the house."

"You and Susan meeting up at the canteen? She sure can dance," Craig teased.

"I guess so." Michael was reluctant to talk about it with Craig. Craig's comment about what a good dancer she was kept running through his thoughts the entire trip home. He couldn't decide if he was excited about getting to spend time with her at the canteen or just scared to death of what she'd think when she realized he wasn't lying—he really couldn't dance.

# CHAPTER 34

Michael was thinking about the previous weekend when he woke on Monday. It was like a dream, and he couldn't wait to tell someone about it. Jesse was his first choice, but he knew there'd be no way they'd have any time together. Tommy was a consideration, but he was always being interrupted with work. Then it hit him: Mrs. Farmer was perfect. While he was eating breakfast, his mother told him she'd used the last of her kindling. "Cut up one of those dead chestnut logs Jesse gave your daddy," she instructed.

"Yes, Momma." He made quick work of eating and headed to the woodshed. He placed one of the logs in the sawhorse and cut four sticks about ten inches long with the bucksaw. In less than an hour, he had two piles of kindling. He used the first one to fill the box in the kitchen and placed the second pile in a toe sack. He called out to his momma, "I'll be back later."

She yelled back, "Be home in time for supper."

He was so excited he ran most of the way to Mrs. Farmer's house. She was sitting in her rocker and greeted him with her sweet smile. "Howdy, Buck. What've you got in the bag?"

"I cut some kindling for Momma and thought you might need some too."

"That's awful thoughtful of you. I do need some. Come on in; you know where to put it. You got time to eat a biscuit?"

He smiled. "Got any apple butter for that biscuit?"

"I might be able to find some," she said with a wink.

They sat at the table as he filled his biscuit. She watched him in amusement; she could tell something important was on his mind. She had years of patience under her belt, so she just settled down to wait until he was ready. A while later, he still seemed to be having trouble working up to it, so she finally prompted him, "I can tell you've got a bee in your bonnet. You've seen Susan, haven't you?"

He was so relieved she'd brought it up.

"Does she like you? Did she remember you?" she prompted.

"Yes, ma'am. She came looking for me at the lake."

"Well, Buck, tell me more. Does she live near here?"

"Lakewood; she goes to East Fannin High School," he offered.

She watched him sweat over her questions for a moment and then reassured him, "Well, if she came looking for you, you must be her beau."

For the next couple of hours, Michael regurgitated every single detail of the weekend. Listening with attention the entire time, she finally asked, "Buck, do you have a driver's license?"

She watched as he tumbled off the cloud he'd been on. He shook his head in sorrow and answered, "No, ma'am, not yet."

"Looks like you'll need to get one, since you're in Blue Ridge and she's in Lakewood. I can't think of any other way you two can see each other."

The conversation dried up after that, and he promised he'd return soon. He had a solution in mind before he crossed the highway. He came through the back door asking his momma, "Can you teach me how to drive so I can get my license?"

She laughed and said, "Well hello to you, too, and how was your day? Why don't you ask your daddy? He's much better at it."

Michael frowned and started outside. "Yeah, right. He doesn't have time for me. I'll ask Uncle Jesse," he said, slamming the back door.

In bed that night, Martha took a deep breath and sent up a silent prayer before suggesting, "Michael wants you to teach him to drive so he can get his license."

"He's just a boy. He doesn't need one. That darn Craig has put that idea in his head. He's not even old enough, and this post master job is almost more than I can handle. We're short two people at work. It's hard to believe no one wants to work anymore."

Realizing she needed to solve Mike's problem before she continued to plead her son's case, she patiently asked, "Where would they work?"

"In back sorting mail and moving packages around."

She said, "That's got to be one boring job. Maybe you just need to find the right person."

He continued to complain. "Every time I tell a new hire what to do, the next day he quits. What's wrong with kids these days? Don't the parents teach them they have to work to get ahead in life and that they might not always enjoy it?"

She snapped back, "Guess their daddies were way too busy to teach them," and then turned over to sleep.

Mike knew he'd screwed up, but he didn't know how. One thing was certain though, his woman was mad.

At breakfast, Michael asked, "Where's Daddy?"

"He decided to go in early," Martha said. She was still irritated, and as usual Mike had taken the easy way out and left.

"Boy, that's not like him. He's always said breakfast is the best meal of the day," Michael scoffed.

"Well he did. I've been thinking about your driving lesson. Why don't you go over to the state patrol office, pick up a booklet, and start studying so you can pass the written part of the test?"

Excited, he said, "I don't know where that is."

"It's the road just past the Swan Drive-In. When you learn the book from cover to cover, I'll teach you to drive. Is that fair?"

He jumped up and hugged her. "Momma, you're an angel."

"Maybe you should remind your father of that," she mumbled. "Hurry up and eat. Margaret and her friends are coming to make brownies."

Walking through downtown Blue Ridge, Michael avoided the post office. He knew Craig would give him a ride, but he wasn't willing to suffer the interrogation and teasing he'd have to endure. It didn't take as long as he'd thought it would to get to the State Patrol Headquarters. He grabbed a pamphlet, approached the clerk, and asked her to describe the procedure necessary to obtain a driver's license. She gave him her usual reply: "It's first come, first served. First you have to take the written test, then the driver's portion. We're open five days a week."

He thanked her and began his walk home. As he passed the Tastee Freeze, he noticed some of his friends were there and decided to join them.

Ironically, they were there celebrating one of them receiving his license. He spent nearly an hour picking his friend's brain on how he'd passed and what it had entailed. The other two buddies listened with interest, as they all knew the process was ahead of them. By the time he left, Michael realized it was OK that he didn't have a license yet. Relieved, he walked by the canteen building. The white, single-story wooden building looked nothing like he'd expected. It was about fifty feet wide and eighty feet long. He kept walking and looked at his watch so he could time how long it would take him to get home.

The rest of the week was spent studying the pamphlet. Friday morning, he asked his momma to test him on some of the questions. It appeared he'd been studying the wrong things, so he was grateful he'd taken the extra step before trying the actual exam.

The next morning, he was too excited to study and began doing routine chores to pass the time—stacking wood, splitting kindling, and cleaning out the ditches next to the driveway. Martha stood at the window and watched him. Her motherly antenna was up, and she knew he was up to something. When Margaret knocked quietly on the door, Martha quizzed her, "Do you have any idea what's going on with Michael? He's up to something."

Margaret flushed. She didn't want to rat out Michael, but the one person she trusted and depended on the most had just called her bluff. She hesitated for just a moment, and then caved. "Mother Barkley, he's got a girlfriend. He met her at the lake."

Martha nodded. "Well, that explains a lot. Don't worry, I won't tell him you told me. Now, what's her name?"

"Susan, but I don't know her last name."

Martha laughed in relief. "I've been wondering what the big hurry was to get a license. Now I know."

Margaret pleaded, "Please don't tell him I told you. I don't want him to be mad at me. I love coming here."

"It's OK, honey, don't worry. He's never been able to keep a secret from me for long."

Supper was entertaining for Martha as she watched her little boy being "cool." Mike, as usual, was oblivious to what was going on under his own roof. She was frustrated and disappointed that Michael was entering this new phase of his life without the guidance and reassurance of his father.

Michael was nervous as he entered the canteen. A nice lady had him sign in, then she cautioned him and gave him the rules—if he left he couldn't come back inside. He walked around her table, past the restrooms, and into a large, open room. It had folding metal chairs against the walls. Less than half of them were occupied, and about ten people were dancing. On the left side of the room was a stage about a foot high that held a small record player surrounded with stacks of 45s. He didn't know what he'd been expecting, but it certainly wasn't this. He walked over to an open space with chairs, sat down, and scanned the crowd looking for Susan. He was disappointed she wasn't there yet, but he was also relieved because it gave him time to study the brave souls on the floor to see if he could pick up some tips on what to do. As he watched, he noticed that anyone could select the next record to play, but the pattern he discerned was two fast songs and then one slow.

When the music stopped, a tall blonde called out, "I've got 'Hand Jive.' How many of you have seen it on *Bandstand?*"

About half of the crowd held up their hands and she said, "OK, then. Ready to give it a try?"

The crowd was game. Michael watched them for a while and felt sure he could do better than some of them. His nerves began to fade. The blonde stopped the record and said, "Everybody line up and let's try it again."

Michael couldn't help himself; he stood and moved quickly to the middle of the line. The more he tried, the more confidence he gained. When the record stopped, he went back to his seat for the slow song. He watched the best male dancer very carefully. He was so engrossed, he didn't notice a girl approach and ask him, "Can I have this dance?"

Surprised, he looked up at Susan. Trying to be cool, he stuck out his hand, "Yes, ma'am, I'd be delighted."

He took a couple of steps onto the floor, and she grabbed him and pulled him to her. He responded by putting his arm around her waist and sighed with satisfaction at the feel of her in his arms. He wasn't experienced enough to tell she was leading. Before he could blink, the music had stopped. Susan didn't rush to step back. That was a nice surprise. Several dances later, her older brother came and picked her up. Michael stood back watching her leave; he had never felt so helpless in his life. With nothing left of interest at the canteen, he headed home. As he walked outside, he heard Craig's voice yell, "Hey buddy, where you going? The party's just starting."

He really didn't want to spend time with these older guys, so he said, "I can't go back in. I've already signed out."

"Sorry about that. Heading to the lake next Saturday if you need a ride," Craig offered.

"I do, thanks," Michael replied.

# CHAPTER 35

On the way to church, Martha casually mentioned, "I need the car a couple of days next week."

Without thinking, Mike snapped, "What for?" He could feel the air in the car shift and he knew he'd screwed up again. It wasn't what he'd said, but his tone that kept getting him in trouble.

"Mike Barkley, I am not one of your employees. If you expect me to cook, I need to get groceries. Fine! Forget it. I'll find another way."

Sitting in the backseat with his head swiveling between his annoyed parents, Michael tried to be as quiet as a mouse. His dad was silent the remainder of the trip. He knew he'd pushed his lovely wife just a smidgen too far. You could cut the tension with a knife, and he was almost relived when after church she said, "Don't worry about the car. Mother said she'd take me wherever I needed to go."

Mike shivered, unconsciously, as he always did when her mother was mentioned. What on earth had he done? She was acting just like Jesse had when he was a kid. Mike figured it was time to ask for his momma's help in navigating his way out of the doghouse.

He decided to keep a low profile the rest of the day and give her time to settle down. "You can tell your mother she's off the hook as far as hauling you around," Mike said as he was getting into bed. "I'll walk to work a couple of days every week. I'm getting a little fat and I guess I can use the exercise. I like your biscuits a little too much to give them up."

Martha just snorted. Her master plan had worked. Even since their truce, the mention of her mother always brought her big old husband to his knees. Still, even though she had gotten her way, she was disgusted. Men attacked the symptoms, not the problem. She wanted him to spend some quality time with their son, as he was growing up every single day. She turned and glared at him, "You're hopeless, you know that?"

Over the years, Mike had learned not to fall into such an obvious trap. He knew anything he said at this point would only fuel some future lesson she would deliver on his being a better husband or father. Deciding to take the easy way out of this mess, he turned over and said, "I love you, sweetie. Good night."

Martha rolled her eyes and wanted so badly to call him a coward, but instead she said, "I love you, too."

He couldn't go to sleep right away. He was getting a little tired of everyone wanting a piece of him. He had a really important job now that required all of his attention, and it was feeding his family. As he drifted off, he wondered why they just couldn't cut him a little slack at home. As Michael handed Martha his plate the next morning, she grinned and said, "Are you ready for your first lesson?"

"Really? Oh, yeah," Michael said with excitement.

As they sat in the car, she had him adjust the mirrors and seat. She was surprised at how comfortable he appeared. He backed up, turned around, and started toward the highway. "Momma, where are we going?"

They sat for a moment while she decided, and then she said, "Sugar Creek Baptist Church. You can practice parallel parking in their lot."

He looked at her in confusion. "What's that?"

She just grinned and said, "You'll see." She was impressed at how smoothly he changed the gears and couldn't resist asking, "Where'd you learn to do that?"

"Uncle Jesse's old truck is really hard and he showed me how to double clutch it," he explained. "But I don't need to on the car." She was so proud of her boy and was sad that Mike wasn't here to see how well he was doing.

After a few more practice days, Michael Barkley was the proud owner of a Georgia driver's license.

# CHAPTER 36

Driving home from work, Jesse spied Nick outside working in the garden. He stopped and yelled out, "What are you up to, farmer? Being sheriff too boring for you?"

"It's not that, but man, some of the things I see drive me nuts. We arrested a guy for beating his wife, and you know what his excuse was? His wife was late putting supper on the table. Now the woman has four kids and the man doesn't work or do anything at home. Sometimes I want to do so much more than just arrest them."

Realizing he couldn't solve the problem, Jesse changed the subject. "You know, your garden is big enough to feed ten people."

"With a baby coming, I need to store up some food," Nick justified.

"Nick, babies don't eat canned beans or corn. Why not just say it out loud? You're scared."

Sheepishly, he admitted, "Is it really that obvious?"

"Bad enough that our women have a bet on who goes to the hospital first, you or Marie," Jesse hooted. He just loved messing with his way too serious friend.

"She's not even going to the hospital. Mrs. Loudermilk is delivering it for us here at home," Nick said, as if that justified his concern.

"See what I mean? She's only four months along and you already have everything planned out. Why Mrs. Loudermilk?"

"She delivered Marie and her sisters," Nick explained. "Marie is deathly afraid of hospitals. Her father and grandmother have convinced her that when you go to a hospital, you die. She has made me swear to her that no matter what I won't ever take her there."

Jesse just shook his head. He loved teasing his friend, but it was really getting kind of crazy how uptight Nick was. "Let me know when your big harvest starts."

Nick stopped him. "Whoa, I haven't seen you in a month. Tell me about the mines."

Jesse hung his head. "Guess if you're looking to make a lot of money, I'm in the right place. They contract a lot of their work. Some guys complete two in one day."

Realizing Jesse was holding back, Nick quietly asked, "Yeah, but what's it like?"

"It's cold, dusty, dark, and lonely."

"Sounds like you don't care much for it," Nick stated the obvious.

"I don't. It's not like jumping from a plane in cool, clear air with a bunch of other fools like me. Guess that's what I miss the most—working with a team."

"Have you told Lorri?"

"Nah, she wouldn't understand. I don't think I've ever seen her happier. Why mess up her world? She's closer to Marie than her own sisters. There's not a day that goes by they aren't up to something together. I wouldn't want to mess with that. You know something, buddy? That wife beater needs his ass kicked. Let me know if you need any help. I'll see you later."

Lorri turned her cheek to Jesse for a kiss when he came into the kitchen. "What have you been up to?"

"Nothing, just spent a few minutes with Nick while he was working in his garden. It's spotless. I didn't see one weed. It's like he's possessed, and I think you're right, he's gone off the deep end."

Lorri laughed. "You're right about that. Marie says he's treating her like a little China doll. It's funny to think a couple of years ago he didn't have a care in the world, and now I don't even recognize the guy."

"I think the Nick we saw that didn't have a care in the world really didn't exist. He experienced so much loss in the army, he covered it up by pretending to be Mr. Happy-go-lucky. Now I know a lot of it was just show. The guy we're seeing now is the real Nick. What's great is I like both of them."

"Me too. Speaking of that, here's a letter from O'Shea," Lorri said as she handed him the mail. He immediately ripped open and read,

Hi, Mountain Boy,

Bet I'm the last person you expected to hear from. Remember when I told you they were reducing the size of the army and would regret it? Well, now they do. Looks like Russia is showing their ass. Would you believe they're trying to build a wall around Berlin? It seems the East Germans are trying to escape to the west, and the guards are even shooting people to stop them. It's crazy. Enough about that. What it means is the army is calling back as many NCOs and officers as they can. When the commander gave us the briefing, I thought of you. Have you and Lorri had enough of civilian life yet? I know one thing: I have an open slot for a tall, skinny mountain boy. Seriously, let me know if you're interested.
O'Shea

"What's he say?" Lorri asked in amusement. O'Shea could always be counted on for a laugh.

The contents of the letter froze Jesse with yearning in every part of his soul. He loved the army life and had never even considered the possibility that it was still there waiting for him. He shook it off, knowing he couldn't uproot his family. Lorri loved it here and had Marie. Danny was happy in school, and the twins thought of Marie as a second momma. But the idea rooted itself deep in his heart as he turned to her and said, "Oh, nothing. He's just bragging about what a wonderful life he has at Fort Benning. Nothing changes with him."

Diverting her attention, Jesse asked, "Did you say Michael had gotten his license? I can't even imagine how Big Mike let that happen." He shook his head and said, "You know, it's like he just doesn't want Michael to grow up."

Lorri agreed. "I think he's growing up in spite of it. Martha tells me he has a girlfriend, but he doesn't want any of us to know about it."

Jesse threw his fist in the air. "Way to go, little Michael! I can't wait to get him alone and get an update. You know, I really miss those Sunday dinners at Momma's."

Looking at him pointedly, she said, "Are you saying her cooking's better than mine?"

"Nah, it's more like I've been deleted from the gossip chain in the area, and boy do I miss that. You can always count on these mountain people to keep you entertained."

She stared at him for a moment and frowned. "Admit it, you really don't like working in those mines, do you?" She could tell something was up with him, but she couldn't quite put her finger on it. Still, she was determined to get to the bottom of it.

After hesitating for a moment, he looked her in the eye and just held her gaze. Then he said quietly, "Is that wrong of me?"

# CHAPTER 37

When he got his license, Michael had expected all his problems to be solved. But he was getting his first lesson in adulthood, as solving one problem unearthed a few more. He could drive now, but how on earth was he going to convince his daddy to let him have the car? His first approach was tentative and didn't go too well. Realizing nothing was going to be accomplished, he gave up and walked out the front door, slamming it behind him. Watching from the kitchen, Martha shook her head in disgust.

Mike came storming into the room and demanded, "Did you know that boy has his license?"

She wiped her hands on a towel and folded them across her chest. Instantly, Mike knew he'd messed up and patiently waited to discover exactly what he'd done.

"Yes, I knew about it. In fact, I took him. If you weren't so busy, you might have noticed how good he is at it. Mike, if you don't start taking more of an interest in him, you're going to regret it one day." She was so annoyed, yet full of sadness. She had never even imagined Mike would allow himself to miss out on Michael's young life—especially after the way he and Jesse had been treated by Amos.

In defensive mode, he tried to justify his behavior: "Martha, I'm too busy at work; I just don't have time for this stuff."

"Quit trying to fool yourself and tell that BS to somebody who doesn't know you better. Ever since you got promoted, nothing else in your life matters. You don't have time because you don't make time. Have you noticed Jesse's the only person who can call your bluff and get you to do anything? Why is that?"

On the last weekend before summer ended, Michael was one frustrated teen. James Edward had gone home to Jasper a week after they'd met and his absence meant Susan didn't have a reason to be at the lake. At first, he'd go over and fish with Mr. Harper for the day. He'd tease him when he'd notice Michael constantly looking over his shoulder trying to catch a glimpse of her: "Boy, is the law looking for you? You know I'm old and can't afford to be caught with any bank robbers. Mrs. Harper would be really lonely if they put me in jail."

He liked Mr. Harper, but he didn't feel comfortable confiding in him. He was so naïve he didn't even realize Mr. Harper already knew what his trouble was. One good thing was he was learning to love fishing.

The only bright spot in the summer was Saturday nights at the canteen, but with the rules in place and the crowds, they never had any time alone. Her brother brought her and picked her up at closing. Everyone knew they were a couple, and Susan was so popular that their friends surrounded them as soon as they sat down in the old metal chairs. Boy would they be shocked to know that Michael and Susan had never even kissed.

The anticipation of that kiss consumed Michael. He dreamed about it every single night until it became larger than life in his mind. What if he messed it up? He'd never kissed a girl before. He decided on a simple plan—get his daddy's car, take her home from the canteen, and kiss her on her front porch at the end of the night. He was so desperate to be alone with her that he decided to confide how he felt that night. He would tell her that he was getting the car, even if he had to steal it, so they could be alone. No way was he going to let her to fall in love with some stupid football jock from school next week when she returned to East Fannin.

Susan arrived first and was waiting for him when he entered the canteen. She gave him a little wave, and he glanced around and noticed that their friends hadn't arrived yet. It was the perfect time to share his plan and seek her approval.

"Susan, we need to talk before the others get here. I got my license and I am getting the car next week so I can take you home. Can you tell your brother?'

She slumped back against the chair and looked at him in dismay. "Michael, I can't do that. Daddy won't let me date until I'm sixteen, and that's not until November. If it wasn't for Momma, I wouldn't be allowed to come here at all. My brother hates having to pick me up. He's not the problem, though, it's my daddy. You have no idea how strict he is."

Michael nodded in sympathy. "Oh, yes I do. That's my daddy too. When am I ever going to kiss you and ask you to go steady?"

She turned to him, placed her hands on both sides of his face, and pulled his lips to hers. She held the kiss as long as she could hold her breath. Afterward, she took a couple of deep breaths and said, "Yes, I will go steady with you, but it has to be a secret until December."

The decision was made to have Susan's sixteenth birthday party on the Saturday following her birthday on the eighth. Since she was on the school basketball team, she had a lot of friends, and she didn't want to leave anyone out. She needed to give her mother a list of how many would be coming. When she handed it over, her mother noticed some of the names had "plus one" written beside them. She frowned. "What exactly does this *plus one* mean?"

"Those girls want to bring a boy along."

"I notice you've left someone off," she teased.

Susan was confused. "I think I put down all the relatives that could come, and the coach said he couldn't come. There's not anyone else at school I want to come."

Her mother grinned. "How about Michael Barkley?"

Susan was shocked. She ducked her head and tried to come up with something to say. She had no idea how on earth her mother knew about Michael. What mothers everywhere always threatened must be true—they really did have eyes in the back of their heads.

"Susan, if you're going to try to keep a secret from me, you'd better warn your friends," her mother chided. "It's clear they all think he's pretty cool, as you kids say."

"Momma, are you mad?"

"Why would I be mad? We told you that you weren't allowed to date, but we didn't say you couldn't talk to a boy or dance with one. Besides, your brother really likes him."

"He knows too? Does Daddy know?" Susan wondered, horrified.

"You know your daddy. He's only interested in hunting and fishing. I would recommend we keep this between us, though, until your daddy actually meets this young man."

Susan hugged her in relief. "Momma, I love you so much."

Michael couldn't wait to attend the party. Wednesday at the supper table, he asked, "Daddy, can I please have the car Saturday night? I want to go to a birthday party in Lakewood. Please, I won't ask again the whole year. It's that important to me."

Mike sat with the fork to his mouth and watched his son beg. It was like time stood still, and in his mind all the emotions he'd had as he had begged Amos for the truck so he could see Martha swirled around him. It was an epiphany for him, and he glanced over at Martha for guidance. All he could think was, oh my God, I've turned into Amos and I didn't even know it was happening. He was no longer hungry and withered under the look Martha was throwing like daggers his way. He knew his own life hung in the balance and depended upon the answer he gave their son in the next moment. He tried to throw her a reassuring grin to let her know he finally "got it" before turning to Michael and saying, "Of course, son. I won't need it. Do you have the money to put gas in the tank?"

# CHAPTER 38

It was just after midnight when Marie shook Nick awake. "Go get Lorri; I need her."

"Is it the baby? Do you want me to go get Mrs. Loudermilk?"

Marie just sighed. "Relax, Nick, I'm just having a little pain. Lorri will know what to do. Now please go get her."

Nick took off down the little path to the Barkleys' house. He ran up the stairs to the kitchen door and banged on it. Jesse opened it a moment later. "What's up?"

Nick stammered, "Marie wants Lorri. I'm afraid she might be having the baby."

Lorri poked her head around Jesse. "I'll get dressed and be right there. Now you go home and stay with her."

Lorri went straight to the bedroom. Nick went into the living room and turned on the television to try to calm himself down. As it warmed up, he realized that the only thing on was the test pattern. He turned on the radio and turned the dial, looking for a station. A voice finally came on, saying, "This is Dick Biondi, coming to you from WKBW, 1520 AM in Buffalo. Let's listen to my friend, Paul Anka." Nick sat down to listen. He really liked this new rock and roll music. After a few songs, he heard the women laughing back in the bedroom. He stuck his head in the door and asked, "What's so funny?"

Marie waved him in. "It's a false alarm. It was just indigestion."

Lorri added, "Nick, you can't let her eat a whole jar of pickles before she goes to bed."

He apologized, "Oh, man. I'm so sorry I woke you guys up."

"That's OK, turnabout is fair enough. Can't tell you how many times I've gotten her up with the twins. That's what friends are for."

Michael wolfed down his breakfast Saturday morning so he could wash the car. It was a beautiful, clear day, though it was a little cold. The party would begin at six o'clock, but Susan had invited him to come earlier and help set up. That was perfect. He would be able to give her his gift without a lot of witnesses. He'd had a hard time coming up with an idea, but after listening to her talk about her love of basketball, he realized that was the solution. He left home at two o'clock and prayed the entire way he wouldn't get lost. He'd studied the map until he'd memorized it. There were only two roads in Lakewood. One went to Mineral Bluff and the other to Morganton. When he turned into her driveway, he watched as an older man put camping gear into an old truck. Michael got out and asked, "Sir, is this where the birthday party is? I'm supposed to help."

"You've found it," the man replied. As they talked, he picked up an old army field jacket. Michael immediately noticed the airborne wings and said, "My uncle Jesse was in the airborne. He jumped in at Normandy."

The old man stood a little straighter. "A lot of us did, son."

"Uncle Jesse was an instructor at the school at Fort Benning. I plan to join the army as soon as I graduate. I want to go to airborne school, too. My goal is to make it a career."

"Sounds like you've thought about this a lot," the man replied. "When I first got back, I thought about making it a career myself, but my high school sweetheart had other plans. Sometimes I regret not staying. Watch out some girl doesn't talk you right out of your plan."

Michael couldn't imagine that ever happening, so he changed the subject. "Where are you headed, sir?"

"Me and about eight of my buddies always camp out at Coopers Creek during deer season. In between playing poker, we sometimes hunt. Next week is doe season, so we should be bringing back some meat for the freezer. You deer hunt?"

"No, sir. I hunt squirrels and rabbits, though."

"I used to like tracking rabbits in the snow. You ever do that?" the old man asked.

"Yes, sir, a couple of times."

The man stuck out his hand "I'm Claude. What's your name?"

"Michael," he replied, sticking out his hand.

"Nice to meet you, Michael. Let me make a suggestion. Before you knock down airborne school, I'd check out if you can be a pilot those newfangled things called a helicopter. If I was your age, I'd jump at that chance," he said as he got into his truck and drove off.

Susan had been on the front porch, where they couldn't see her watching them talk. As Michael climbed the steps and approached the front door, she came out behind him and put her hands over his eyes, saying, "Surprise." Before he could react, she turned him around and kissed him. They held each other for a minute and savored the moment. Finally, her curiosity won out and she asked, "What did you and Daddy talk about?"

Michael could have slapped himself—boy was he stupid. He'd had no idea that old man was her father. "We talked about hunting and his time in the army."

She was surprised. "He actually talked about the war?"

"Yeah, why?" Michael asked.

"Because he won't ever talk about it to us. He just says it's in the past," she explained.

"Did you know he jumped out of planes?"

"Are you serious?" she asked, wide-eyed.

"Said he jumped at Normandy."

She tugged on his arm and pulled him into the kitchen. She asked her mother, "Momma, did you know Daddy was at Normandy?"

"Yes, but he doesn't like to talk about it," her mother warned as she looked at Michael. Susan saw her watching him and realized she'd forgotten her manners.

"Michael, this is my momma."

He stuck out his hand. "Nice to meet you, Momma."

She grinned and said, "Nice to meet you too. It's OK for you to call me that, but most people call me Thelma. OK, kids, we've got a lot of work to do. Ready to get started, Michael?"

He relaxed. "Yes, ma'am, just tell me what to do."

Working with Susan was fun. They made it a competition, and Susan's mother was laughing to herself as she watched them banter back and forth. She liked Michael and didn't know if they would last, but she knew her daughter would learn a lot from that boy—trust and respect.

When he finally glanced at his watch it was almost five o'clock. He slipped away and got her gift from the car. Handing it to her, he said shyly, "Hope you like it."

She opened it and made every effort to preserve the paper. She pulled the top off the box and said, "I love it!" She pulled out a bracelet that had a charm of a tiny basketball hanging from it. She hugged him tightly until she noticed her mom was watching.

By Thursday, Mike had finally arrived at what he thought would be the solution to the problem of Michael dating and wanting the car. That evening, he tentatively approached Martha, saying, "Sweetie, if Michael is going to be using the car, he's going to need a way to earn some money. How about telling him I heard the owner of the Red Dot Grocery Store hires high school boys to bag groceries? He pays ten dollars for the weekend. He could work Friday evening and all day Saturday. That should be more than he needs to buy gas."

"Why don't you tell him?" she asked, exasperated with the entire situation.

"I'd really like to, but I'm afraid anything I say to him right now would be thrown back in my face. That boy is really mad at me."

She thought about it for a moment and sadly said, "It's a shame, but you're probably right. I think the best solution would be for me to tell Margaret and let her suggest it to him. That way he'll think it's his idea."

He stared at her in wonder for a moment and then shook his head. "Sweetie, do you do that to me?"

She just grinned. "Now would I do that?"

# CHAPTER 39

It was the second week in December as Nick rushed to the Barkley house in the middle of the night again. This time he was driving the car with lights flashing and blowing his horn. Lorri met him on the porch. "Is it time?"

Frantic, he stuck his head out the window and yelled, "I'm going to get Mrs. Loudermilk. Will you watch her until we can get back?"

"You know I will," she agreed. Worried by his state of mind, she shook her finger at him and warned, "Nick, please try to calm down. Don't you wreck that car going after her in such a hurry."

"Lorri Barkley, you sound just like my sister."

She just waved and yelled back, "Yeah, and I bet she's pretty darn smart, too."

Lorri assessed Marie when she entered the bedroom. She was soaked in sweat, doubled over in pain, and panting like she couldn't catch her breath. Lorri immediately sensed something was horribly wrong. The pain wasn't coming every few minutes as it should, but constantly, and it seemed to be building in strength. Shoving back her panic, she reached out to Marie, brushed her hair back from her face and wiped her brow. "Did you eat another jar of pickles?"

Marie looked at her in fear and groaned, "No, I haven't eaten, and Lorri, I'm really scared."

"Just relax, Mrs. Loudermilk will be here soon, and she'll know exactly what to do," Lorri pleaded. "Can you lay back and straighten out some for me?"

"I tried, but it hurts too badly," Marie whimpered.

Hearing the sound of a car approaching, Lorri sent up a silent prayer, trying not to let Marie see how anxious she was. "Hey, they're here already." In her heart Lorri knew it was bad and cautiously asked, "Marie, are you absolutely sure you don't want to go to the hospital?"

Panting through the pain, Marie insisted, "No! I'm not going. Everything is going to be fine."

But things weren't fine. Eighteen hours later, Marie was still in labor and showed no signs of delivering the baby. Lorri was frantically trying to reassure Nick that Marie and the baby would be fine, when suddenly the door to the bedroom opened and Mrs. Loudermilk entered the living room crying. She looked at Lorri and then shook her head slightly. Then she turned to Nick and said, "Nick, I'm so sorry. She's gone, and I couldn't save the baby."

The funeral was difficult for the entire community. Nick had quickly become a favorite and everyone was devastated with his loss. Nick got through the service and then withdrew, asking everyone to just leave him alone for a while.

About a week went by before Lorri pulled Jesse aside and told him, "You need to stay with Nick for a while. He's been in that chair all day long. He's not eating, and I don't think I've ever seen anyone so depressed. I'm afraid he might do something to hurt himself. I'd love it if you could get him to come and stay with us, but if not, then you need to stay with him for a while."

Jesse walked up and called out, "Hey, buddy, how are you doing?"

"Sarge, do you think I was punished for being too happy?"

Floored by the question, Jesse wasn't too sure how he should answer. He thought about it for a moment and then gave it his best shot: "I don't believe you lose people you love because you're being punished. It's just life, and life is hard sometimes, Nick. As hard as it is, try to focus on how happy you were and the time you were able to share together."

Nick said, "I'll never forget the day I first saw her. I knew she was an angel on earth and the most beautiful woman I'd ever seen. In the first few minutes we talked, I experienced the most warm, secure feeling, and it lasted the entire time we were married."

Jesse advised his friend, "Nick, try not to forget that. Most people aren't lucky enough to experience what the two of you shared. Now get up and let's go eat supper. Lorri's waiting on us."

Nick protested, "I'm a mess. I haven't shaved or showered."

"Soldier, that sounds like an excuse to me."

"OK, you made your point. Let's go," Nick said.

As they came through the door, the twins spied Nick and yelled in unison, "Uncle Nick, give us a horsey ride."

Normally Lorri would scold them to leave him alone, but today she watched with pride as she saw their unconditional love and innocence put the first smile on Nick's face in over a week. He sat in one of the chairs and crossed his legs. "Who's first?"

They both yelled, "Me!"

He took a coin out of his pocket, put it behind his back, and let them select which hand. They both chose. Mindy chose the hand with the coin, and Nick said, "Hop on, Mindy, let's go for a ride."

After about two minutes, Jesse could see he was tiring and interrupted, "I believe it might be Cindy's turn."

Lorri watched for a moment to give her daughter equal time and then pretended to scold them, "OK, you two. Let your uncle eat his supper."

By the New Year, Jesse was really getting worried about Lorri. He needed some advice from the one person who would tell him the truth, so he drove to his momma's house. "I'm really worried about her, Momma. Ever since Marie died, she won't talk or go anywhere. All she does is clean. She even took down the Christmas tree on the twenty-sixth. She's never done that. She always strings out the holiday as long as she can. What on earth do I do to make it better?"

"Son, there's not much you can do. I know it's hard, but you've got to be patient. She lost the one person besides you she was closest to, and that's hard. They were like sisters. Give it some time, and after a while try to come up with something for her to do. Right now everything she does reminds her of Marie. I know you, son. You want to fix it, but you have to give her some time and space."

"Thanks, Momma."

"Get over here and give me some sugar. Things will get better," she promised.

Driving home slowly, he realized he just couldn't follow her advice. He noticed a young soldier on the side of the road just before he got to the house. He was wearing jump boots with his pants bloused at the top of the boots. He made a U-turn and stopped, asking, "Where are you headed?"

"Ducktown, sir."

"Hop in and I'll take you. Does the family know you're coming home?" Jesse asked.

"No, sir, it's going to be a huge surprise."

Jesse asked, "When did you graduate jump school?"

"Last week," he said, surprised. "How'd you know?"

"Your boots and wings. Did you happen to meet a Sergeant O'Shea?"

"I saw him, but I stayed away from him. That guy was always looking for a reason to make you do pushups."

"Sounds like him to me," Jesse chuckled.

"Do you know him?"

"Yeah, we went through basic together. His bark is worse than his bite."

Jesse pulled up to the soldier's house and noticed someone peeking out of the curtain. As the soldier got his duffle bag out of the trunk, his family rushed him. Jesse smiled and waved, "Good luck, private. Enjoy your leave."

On the way back home, Jesse decided it was time he wrote O'Shea.

Michael really liked his job at the Red Dot. Today the owner had him dusting and straightening the merchandise on the shelves. It gave him time to reflect, and he realized Margaret's suggestion about the job was a Godsend. She was around so much she'd become part of the family, and that made him think a lot about his sister, Betsy, who'd died when he was a baby. He wondered what his world would have been like if she'd lived. If she was like Margaret, she would have been someone he could have shared his secrets with; he felt sad he'd missed that. He decided when he married he would have at least two kids, hopefully more.

In the middle of daydreaming, he noticed a pair of shoes planted right beside him, and as he looked up he saw the beautiful blue eyes he'd fallen in love with. She asked, "Can you help me find the hairspray?"

He smiled, "I sure can if you'll follow me." He led her to the back of the store and gave her a quick kiss behind one of the displays.

"When do you think you'll get off and make it to the canteen?"

He reassured her, "I should be there by eight at the latest."

She pouted. "Does it have to be that late?"

"Yeah, I have to walk home and get the car from Daddy first. Tell your brother I can bring you home tonight."

"He'll like that," she said.

"I sure hope so; he's a really big guy," he teased.

"And he loves his little sister, too. I'll see you later." She gave him a quick grin and wave as she sashayed back up the aisle, winking at him over her shoulder.

# CHAPTER 40

A week after Jesse had the talk with his momma, Lorri surprised him by asking if they could go visit her family in Marietta. He was tickled to death to get them all out of the house. Saturday morning, they had a quick breakfast and hit the road. The day went by quickly. Lorri's parents were competing for time with the kids, and Lorri stayed busy in the kitchen cooking dinner and some pies. All Jesse had to do was relax and make a little conversation with his father-in-law.

The kids crashed as soon as they got in the car. To break the silence, Jesse asked, "Remember last week when I was late getting home? I saw a soldier hitchhiking near Epworth and I took him home to Ducktown. He'd just graduated from jump school and was taking some leave. Would you believe it? He actually knew O'Shea and said he avoided him because he was always making them do pushups."

She laughed. "The old rascal hasn't changed at all, has he? You know, I actually miss him."

A few more miles down the road, Jesse said, "You know, Lorri, I'm thinking about going back in the army."

She stared at him for a moment and finally asked, "You really do hate your job in the mine, don't you?" They rode in silence for a few minutes and then she said, "We did have a good life at Fort Benning, and we had a lot of friends there."

Jesse sat silently and let the idea marinate with her. He was holding his breath in anticipation of how she'd respond. After a moment, she asked, "Could you just go back in? What would we do with the house and farm?"

"I've got an idea about that and wanted to see what you thought. Daddy is about to retire, and you know he's paying rent on that place now. I'm sure it will take most of his pension to cover that. What if they moved into our place until we retire from the army?"

She looked at him in awe and then accused, "Just how long have you been planning this?"

"Ever since I began working in that dirty, dusty black hole," he said in disgust.

She just nodded in agreement. "Well, then, it looks like the Barkley family is about to go on another adventure."

He drove for a long time in silence as they both thought about the situation. "If you're certain, sweetie, I can make it happen."

She placed her hand on his leg and said, "I'm ready; let's do it. I can't bear the thought of you being so miserable. I wish you had talked to me about it before, though."

Friday after supper, Lorri was doing the dishes when she heard Jesse up in the attic. Twenty minutes later, her curiosity got the best of her and she went to see what he was up to. She climbed the stairs and peeked in. "What are you doing?"

He was busily throwing stuff left and right out of her neatly packed boxes, and the more she watched, the more she frowned. "Do you know where my jump boots are? I've got to get back into shape. Thought I'd start running in the morning."

Angry and frustrated at the mess before her, she demanded, "Why didn't you just ask me where they were before you decided to come up here? I put them in the bottom of your clothing bag with your old uniforms."

Sheepishly, he said, "Would you believe me if I told you I didn't want to bother you?"

"Try again, mister. That dog doesn't hunt."

He knew he'd dug himself into another hole and gave up. "You know I really do love you more."

"Clean up that mess before you even think about coming back downstairs. I'll get your boots."

Sitting at the family dinner table on Sunday a few weeks later, Michael realized he was bored to tears. He and Danny decided to find something to occupy their time while the adults talked. As they walked to the barn, Danny said, "Daddy should be here in a little while."

"What do you mean? Your momma has the car," Michael asked in surprise.

"Daddy runs now. He runs every day. I tried to keep up with him but he runs too fast and too far."

Michael couldn't believe his ears. "How far does he run?"

Danny responded, "He says about ten miles."

"Why on earth would he do that?"

"He's going back in the army," Danny explained with pride.

So many questions began running through his head that Michael didn't even know where to begin. He just walked around the side of the barn watching for Jesse. Danny was obviously bored as he threw rocks at the door to the pig pen. Just as Michael started to tell him to stop, he noticed a tall, lean man in jump boots running toward them. Danny jumped up and down. "See? Told you he'd be here soon. He runs all the time."

Michael was in awe of his uncle. He looked so comfortable with his long stride and speed. When Jesse saw them he jumped the fence and ran over to them. Michael was stunned; Jesse wasn't even breathing hard. He asked, "Can you teach me to run like that?"

"Sure; if you're going to be a soldier, you'll need to learn."

Michael hopefully asked, "Can I run with you today?"

"Sure, but I need to talk to Momma and Daddy first. Can you give me a minute?"

As Jesse entered the house, Mike said, "Little brother, why on earth are you playing soldier?"

"Because it's something I'm good at. Believe it or not, the army wants me back," Jesse said quietly as he looked over at his momma.

She took a deep breath, placed her hand over her mouth for a moment, and then timidly asked, "Son, are you serious? You're going back in?"

"Yes, Momma, in two weeks," Jesse said. He moved to the table and took a seat, looking around at his family to gauge their reactions.

Amos just shook his head in disgust. "Boy, you've done some stupid things, but I think this takes the cake. You're too old to be a soldier, and you've got a family. Get that nonsense out of your head."

Jesse met his father's eye and firmed up his posture. "It's too late, Daddy. I've already signed up for four years."

Mrs. Barkley asked, "What about Lorri and the kids?"

"They'll stay here until I get settled and find a place to live, and then they'll join me. Momma, I have another favor to ask. With us gone, Nick is going to be completely without a family. Would you take him under your wing for us?"

Amos snorted, "Hell, boy, she'll just adopt him. Just you wait and see."

Mike just sat there dumbfounded. Jesse could see the arguments racing through his brother's head as he tried to come up with the one that might talk Jesse out of his decision. Finally he asked, "What's going to happen to your place?"

Jesse smiled. "I was thinking Momma and Daddy could live there and keep an eye on the place for me, rent-free. What do you think, Momma?"

Mrs. Barkley's face lit up with excitement and worry at the same time. She began to pace and wring her hands, all the while glancing over at Amos with hope in her eyes. "I don't know, son. It's whatever your daddy thinks."

As he usually did when faced with an important decision, Amos just sat and groaned. He did not like confrontation of any kind and would avoid it at all costs. His usual response was to bark back, hoping he would scare the problem away. Everyone just sat waiting for his decision. The only noise was the creaking of the swing on the front porch as the wind moved it.

Finally, Jesse had waited long enough. He looked over at Amos. "Well, Daddy, will you take care of the farm for me and live there rent-free?"

"When do I have to move?"

"Not for a while. It should be a few months before Lorri and the kids come to Fort Benning," Jesse stated.

Amos looked at his wife. "Momma, if you think it'll be OK, I guess we can do it."

Lorri shook her head in disgust. She had Amos' number. No way would he set himself up to be responsible if things didn't work out. Once again, he'd placed the ball firmly in his wife's lap. Lorri was hoping he'd at least be grateful for the opportunity and allow Mrs. Barkley to have a little joy in having her own place. She looked over at Jesse, who was watching her closely, and just rolled her eyes.

Jesse looked at his momma and said, "Well, then, it's settled. Michael wants me to teach him how to run. I'll get him home, so don't worry about him, big brother."

As Jesse approached, Michael looked over at Danny and asked, "Do you want to go too?"

"No way! I'm riding home with Momma. Daddy runs too fast," Danny protested.

As Michael and Jesse walked to the end of the road, Jesse suggested, "Let's go up the road to Pleasant Grove Church and run on Old Copperhill Road." He moved to Michael's left side and instructed, "You set the pace and I'll just run next to you. Are you ready?"

Michael took off at a jog and due to inexperience he ran as fast as he could. He was pushing himself, but Jesse just chuckled because it was an easy pace for him. After about a quarter of a mile, Michael was gasping for breath and so red in the face he resembled a beet. Jesse just calmly instructed, "Don't sit down; just walk until you get your wind back."

Bent over at the waist, Michael couldn't even catch his breath enough to speak, so he did as he was told. After a few minutes, Jesse asked, "What do you think you did wrong?"

"I don't know; I was OK until all of a sudden I couldn't catch my breath."

"You were breathing too hard and too fast. They call that hyperventilating; your body was telling you it needed more oxygen because you're out of shape. Another mistake was you started out at full speed. We need to build your endurance before we try to win a race."

As they walked up the dirt road, Michael asked, "Uncle Jesse, why didn't you tell me this before we started?"

"I've learned experience is a much faster teacher than just telling somebody, and I've found the student doesn't usually question me after that."

Michael was a little embarrassed. "Is that the way you do it in the army?"

"Sometimes. Now, let's trade places and I'll set the pace this time."

Michael did as he was told and matched his uncle step for step. He didn't realize Jesse was constantly talking to him and asking him questions, which forced Michael to talk as he was running. He was so caught up, he was surprised when he saw the church just ahead. "Uncle Jesse, we're already at the church and I can still breathe."

"Michael, when you first start to run, it's ninety percent physical and ten percent mental. The more you run and the better shape you're in, those numbers change. If you keep running, one day it will be reversed."

"Where are we going now?" Michael asked.

"To Blue Ridge. You have to get home, don't you?"

"Do you think I can do it?"

"It doesn't matter what I think. It's totally up to you. It's always up to you, Michael," Jesse said.

For the next couple of weeks after school was out Michael would run the mile to Jesse's house. It was a good warmup for him. The more they ran together, the more Michael started to like doing it. Today's lesson was increasing his speed. The power lines followed the little dirt road they ran on. Lined up with one pole, Jesse encouraged him to run as fast as he could to the next pole. Then they'd walk or jog until he was breathing normally again. At the next pole, the sprint would be on again. They decided to do ten of these every other day. Jesse said, "Remember I told you about the mental part? This will get your mind and body used to sprinting, and you'll become comfortable doing it." On their last day of running together, they just had fun. They were running at full speed, laughing, and joking with each other. When they got back to Michael's, Jesse gave him a final piece of advice: "A great man once told me it takes three weeks to make or break a habit."

Michael grinned. "I've just got one more week to go then."

"You keep running, and you won't have any trouble at all getting through basic training. I'm leaving in the morning and will be home by Christmas, so be ready to run." He turned and began to run up Highway 5.

Michael watched him go with regret and yelled out after him, "I'll be ready, Uncle Jesse!"

# CHAPTER 41

Michael was so determined to keep up his running and not disappoint his uncle when he came home that he decided he'd just run home from school every day except Fridays, when he had to work at the Red Dot. Since he couldn't run while working, he made up for it and ran extra miles on Sunday. Susan had mixed feelings about this new Michael. She liked how healthy and self-confident he was, but she didn't like how it came before her in his life. She was hoping she could change that soon.

Even though the new Highway 5 had been completed, Michael still ran the old one—Scenic Drive, as it was now called. His latest routine was running at a constant pace on Mondays and Wednesdays and running the sprinting exercise Jesse had shown him on Tuesdays and Thursdays. Just east of Gravely Gap, he was forced to run on the new highway. He always ran on the left side, facing traffic. One day a car about a hundred yards ahead of him pulled over and the driver got out. He recognized Mr. Haymore, his geometry teacher, who held up his hand to stop Michael's progress.

"Michael, I thought that was you. I didn't know you liked to run. We're starting a track team this year, and I noticed you speed training. We need someone who can run the four hundred or eight hundred meter race for the team. Would you consider trying out?"

"I'm not sure I'd be very good at it, sir. I just love to run."

"Well, think about it this evening, talk it over with your parents, and we'll talk about it at school tomorrow," Mr. Haymore encouraged him.

Michael agreed and began to ponder it on the way home. He decided he'd bring it up to his momma first. Once he'd broached the subject with her, she grabbed him up and hugged him, saying, "I'm so proud of you! It's nice he could see your potential. But what do you want to do, son?"

"I'm excited, but I'm a little scared," he admitted.

"That's normal. What do you think your Uncle Jesse would say about this?"

He rolled his eyes. "He'd tell me to go for it."

"Why do you think that?" she asked him seriously.

"It'll help me when I go in the army."

She didn't like that answer at all, because she still had hopes he'd change his mind before committing to that career, but she did like that he wasn't afraid to try new things. Her heart filled with pride as she remembered that small boy with polio. How far he'd come!

Michael looked at her and pleaded, "Please don't tell Daddy. He won't understand."

His request broke her heart, but she agreed. "I'll let you tell him when you think the time is right."

Tryouts weren't what Michael had anticipated. He had thought he'd have to race against someone in order to earn a spot, but when he showed up, the coach just told him he was on the team and would be running the 880-meter race. There were only ten guys at tryouts, and they were all football players. He assumed they were there to stay in shape for the upcoming season. There wasn't a track at the school either; they ran in the grass on the outside edges of the field. The distance for each race was marked, indicating the number of laps required around the field. Some people were doing the high jump and pole vault. Michael watched for a moment and couldn't see anyone who even remotely looked like they would be successful at those events. He immediately decided he had no interest in doing any of that. Pleased with the way things went, he made the decision to join the team. The coach handed out the training and events schedule, and Michael could see they were required to train Monday through Friday and compete on Saturday. The season ran through the end of the school year. In a panic, he wondered what on earth he was going to do about his job at the Red Dot. It was all he could think about on the run home.

After explaining his dilemma to his momma, he asked, "What can I do?"

Martha hesitated. She couldn't believe how touched she was that Michael trusted her enough to ask her opinion. She could tell he'd really liked what he'd seen and wanted to test his new skill, so she suggested, "You only have two options. You can give up the idea of competing on the team or you can quit your job."

He stared at her in disappointment; he'd already figured out that much on his own. He'd been counting on her to come up with something else. "Momma, I really want to be on the team, but I need to work to earn money so I can use the car."

She asked, "How long is the season?"

"From now until the end of school."

She nodded, "That's only a little more than two months, son. Why don't you ask your boss if you can take off until then and then start working again when school lets out?"

He didn't answer; she heard the back door slamming as he whirled and ran out. Once again she'd answered his prayers and given him a solution. When he talked to his boss, he was surprised to learn he'd run track in college. His event had been cross country, and he seemed disappointed West Fannin didn't have that event. The owner ended their discussion with, "Do me a favor. Let me know when you have meets and where they take place. I'll expect you back to work the week after school lets out."

Michael shook his hand just like he always did with Uncle Jesse. "Sir, you have my word. And thanks for letting me do this."

Long hours of strenuous practice helped Michael form a strong bond with a couple of his teammates, Tommy Hamby and Don Chancey. They all loved to run and challenged each other to excel. Both boys had grown up just like Michael—strict fathers and no extra money. One day, Tommy asked for help on a project he'd agreed to do. His next door neighbor needed a six-strand barbed wire fence across his pasture so he could separate the calves from their mothers. The neighbor had agreed to hire a couple of Tommy's friends to help him. The plan was for all three of them to run to Tommy's house right after practice and work until dark. It was about a five- mile run. They started out together, but Don only had one speed --- fast. It didn't take long for him to create a distance between them. At first, they tried to keep up, but that just inspired Don to run harder. They were running on Highway 5 when Don passed Mason's Tractor on his way to Abernathy's Furniture Store, where the road turned back toward Epworth. Tommy got an idea and pointed to a dirt road just before Mason's, saying, "Let's take this shortcut. It will save us two miles." Thrilled that they were pulling one over on Don, they picked up their pace. When Tommy and Michael got to the pasture, the farmer had already marked out where he wanted the fence. They grabbed posthole diggers and began to work as fast as they could. When Don finally got there, they were just finishing up on their second hole each. Tommy looked up and grinned at Don. "We thought you'd gone home." Tommy was only a sophomore, and everyone knew Don a junior, was the fastest runner on the team.

Don tried to laugh it off, but he knew it'd be a long time before he lived this story down if they decided to share it. He didn't realize that luckily for him Michael and Tommy liked him too much to embarrass their friend.

The day of the first track meet finally arrived. Michael couldn't understand why they had to go all the way to North Whitfield County High School to compete, and Don explained, "Copper Basin, Ellijay, and Murphy don't have a track team. If it wasn't for Coach Haymore, we wouldn't have one either."

Most races were run in the evenings under the lights. Michael was the only runner from West Fannin entered in the 880-meter race. He came in fourth place and was stunned by how fast the other runners had been. He figured the coach would be upset he'd done so poorly, but all he said was, "You've got the endurance; we just need to work on your speed. You'll do better next time."

It had been an exciting day for Michael; he'd run his first race and he'd been on his first trip that far from home. He was beginning to feel like the team was his family, and he couldn't help but admire his coaches. They seemed to put the team first. This was proven when Michael heard a story about one of his team members later that week. The boy was the son of a local farmer and, like many in those circumstances, the family didn't have money to waste on anything but the essentials. He'd been running his races in old worn out tennis shoes. Before practice, the coaches pulled him aside and handed him a box containing brand new white track shoes with four red stripes on the sides. Based on the looks on the faces of his team members as that story was being told, Michael knew every last one of them would run themselves to death for Coach Haymore and Coach Montgomery. The kid with the new shoes immediately put those shoes to use and shaved seconds off of his previous best time. It reminded Michael of something he'd heard from one of his classes: *Give a man the right tools and he will excel.* He'd thought the teacher had been referring to an education, but from what he'd witnessed, the coaches had learned a more realistic way of applying this adage.

When Michael found out the next meet was scheduled in Athens, Georgia, he asked his momma if she and his daddy could attend. Martha didn't give Mike a chance to say no. She just told him they were going and scowled at him when he asked, "Why on earth are we going there now? Michael's got another whole year before he'd go off to college."

"We're going to watch our son run in a track meet."

Speechless, Mike stared at her. He didn't even know his son was on the track team. He knew if she realized he was really that clueless there'd be hell to pay, so he played it smart. "What time do we leave?"

She smiled, nodding in satisfaction. "Around noon. I'll pack a picnic lunch."

"Do you think a peach pie might find its way into that basket?"

His request reminded her of the man she'd fallen in love with before he'd become obsessed with his job. She hugged him. "I guess I can, but if you don't watch it, I'll have to start calling you Bear if you gain any more weight."

He surprised her with one of his belly laughs. It was music to her ears—she hadn't heard one of those in months.

The stadium was impressive. It was an old school and obviously had good funding. The cinder track was marked with bright white lines. From where they were in the bleachers, Martha and Mike had a bird's-eye view of the entire track. Mike couldn't pick out his son standing with the team, but Martha quickly pointed him out. When the 880-meter race began, Mike couldn't take his eyes off Michael as he led the way around the track by a pretty substantial distance. Martha was jumping up and down and grabbed his arm. She looked up at him and was surprised to see the tears slowly running down his face. Her heart seized as she realized her sweet husband was finally seeing their son for the man he was becoming. She looked at him and asked quietly, "Are you OK?"

Mike just started clapping and cheering at the top of his lungs as Michael crossed the finish line first. When the race was over, he looked at her and said proudly, "That's our boy." He looked around at the other members of the crowd around him and yelled, "That's our boy! He had polio! That's my son."

Martha smiled to herself the entire trip home as she listened to Mike recap every single moment of the track meet. It was a given—he was hooked, and they would be attending all of them from now on.

Winning changed Michael's focus; he became totally involved in the sport and trained Monday through Friday with meets on Saturday, which meant he only saw Susan on Sunday afternoons after the family dinner, when the car was available for him to use. Susan was not happy with this new arrangement and drop in her status. She began to fume. The girls were all at the canteen talking about the upcoming prom and what their dresses looked like when one of their friends ran in and announced, "Have you seen the new schedule they posted? Because the West Fannin team won, they're supposed to go to the state meet the night of the prom!"

The girls just looked at each other in horror. They'd already bought their dresses—their boyfriends couldn't possibly do this to them. They huddled up and began to come up with a plan. It was decided that Don's girlfriend was the bravest of the lot, so she should approach Coach Haymore and present their feelings about the meet being on the day of the prom. Everyone agreed it was the best approach they could come up with, and they just hoped he could somehow influence changing the date.

At practice Tuesday afternoon, Coach Haymore approached the problem straight on with his team. He sat them all down on the bleachers. "I have a question to ask you guys. I understand some of you have a concern about the state meet, which happens to fall on the same day as our prom. There's no way you can compete and be back here in time to attend. I'll let you talk about it and decide what you want to do." After a few moments of watching the boys whisper among themselves, he called out, "OK, raise your hand if you want to attend the prom."

All the seniors' and juniors' hands shot up. The freshmen and sopho-more members of the team didn't even bother to vote. They couldn't attend the prom anyway. After he counted the results, Coach Haymore nodded. "Enjoy your prom. You've earned it."

The morning of the prom, Martha said, "Michael, I need the car to run some errands before you start washing it to death."

"OK, Momma, I've got all day to get it done," he agreed.

She was gone almost an hour, and when she returned she handed him a small white box. "Here, you'll need this tonight."

When he opened it, he had no idea what it was. It kind of looked like a flower, but he'd never seen anything like it growing around there. Before he could ask, she explained, "It's a corsage to be worn on her wrist. I got a white orchid since you didn't tell me what color dress she was wearing."

Michael's mouth flew open and all color drained from his face. He stut-tered, "Oh, my! I hadn't thought about any of this. What am I wearing tonight, Momma?"

She just grinned and picked up a garment bag she'd draped over the chair. It said Mull's Department Store. As she unzipped the bag, she pulled out a white sport coat, black pants, and a thin black tie. She also handed him a shoe box containing black penny loafers. He just hurled himself into her arms and hugged her fiercely. She squeezed him back and whispered, "I love you, Michael. Remember when you wrote in your dream book that you wanted to learn how to dance? Well, dance one for me, son."

# OTHER BOOKS BY THE AUTHOR:

<u>The Sugar Creek Series/Historical Fiction</u>

Sugar Creek
Gravely Gap
Hogback
Hoverdown
Talking Rock

<u>Military Fiction/Vietnam</u>

The Ledger
Bear Cat

<u>Nonfiction</u>

Silver Bullets for Managers

28881200R00141

Made in the USA
Charleston, SC
23 April 2014